Surviving To The End

Emilee King

ISBN-10: 1966173021
ISBN-13: 978-1966173021

1

I darted down the darkened hallway, my eyes barely able to make out the shapes of the slick walls around me. Massive picture frames and lopsided fake plants threw lumpy shadows along my path, standing silent, like grave onlookers lined up to watch a grisly execution. I pretended not to notice them, ignoring their judgmental stares boring into my skin. There was nothing in the thick silence—my quick footsteps had been practiced into soundlessness—but I could hear the verdict the shadowed onlookers gave me like the pounding of drums before the guillotine: *guilty*.

A shiver went down my spine without my permission. I pushed it away, willing my fraying nerves to harden and mold into something strong. Indestructible.

Focus, I told myself, scolding, like my brief moment of weakness was a sign of bad behavior. *Down this hallway and take the second right. It's the second right.*

Are you sure it wasn't left? my inner unwanted consultant chimed in, her snarky voice feigning innocence. *It would be such a shame to screw this up. And by a shame, I mean I really want to see you bleed.*

It's right. I'm sure, I snapped back. Except now, I wasn't sure at all.

The uncertainty filled my head like the rising tide despite my efforts to keep it down. She fed off any and all negativity, especially in me, and I felt her rise up. I saw as the grotesque image of her formed in the corner of my head, the image of a nightmare but one that was unfortunately all too real in ways I couldn't explain: nearly a perfect reflection of me. At least, what *used* to be me. Her skin was ridden with scars and torn to expose electric blue flesh, half her hair had been ripped out, and the left side of her face was marred nearly beyond recognition. My right eye looked back at me, but her left was just a brilliant solid blue orb in the socket, and she gave me a smirk with her half-disfigured lips.

Oh, but princess, you sound less sure now.

Shut up, Vanessa. You're not helping.

Whatever you say, princess. After all, I live to serve.

I rolled my eyes at her, trying to ignore her continuous presence. Months back I had named her Vanessa, mostly because I needed something else to call her besides "Monster Me" and thought it was fitting since that was the name of the sea witch in *The Little Mermaid*. At first, she was really annoyed by the name, which was why I kept using it, but now she had embraced it. As she put it, naming her meant I was accepting that she wasn't going anywhere. I always got nauseated at the thought.

Trusting my gut, I continued down the hallway and took the second right. Sure enough, my comrade was there waiting for me, standing against the wall with a loose but alert stance.

"The system's disabled," I breathed, barely audible. "We're good to go."

Micah nodded and straightened up, not hiding the boredom in his bright green eyes that seemed to glow in the dark: radioactive, unstable, and ready to blow. "After you then."

I complied, taking the lead down the corridor. It was two lefts, stairs, and a right—I knew that— but I still found myself mentally running through the map I had memorized the day before just to triple check. Micah didn't allow for mistakes on assignments. That was easy for him until I started accompanying him. Now if anything went wrong it was usually my fault, and I paid for it.

Making my senses focus again, I concentrated on where I was. Feet against shoes, shoes against marble. Musty atmosphere. Faint tropical freshener staining the stagnant air. Micah following close behind, his pace rapid but his breathing even. The shadows that watched us, silently waiting in stoic anticipation for judgment to be passed. Left. Stairs. Right. Never making a sound. Focused on putting one foot in front of the other, leading, tensing, recoiling from what would happen when I reached my destination. The shadows shouted soundlessly at me, exposing me for what I was despite the long sleeves I wore.

A shaky breath escaped me, and I felt Micah's disapproval without even seeing his face.

Stop it, I commanded myself. *Don't think. Focus. You just have to focus.*

I stopped at the immense black double doors with gold letters immortalizing the name 'Laurent Bridges.' How nice of him to put his name on the door, like an invitation beckoning us in.

You don't want us to come in, Laurent. You want to run.

Micah lifted his arm to push me out of the way; I stepped aside on my own. He put his ear up to the door, listened for about twenty seconds, then signaled with his fingers.

Three guards in there, he told me. Piece of cake for us. Poor Laurent thought hiding out in his expensive office with a personal detail would help his situation.

Micah took out his precious knife and started working his magic on the locked handle. Though assignments often made me feel like a spy in need of dart guns, elaborate wigs, and fast cars, my comrade preferred the simplistic approach. Hands-on. For Micah, it's just about him, his weapon, and his target. Anything else—even cool gadgets—

were just unnecessary annoyances. He didn't need them.

I made myself count while he worked. Counting helped in lots of situations. There was something calming about the succession, the order, the absence of chaos without the terror of dreading inevitability. Six came after five, and it would always come after five, and there was never a reason for anyone to be upset that it did. Numbers had such a deep-rooted foundation that even the universe bent around them, allowing them to exist as they were without forcing change.

Twelve. Thirteen. Fourteen. Fifteen. Six—

The handle clicked, my adrenaline spiked, and we stormed in. The look of shock on the guards' faces would've been hilarious in any other circumstance. I knocked out two of them before either could get their guns out; the third got a shot off—I ducked just in time—before Micah took him out.

We both turned to see Laurent sitting at the desk, face pale and clammy, as his entire corporate life flashed before his wide eyes.

"I'll give you anything you want," he blurted, his reedy voice shaky. "Anything. Money? New identities? A private plane anywhere you want to go? Anything."

Laurent continued to attempt a bargain, but Micah couldn't care less for the dead man's last words. He walked toward me and pressed the flat side of his knife against my cheek, too soft to actually cut me but threatening nonetheless. I stopped myself from cringing away.

"You take this one." The hair on the back of my neck stood up at his dark, murderous tone. "Let's see what you can do."

Translation: don't mess up or you die too.

I swallowed myself down, letting a coldness overtake me, numbing me from the core and distancing myself from the situation. Settling into something less Arie but not quite Vanessa, I shifted my glare to Laurent, repeating the thoughts that it was either him or me, and I was stronger, I was more powerful, and I couldn't let myself care what happened to him. This is what I'd come to do, and once I got it over with, it would be done. Just like counting. Six would come after five, and we'd move on to seven.

My muscles tensed as I took steady steps forward, my gaze zeroing in on the target, and he shrunk back into his black leather chair as I got closer. The space between us grew smaller while I climbed onto his desk, keyboards and monitors and paperweights crashing to the floor. I stopped and sat on the edge, digging my boot behind one of the wheels on his chair leg so he couldn't back away from me. He couldn't seem to look away either. Laurent Bridges stared at me, hypnotized with fear because he knew exactly why I was there.

Leaning forward, I rested my elbows on my knees and stared into Laurent's eyes like I'd been taught, like I could reach down into him and crush everything in its wake. A shudder went through him when I parted my lips to speak.

"Where is it?"

Each word was its own cold thing, my voice sharp but lifeless, like a dead snake's fangs still dripping with venom. Empty but no less dangerous. I barely even recognized my own voice because it wasn't really me. For these tasks, I had to become something else entirely.

It took Laurent twelve seconds to answer, and even then his words stuttered and faltered and tripped over each other. "I, I don't...I don't know...I don't know what you mean."

My eyebrows rose at his bold decision, and he flinched.

This'll be too easy.

Child's play, Vanessa echoed. *It's almost not even fun.*

Faster than Laurent could follow, I jerked my hand out and snatched the closest weapon to me— a long silver letter opener, sharper than was safe— and drove it into Laurent's leg. His scream ricocheted off the walls of the spacious office, and I found my mouth twisting with disgust. This man had no concept of real hurt.

"Where is it?" I asked again.

Laurent was already crying—seriously?—and blubbered something in response. Not an answer, though. Not what I asked for.

Lifting my free leg, I slammed the heel of my boot down on his good knee, just like I'd been taught, and heard a deafening cracking sound. Laurent shrieked and doubled over. I leaned forward further, clasping my hand around the letter opener, and Laurent screamed again before I even moved it.

"Laurent," I said, forcing the name off my tongue because I hated the taste of it. "Do you know who I am?"

Laurent looked at me through his tears for a moment before finally nodding.

"So then you know who sent me."

Another cry burst through his teeth, and he nodded again, miserably.

I held his gaze with a warning glare. "Where is it?"

I gave him thirty seconds to answer, which was generous—I heard Micah huff in impatience behind me—but when Laurent stayed quiet, I jerked the letter opener around, and he howled in response. Something inside me winced when I saw his hands clutch the armrests, like my soul was reminding me that I'd been the one in the chair too, screaming through number six and begging for seven. For the counting to keep going. For the pain to stop.

Please make it stop.

The thought made me slip, a lapse in the charade, and I had to shake my head to focus. That's when I saw it. Subtle, but still there: the shift of Laurent's eyes away from mine. Just for a split second. Just enough.

I straightened up and raised my voice a notch, so Micah would know I was talking to him. "It's somewhere in here. He wouldn't part with it."

A crashing sounded, then a smashing, clattering, more crashing, as the tornado that was Micah tore through the place. I didn't flinch at the chaotic symphony, but Laurent did, wet eyes wide while he watched Micah destroy the beautiful office that stood for his success and had probably cost a fortune on its own.

"Better tell me now," I said softly, too low for Micah to hear, and Laurent's gaze snapped back to me. "Give yourself a chance."

It was getting warm in the office—uncomfortably warm. Sweat beaded down Laurent's face, his cheeks flushed, as he'd probably never been uncomfortably warm in his life. He opened his mouth, hopefully to speak, but a last crash from Micah sent the words back down his throat. I turned to look. Behind an abstract painting Micah had torn off the wall, there was a cutout nestling a small black safe.

I actually snorted, a chemical reaction between the two sides of me that were never meant to go together. "Behind a painting? Seriously?"

Micah snapped his fingers at me while he inspected the safe. "Code?"

I turned to look at Laurent, and he recoiled under my gaze. Taking a breath, I steeled myself, preparing to go deeper and darker than some flimsy little letter opener, because I was trained to do much worse.

Laurent must've finally got his head screwed on straight because he let it all out in a gust of painful breaths. "One, nine, nine, one, one, six, one, two, five, six."

That was it. Micah must've put in the code because I heard a pop and turned to see him holding up a black plastic rectangle with fancy silver embellishments. A flash drive. Neither of us knew what was on it, but we weren't supposed to. Assignments were for what, not why.

Micah pocketed the drive, then turned around to face us, jade green eyes locked on Laurent. I stood just as Micah stepped forward.

"We have it," I said, trying to bring the cold cruelty back to my voice. "Assignment complete. Let's go."

Micah shook his head and jerked his chin at Laurent. "No, *he's* the assignment. Anything else is just extra meat."

My mouth went dry. "We have what we came—"

"Arie," Micah growled, drying the rest of me up, and I actually took a stumbling step away, nearly tripping over the end of the desk. A flash of surprise went across Laurent's glazing eyes at my fear. I wasn't supposed to be scared. I wasn't supposed to care whether he lived or died.

In fact, I was supposed to kill him.

Gripping the knife, Micah gestured to Laurent, a mocking invitation. I summoned up some courage from somewhere, shaking my head and folding my arms. He scoffed before walking toward us—toward Laurent—steps slow and deliberate, mounting his target's terror, and I had to force myself to hold my ground.

Laurent let out a small squeal as he held his hands up, partly in surrender and partly in defense. "Please, you can't do this. I gave you the code. I was willing to cooperate." His searching eyes turned to me. "Please, I have a family. A wife and two kids. Don't do this, please, I'm begging for your mercy."

A choking sound caught in my throat just as Micah reached Laurent. I forced my eyes to go out of focus, catching one last look of Laurent's terrified yet somehow accusing gaze before he and Micah became a blur. The accusing gaze stayed with me as Laurent's scream echoed with breaking and squelching sounds that used to make my toes curl.

An irrational urge came over me: the urge to tell Laurent everything. Even as I stood there, watching him die, I felt the need to speak, to explain myself. To defend a losing case. My poisoning guilt wanted him to know all the times I was the one in the chair, all of the horrible things I'd been forced to sit through to condition me, so I could stand here stoically and watch him be ripped apart and not blink an eye.

I stayed quiet. Then I sensed his presence leave the room, and an eerie stillness settled over the destroyed office.

It was over.

I had to take a few silent deep breaths through my teeth to keep myself in check. Of course, Micah wasn't fazed at all. He wiped his knife and hands on his black pants, smearing Laurent's blood, then grabbed his gun and aimed it at the mangled corpse.

"He's dead," I said, able to keep my quiet voice from cracking. "Leave him alone."

Micah froze, then turned his glare to me with a raised eyebrow. I had to remind myself to breathe. Most people looked at Micah and saw their nightmare, their darkness, their end—the young Grim Reaper with olive skin and black hair. I continued to look for my best friend buried underneath the heartless murderer, but—especially on assignments—I often couldn't find him. Like me, he had to turn into something else, something less than human, to get these jobs done, though his transformation was on a much larger and more dangerous scale.

He stalked up to me and grabbed my jaw in one hand, then spun me around so my back was to him and I was facing what was left of Laurent.

"Whose op is this?" Micah demanded in my ear, the edge of his tone sharp enough to cut me.

I waited, deciding which angle I should take. His hold tightened on my jaw.

"Whose op is this?" he asked again. He wasn't going to drop it, like I was hoping. He was going to make this a teaching moment.

Lovely.

"Yours," I finally consented through my teeth. I didn't want him to break my arm or rip off my jaw. He was fully capable of doing both.

"And who makes the decisions? Whose judgment do we trust here?"

Laurent's dead hazel eyes stared back at me. "Yours."

"And who needs to learn to shut up when she doesn't know what she's talking about?"

"I do."

Good girl! Vanessa applauded.

Still holding me against him, Micah grabbed my hand in his other one so we were both touching the gun, then raised our arms to Laurent. He pulled the trigger. I flinched when the bullet hit the corpse. He fired again. I stayed still. A third time. I didn't move. I braced myself for a fourth, not sure if I could handle another vibration up my arm, staining me, but Micah dropped my arm and squeezed my jaw so tight I thought all my bottom teeth would pop out.

"This is the business, Arie." His breathing was still steady and even. Like this didn't even matter. Like it was just an assignment. "You should be used to it by now."

He mercifully released me, and I immediately jumped on my next duty before he decided I needed another lesson. Pulling out a gritty cloth from my pant pocket, I spent sixty seconds wiping everything down, erasing fingerprints. Micah didn't have a real identity, so he never had to worry, but the threat hung over me: if my DNA was ever found at a scene like this, my identity would be deleted from public record. I didn't know why it mattered so much to me that I wasn't erased since I was never going back to the real world anyway. False hope was such a powerful drug.

Micah stalked out the door as I finished, neither of us sparing a glance for Laurent Bridges. I tried but couldn't, more out of shame than anything.

I'm so sorry.

Yeah tell that to his family, Vanessa said snidely. *Being sorry doesn't fix anything.*

I stepped outside the office and shut the doors, as if sealing off a burial ground, then wiped off the handles with my special cloth. The unlucky guy who would open them tomorrow was in for a scarring experience. It would leave its mark though. Those who were important enough to know what Laurent Bridges really did with his money would know exactly who it was that stole his life in the dead of night, and the warning would be sent, crystal clear.

A scuffling sounded from down the hallway, which was weird; Micah knew better than to make unnecessary noises. He must've found a straggler.

Oh no.

I raced down the hallway and around the corner where Micah had gone, screeching to a halt when I found him standing over two guards in suits. Both of their necks were broken.

I dropped my head, clenching my fists. "You don't have to kill them, you know," I muttered.

Micah turned around. "Excuse me?"

Biting my tongue, I stepped over the bodies and kept walking. I was more than ready for this to be over.

"Yeah, that's what I thought you said," he called after me. Arrogance oozing like slime, he pushed past me and led the way out. Because there was just no way I'd be smart enough to get us out, despite being the one who memorized the map.

We exited the building and I gave a last thought to Laurent Bridges. We were never told why a target needed to be eliminated—Micah didn't care anyway—which never offered much closure. I could only justify it by hoping that Laurent and all the others were nasty people. Maybe the world was better off without them.

That's a stupid excuse, Vanessa told me.

You think I don't know that?

Oh, I know you know. I was just reminding you.

Micah put his gun away, oblivious to the fact I'd been having an internal conversation and gave me the 'aren't you paying any attention?' glare. "We're done. Let's go." Then he took off running into the night.

That's another problem with Micah: he runs everywhere. He gets called on assignment, a plane drops him somewhere in the vicinity of his target, and then he's on his own. He never has cash or any kind of assets—just himself and his few weapons. He has a time period to make it back to the plane. If he misses it, then even more running. My first assignment with him, I suggested getting a taxi or even stealing a car. He just laughed and left me in the dust. The guy was fast.

I never pretended like I could keep up with him. I worked my butt off in training to be an even match, but the day that I passed him had yet to come.

Of course, there were times—like tonight— when we went through a big city, the kind that never truly went to sleep. That's where I excelled. Micah had to go out of his way to keep his bloodstained assassin self out of sight, but I was a pro at walking down a busy street and being utterly invisible.

Tonight, my chameleon skills were much needed. I went down the sidewalk at a fast but still natural pace, knowing that Micah would only wait so long for me if he beat me. At the same time, I tried to enjoy the small amount of time I had in the outside world. The city lights blew up the night sky, the sparse car headlights adding to the illumination, as a few people walked in and out of the small number of bars and stores that were still open. It would've been near perfect weather—not too cold, not too hot—if I hadn't been wearing black pants, combat boots, and long sleeves, all concealing weapons and blue tattoos. The lines from the blue symbol on my wrists had grown up past my elbows, nearly to my shoulders, and continued to scald itself on me every second of every day. I'd learned it was better to keep them hidden. For some reason people tended to not react well to them.

Vanessa laughed at that. *Yeah, I wonder why. Not quite the conversation starter you're looking for, huh?*

I rolled my eyes. *Well, I can't exactly start with you, now can I?*

You know I'd love that. I believe the world should see just how truly messed up you are.

I've noticed.

To my annoyance, she didn't stop talking. *Is that why you're so sad tonight?*

I sighed. Playing stupid is pointless when your correspondent knows your every thought, but I was often still stubborn enough to try.

I'm trying to focus here. Be quiet.

She laughed. *Poor Princess Arie misses her family. Or what's left of them, I guess. It's not like you would know. Is that where all the doom and gloom is coming from? Or I guess it could be from the murder you did nothing to stop.*

Shut up.

Are you sure?

I'm not even sad.

You look sad.

You can't even see me.

I can sense it. It's desolate in here.

Well, you're welcome to leave anytime. My feet came down harder on the cement as I picked up my pace—as if I could possibly run away from her.

Don't pretend, she said, her voice dripping with sickly sweetness. *You love me.*

I rolled my eyes. *Oh yes, I just love being alone with only you to keep me company. Please continue to mess with my emotions as you wish.*

I then made the executive decision that the conversation was over. It was *my* head, after all. I was the one who should be in charge. Vanessa smiled smugly as I shifted my focus from my head to my surroundings—Micah would kill me if he knew I was so distracted on assignment—and figured out where I needed to go.

My steps were silent as I ran across the barren field and down the abandoned road to where the plane was parked. My feet pounded up the six stairs into the cabin only to see Micah already inside. He was leaning up against the far wall, glaring at me as I appeared in the doorway.

"It's been five minutes," he stated, annoyed.

I decided to take a leap and raised an eyebrow. "Please. It's been two."

He let out an irritated breath. "Fine, it's been three. But two more and I would've left."

I rolled my eyes, secretly relieved, and made my way inside the cabin. "Sure."

The plane wasn't comfortable by any means: it was small, steel and dark, three red bulbs on the ceiling being the only light, and no seating. It was meant to be a cargo plane, to transfer boxes rather than people, and had no place for me. Like Micah, I spent my traveling time sitting on the floor.

The stairs folded up into the plane as the engines started automatically. The whole plane was run by some automated system manned by a distant cell tower, erasing the need for a pilot and making me queasy at the thought of our trips. Nothing ever malfunctioned, though, which was a good track record, I guess.

Micah sat opposite of me, rummaging through his backpack of extra supplies kept in the plane. He dug out a radio and slid it across the floor to me.

"Call it in," he ordered without giving me a glance.

I tapped my teeth together a few times and stared at the black box before picking it up. I never understood why reporting seemed to be one of the hardest parts for me.

My finger pressed the small button as I brought the device to my face. "Nolan to base," I said, my voice hard and professional. I was supposed to be a killer, after all.

Only a second passed before a man answered. "Go ahead, Nolan."

"The assignment has been completed. Laurent Bridges is dead."

A hiss of disapproval came from Micah. He hated using names—I always snuck them in to try and awaken some humanity in him. It never worked.

I cleared my throat. "I mean, the target has been terminated. We have made it to transport and are en route to the Compound."

"Copy that, Nolan." And then the mystery man was gone.

I tossed the black box back and forth in my hands a few times before sliding it back to Micah. He caught it without looking and stowed it back in the bag, then zipped it up.

"Did I pass?" I muttered.

Micah scoffed. "Barely. If that's what you want to call it. How long are you going to pretend you're actually doing this right?"

"There is no way to do this right. It's murder."

"Arie." He sucked my name in through his teeth, emphasizing his frustration. "You know, eventually you're going to get caught."

I shrugged. "Then eventually I'll deal with it."

"How stupid can you possibly get?" he demanded, and I flinched at his rising anger. Why hadn't I shut up? "I hope you get caught in your pathetic charade. You couldn't even get the guy to give anything up—do we need to practice torture again?"

A shudder went through me at the memories— nobody cared how I learned the art of torture, whether I practiced on others or they practiced on me—and I shook my head too fast.

"No. I've got it. I'll be better."

Thankfully, that was enough to get him to back off. Micah closed his eyes and fell asleep sitting up straight, per usual. I was conscious of my every move though, including breathing, because he'd jolt awake at the landing of a fly.

I rested my back against the wall of the plane, cooling my sweaty body with the cold metal, trying to relax every muscle. Sleep would be a lost cause for sure. I never understood how Micah could just go to sleep after a night like tonight.

It's over, I repeated to myself as I breathed deeply in and out. *It's over.*

Tonight was the fifth assignment I'd been sent on with Micah, and I remembered the names of every single target: Nikolas Spader, Natalie and Trigger Tonks, Mycroft Poulsen, Misha Ramierez, and now Laurent Bridges. Everyone except the couple knew it was coming. Everyone except Nikolas ended up begging for their lives.

The plane hit some turbulence, making me clench up and hold my breath. I'd never been actually scared of flying, but this plane really freaked me out. It was too easy to imagine it malfunctioning and us plummeting to our deaths.

Maybe that's what you deserve, Vanessa mused to herself but really to me.

I let out my held breath slowly and rested my head in my hands, ignoring her and trying to bring myself back. I was almost there—almost completely Arie again. It took time and energy for me to shift in and out of that thing that hurt Laurent, but I reminded myself to be grateful I could still go back and forth. The idea was, eventually, I'd morph into something much worse and never come back out.

Don't think about that now. I obeyed myself. I counted instead.

Travel time flew by, probably because I really didn't want to get back to the Compound. Time was never on your side when you were headed exactly where you didn't want to go. I spent the flight in the same spot on the floor, curled up with my head in my hands, trying and failing to block the last three hours from my memory.

Micah woke up right before we landed, and the sleep seemed to thaw him out too. He stood as the plane came to a stop, picked up his backpack, and walked over to me. Cautiously, I lifted my head to see his hand outstretched, his eyes still jade stones but with rounded edges—less a killer and more my friend.

Relieved, I took his hand and he pulled me up before getting off the plane. My body whined, so I stretched my arms, cracked my neck, and bounced on the balls of my feet a few times before following Micah.

The warehouse that the planes were kept in was huge and airy, every single sound echoing for seconds afterward. Our nearly silent footsteps still resounded throughout the hangar as we made our way past the second parked plane, through the door, and outside.

Micah always took huge steps even when he was just casually walking. It added to his powerful and driven demeanor, standing as another reason people tended to scramble out of his way. Thankfully he wasn't that much taller than me, so I was able to match his steps and flank him as he'd taught me while we went across the Compound.

The Compound was like a mini city encapsulated by a fifty-foot slick wall that was manned twenty-four seven. We had our own leadership, businesses, workers, social class system, economy, and even weather. Guests from around the world—most drowning in cash—stayed and were entertained here, like a glorified vacation resort. The more I sniffed around, the more I discovered how many of them were dirty or involved with infection practices in some way. 'Employees' like me—almost all of us infecteds—were worked into the ground in order to keep the Compound running smoothly. We all had different ranks, therefore different jobs, and were separated into groups based on that. Different groups rarely interacted with each other, and a competitive spirit roamed through everyone. For the inferiors, the Compound was all about survival of the fittest.

Micah was the highest-ranking infected and very few in the Compound had the power or the guts to tell him what to do. Everyone was well aware of what Micah was capable of, and he reminded doubters often.

I was ranked right under Micah, giving me authority over every other infected, and—thanks to my notably false reputation—they were scared of me too. The ridiculous rumors that flew around were hard to refute, though, because they usually stemmed from truth. After all, I was the Golden Girl, Arie Nolan, the key to the formula who flanked Micah the executioner. It only made sense that I was a soulless monster who drank the blood of my prey as everything was handed to me on a silver platter.

It was afternoon now, so the Compound was bustling with life. We were on the south end—the inferior end—working our way north, passing by the labor groups hard at work. At the Compound there was *always* something in need of remodeling, rebuilding, or renovating, so the labor groups never ran out of work to do. Those who weren't in construction worked in the fields, orchards, and vineyards, providing the resources to keep the Compound going, while other luckier souls (depending on who you asked, anyway) worked security, service, or administration indoors. The workers must've been doing a good job today because the temperature was a good medium for hard labor. Sweat and sawdust sticking to the air, I kept my eyes forward as Micah and I passed them, ignoring the comments and whispers that would be shared after we were gone.

We reached the halfway point of the Compound, the invisible line between inferiors and guests, where dirt, gravel, and debris turned to luscious grass, beautiful plants, and smooth roads. There wasn't a fence of any kind to further mark the divide: we all knew the conduct expected from us and, more importantly, the punishment of acting out of accordance. Instead, the giant administration building stood as a marker separating the two worlds. It was our version of the Capitol Building, where important information was kept, vital decisions were made, and our main leadership was housed.

I followed Micah up the brilliant white marble stairs and through the back door into the administration building. 'Immaculate' couldn't really cover it: the building was gorgeous, white, sleek and smooth, not a speck of dirt in sight or a thing out of place. The reception area was as big as a house on its own, and that didn't account for the hallways that spread out in every direction like spindles on a wheel.

We stayed near the backside, going through a password-protected door that opened to a golden elevator. Even then, we both had to press our fingers onto the pad on the wall for a scan to make the elevator go up—only a handful of people were allowed on the second floor and security was top priority.

I stood on Micah's left, staring ahead as the elevator took us up, mentally preparing myself.

This is five, and six will come right after, and then we'll get to seven.

The elevator opened and we stepped into a room just as large and clean as the reception area downstairs. It was subtly drawn into thirds: the right side housed a long white conference table with white leather chairs; the left a large white wooden desk, nothing on it except a glass cup holding three pens that stood at the perfect angle from each other; the middle section was empty besides an oversized white leather chair that stood on the opposite side of where we entered. The back of the chair was to us, but I could see a man's elbow resting on the arm of the chair. He was watching life in the Compound from the comfort of his chair, as every wall was one-sided glass: he could see the world, but the world couldn't see him. And it only took a button on a remote for one of the glass panes to turn into a screen that played footage from any security camera in the Compound. He held the highest ranking—king of this little world.

Micah and I walked in unison to the center of the room, stopping and waiting with hands held behind our backs.

Here we go.

The chair turned around to reveal our sovereign. He looked even smaller when sitting in the oversized chair, his hunched back only exaggerating the effect. A deformed grin spread across his lips when he saw us, slightly animating the four scars that pinched up the left side of his face, while his bouncing green eyes moved every which way—as if he could see everything.

"My dear Arie," Cyrus said, raising his hands in delighted presentation. "You've returned." His voice hardened slightly when he addressed Micah. "I take it your assignment was a success?"

Micah gave a stiff nod and handed over the flash drive. "Yes, sir."

"Excellent." Cyrus shook his head, almost as if in pity. "Laurent was causing too many problems. Quite a tragedy. I'll have to send flowers to his family." He turned his attention back to me, noting the blood on my fingertips. Those eyes of his saw everything. "So how was the trip, dear? Have your skills excelled with your continued participation?"

"Yes, sir," I answered without missing a beat. Once again, Micah didn't refute me, which was dangerous for him but my saving grace. Cyrus was under the impression that I assisted Micah in the murders to improve my own craft. He would be furious to know I actually tried to keep Micah from killing people instead—especially if he knew Micah was covering for me.

"Well done." Cyrus tilted his head toward Micah, his voice taking on a deliberate tone. "You are learning from the best, you know. I imagine it won't be long before you're an even match for him."

I kept myself from scoffing. That was his passive aggressive way of saying, "I've seen your training stats and you should be better." There was no way I was even close to taking on Micah and walking away from the fight.

But I nodded because that's what Cyrus wanted me to do. You always did what Cyrus wanted you to do.

Cyrus settled further into his chair. "Now I'm sure you both have duties to attend to. You're dismissed."

"Yes, sir," Micah and I said in unison. We turned and walked back to the elevator.

"Arie?" Cyrus called.

My nerves stiffened. I stopped and turned around, Micah holding the elevator door for me.

"Sir?" Somehow I kept my voice smooth.

He knows I lied about the assignment. He totally knows.

"What flowers should I send: roses or tulips?" Cyrus thought for a moment. "Or maybe daisies?"

I breathed a silent sigh of relief. "Um…roses. That's what I would send."

"Excellent choice." He turned his chair back around, a last dismissal.

I shook my head at his oddity and took the last step into the elevator. Micah let the door slide shut and we began our descent.

He surprised me by breaking the silence. He sighed. "He's going to figure out you're lying to him. This is a stupid plan."

"I never asked you to cover for me," I reminded him, hoping he wouldn't listen to me. "You can stop any time you want."

"I'm just saying it's a bad idea." The door opened and he slipped out.

I know.

He was gone by the time I got out of the elevator, but it didn't really matter. If I had something else to say to him then I could tell him tomorrow at training.

I exited the administration building and walked the quarter mile to the production building. I wasn't sure exactly what time it was, but with my luck, I was probably late to rehearsal. Hopefully I would be able to change and slip in without anyone noticing.

The production building was exactly that: a production. Like every other building in the Compound, it was huge, beautiful and white, but it was in a class all its own. It could be transformed into nearly anything, with countless stages, pyrotechnics, seating, and flooring. It was mostly used as a venue for fundraisers Cyrus threw for special visitors, or the concerts and dance parties held for all guests. The bar, kitchen, chefs, and staff made the production building the ultimate party scene, especially for the kids staying here with their rich parents.

A production team had been put together—infecteds who had a knack for singing, dancing, or stage management—and, of course, Cyrus added me to the team the second I arrived. It was arguably the most humiliating thing I'd ever been forced to do, like a performing monkey, but the humiliation didn't compare to the crushing anxiety. Thanks to my rank, and Cyrus' insistence, I'm sure, I was appointed the female lead, which was the worst thing that could've happened to me. Every performance nearly stressed me to the point of combustion.

Naturally, a strange girl coming in and stealing their thunder caused some resentment between the production team and me, but it wasn't too bad. They were some of the only people in the Compound who were remotely nice to me—or at least talked to me—mostly because they were sheltered from pretty much everything besides the stage.

I dashed through the back door into the empty dressing room, ducking into my changing cubicle and stripping off my combat clothes. My production wardrobe consisted mostly of fancy but flexible dresses and heels—the full out costumes were reserved for the dancers. I didn't have much say in what I was forced to wear except the rule that everything had to be long sleeved. It only took one conversation with the designers for them to agree with me.

For rehearsal I just threw one of the dozens of black dresses that I wore to every occasion I had to dress up for. The design was simple, the fabric was comfortable, and I was able to run in it if disaster struck. My kind of dress.

I had to take the time to wash myself of blood, so I couldn't spare a second to fix my hair in a travel-tossed bun or lack of excessive makeup. The base layer of thick foundation I always had on, plus the rogue mascara from yesterday, would just have to do.

Oh well. We can't have everything.

Taking the stairs two at a time, I made my way out of the dressing room and up on the stage, hanging in the back to survey the scene.

There were twelve girls and twelve guys, plus Elijah, the male lead, and me, making the team stand at twenty-six. Everyone was standing around loosely on the stage, aimless chatter fluttering around. I guess I hadn't missed much.

"Just in time, Arie," Elijah said quietly as he walked up to me, and I caught myself fruitlessly trying to fix my hair. It was hard to describe the way Elijah moved—it was smooth and flowed like a river, almost like a ballerina but not feminine. Just graceful. He had total control of his body and a killer voice to match.

"Did I miss anything?" I asked, adjusting my dress before realizing what I was doing, then dropped my hands.

I rarely admitted to myself the tiny crush I had on Elijah. Rarely. It would never work, plus I'd have to stand in line with every other girl in the universe. But sometimes when we were performing together, singing some sort of love song, and he'd look into my eyes while his gorgeous voice claimed I was the most beautiful thing he'd ever seen, I'd catch my stupid heart fluttering. Then the song was over, the part played, and he'd snap back into his old self, and I'd hide gallons of mortification that I fell for his magic again. Nothing would ever happen, I knew, nor did

I want it to really, but I always found myself wanting to please him in spite of myself.

Elijah shook his head. "Not unless you call Miss Welch chewing Sadie out for breaking a toenail anything."

I shrugged. Better her than me.

Miss Welch was the Director of Production, a title that she snuck into every conversation she could. Once it had slipped that she was fifty, but she didn't look a day over thirty—I suspect lots of Botox—however every once in a while you could see her age shine through in a wrinkle that usually disappeared the next day.

She epitomized the classic high school student teacher: she seemed nice and cool until she was put in a leadership position, then her true colors came through. She loved her job because she could exercise power over others, punishing them for the things in her life that had gone wrong.

"Has anyone seen Arie?" Miss Welch barked—literally. Her surprisingly deep voice was the human version of what an angry Chihuahua with a nasty cold would sound like.

I weaved my way to the front of the stage and gave a half bow. "I'm here, Miss Welch."

Miss Welch stood on the ground to the right of the runway, her strawberry blonde hair up in a messy bun with her bangs held back by a headband, making her suspicious glare perfectly visible.

She clicked her tongue sharply. "And what's wrong with your face?"

Appearance was everything to her—everything about her look was always flawless, but there was a weird hippie meets the nineteen eighties-ness about her, as though she'd peaked in another other era and couldn't quite let it go.

"I'm sorry, I didn't have time for the makeup chair today," I explained, tucking a piece of rogue hair behind my ear. It was the truth, but around here it was really just a pathetic excuse.

"Uh huh. Team?" she called. "What's our policy on presentation?"

Twenty-five people called back in unison. "Presentation is the key to success."

Miss Welch nodded, her hoop earrings shaking, then gave me a stern look. "See that it doesn't happen again."

My nod was too fast, heightening my self-consciousness. "Yes, Miss Welch."

"Okay, we're going to finish blocking the new number for tomorrow night." Her voice rang out, bouncing off the walls. "Arie, Ezra and Zoe, you're on point. The rest of you fall back into position. Let's go."

The next few hours were filled with music, sweat, and the ever-constant barking of Miss Welch.

"Ezra, are you *deaf*? Do you hit notes or just shatter them with a baseball bat?"

"Point your toe, Isaiah, you're ruining the mood!"

"See, Lani, maybe if you lost a few pounds you could actually land that right!"

"I swear on my nana's grave, Sadie, if I see another drop of blood from that toe of yours you will be on red card for a week!"

"Oh, for the love, Mesa, just get behind Zoe—your ugly face is just slaughtering this cow carcass you all call a performance."

Mesa's face went pink before she ducked behind the goddess that was Zoe, who promptly flipped her flawless golden hair and stole the attention Mesa's shame had garnered. Zoe used to be the female lead until I came along, and there was no way I'd ever fill her immaculate and talented shoes—a fact I was reminded of every time we shared the stage.

By the time rehearsal had ended and Miss Welch finally let us go, my dress was caked with sweat, and I was dying for water. We filed to the dressing room, only too eager to get changed and get out. Rehearsals left everyone completely drained. Miss Welch would withhold food, water, and sleep until we got everything right.

"Remember that the show starts at eight tomorrow night," she called after us, as she did every single day despite the time never changing. "Be here getting ready by six-thirty!"

I shut myself in my cubicle and sagged against the door with a tired sigh. Then I noticed the water bottle on my shelf and snatched it up, draining the water easily.

"It's been a long day," Elijah called from his cubicle next door. "I'm ready to go relax."

Wiping extra water off my lips, I laughed once to myself as I gathered my combat clothes from the pile on the floor and put them in a duffle bag. "I know what you mean." Slinging the duffle bag over my shoulder, I headed out the back door. "See ya tomorrow."

"See you, Arie."

It was dark outside now, a chilly wind blowing my dress in between my legs as I walked barefoot down the even cement. There wasn't a soul in sight—most everyone staying in the north end was inside enjoying a feast or having one last activity before bed. The quiet was nice after the blaring of music and Miss Welch's aggravated shouting.

The wind whooshed through my disarrayed hair, drying my sweat and cooling me down. I walked past the administration building, unconsciously standing up straighter, walking better and with more purpose, stomach churning at the thought of Cyrus sitting in his big white chair and watching me from his window.

I crossed the line to the south side. Gravel dug into my feet, but I didn't feel it much anymore. Besides my combat boots for training and heels for performing, I wasn't given much in the way of footwear, causing me to go barefoot most of the time. It hurt at first but now my feet had toughened to the point where it hardly bothered me.

Any route I took would force me to pass a labor group—they were everywhere, especially on the south side. Every few months Cyrus would order the complete rebuilding of a housing building, creating work for laborers and forcing hundreds of infecteds to move to another building while theirs was being rebuilt. It kept people busy and on their toes, as they were never able to get truly comfortable with where they were living.

Our material status shows our status as individuals, Cyrus would say. *We can be better than this. We must be better than this.*

Toward the end of the south side was the maintenance building, which housed supplies as well as the generators that powered the Compound. The backside of the building had a forgotten fire escape I would use to get to the second floor.

I adjusted the duffle bag on my shoulder before climbing up the ladder, wincing at the creaking of the metal with every step. At the top was a window. From the ground it looked as though the window didn't open, but I'd debunked that theory a long time ago. Gritting my teeth, I forced the window up and climbed through, then secured it back in place.

The second floor held the generators: about twenty silver boxes ten feet tall and ten feet wide, strategically placed so there was a narrow hallway between them you could walk through. I'd learned the hard way to not touch the metal because they were hot enough to fry your skin. The floor and ceiling emanated freezing air to keep the generators from overheating, creating an odd mix of cold and hot air. Being in there for an extended period of time made me feel like I had a fever. Hot then cold then hot again.

Home sweet home.

I discovered the place shortly after I arrived at the Compound. Cyrus allowed me to make it my living quarters as long as I didn't tell anyone—after all, everyone thought I was put up in a five-star hotel—which I was fine with. The place wasn't homey by any means, but it was better than the damp hole they gave Micah, similar to the hole they were going to give me. There was a reason he could sleep so soundly sitting up and there was no way I would allow myself to be reduced to the same thing.

My corner held my few belongings: a pair of leggings, a t-shirt, three long sleeved shirts, three hoodies, and two pairs of jeans made up my collected wardrobe that I'd purchased at the supply depository. I also kept a piece of chalk for recording purposes, a kitchen knife for defending purposes, and a pillow and a sheet for sleeping purposes. Inside my pillowcase were the hair elastics I'd managed to steal from the production building—they always seemed to disappear, and with my hair falling halfway down my back now, I was always in need of a ponytail.

Each generator had a backlight that created odd shadows across the walls, but it was enough light that I could get to my corner without running into anything. I dropped my duffle bag and plopped on the floor. I was tired. I changed into my leggings and t-shirt, the blue on my arms seemingly brighter in the dark, and pulled my hair out of its bun, running my hands through it a few times. Then I wrapped my sheet around me and stared at the wall.

"It's been a long day," I said to myself. Sometimes the best person to talk to is yourself, which was good because often I was the only one I had to talk to. "It's been a long day and now it's time to forget it all and go to sleep."

That was my nightly pep talk in an effort to keep myself from having nightmares. I'd gotten better at containing my reactions, but that made them no less terrifying. I tried to give myself a rundown of every day so that when I went to sleep my brain would be bored of thinking about it and my dreams would be about rainbows and peach cobbler instead.

"You went on an assignment today." I stopped for a second and cleared my throat. "You saw a man die." I stopped again, longer this time. My clammy hands pulled on the sheet around me. "You saw a man die, but it's over now. You've got to just go to sleep. The day is over now and there is nothing you can do. Time to go to sleep."

Vanessa smirked. *Yeah, just to do it all again tomorrow. What a charmed life.*

I couldn't stop the groan that came at the thought. Again. I'd have to wake up and do another day *again*, plus all the days that came after that.

If your life is so horrible then just leave. Vanessa gave me a knowing look. *Or is that just too much for you too?*

I gritted my teeth. *You of all people know why I can't leave.*

Vanessa shrugged. *Combust in here, combust out there—who really cares?*

Thoughts of real explosions, threats, and blue veins filled my mind, jumbling the logic of whether I could really leave or not, of what could possibly be out there for me when I was in this state. I just couldn't help myself: I wondered about Sark, Alaina, Brennan, Peter and the others, where they were, what they were doing, if they were okay. If they wondered about me.

Of course, they were probably doing okay. After all—whether they knew or not—Alexis was dead. His organization was probably in a mass panic with the fall of their leader, rendering them unable to hunt Sark and the rest of the infecteds. That had to count for something, right?

I wondered what they would think if they knew where I was, if they knew what I did. What would they say if they knew I'd witnessed a murder today and did nothing to stop it? Would they understand the situation or would they assume I was becoming the key, the monster I was eventually going to turn into?

"Would you still love me," I imagined asking Sark, "if you knew what I was becoming? If you knew what they were training me to be? If you knew that when I stand there as Micah goes for the kill, some instinctual part of me wants it too? It scares me, Sark, that I'm beginning to feel the lust for blood, the crazy desire to kill something. I don't want to be a monster. I don't know what to do."

I sighed and shook my head violently as if to empty it. That was a dangerous road to go down, especially right before bed. It was better to bury everything, go on with life, and deal with it another day. 'Another day' hadn't come yet. Part of me hoped it never would.

"All right, time for bed," I told myself. "We just need to be done."

I grabbed my stub of chalk and turned to the wall next to me covered in a ton of faint chalk marks. My hand shook slightly as I drew another crooked line.

"Day one hundred and nineteen at the Compound," I murmured before putting my chalk back in my corner, dusting off my hands, and settling in for a long sleepless night.

2

My alarm on my radio went off at four thirty, the deafening blaring like a fire alarm alerting all of danger: *Warning! Another day is here!*

I groaned, blindly reaching for my duffle bag. It took me four tries to get the zipper open, then another twenty seconds of racket before I finally found the button to turn the alarm off. Rolling on my back, I stared at the ceiling, which looked exactly the same as when I fell asleep. It was still dark outside, nature's way of telling humans they shouldn't be awake yet.

Half of my body felt frozen from lying on the cold floor for so long, while the other half was warm from being just a foot from a generator. I stretched myself out, cracking some joints, and yawned before lying in denial. Like every morning, I *really* didn't want to get up.

"You're going to be late," I told myself, as if my moaning could motivate me. "Get up or you'll be late."

Late was definitely something I didn't want to be, but my priorities were all messed up. Right now 'pillow' was more important than anything.

My body seemed to weigh tons as I forced myself up, rubbed the sleep out of my eyes, and changed into my wrinkled combat clothes. They smelled worn, so I figured I'd have to get new ones soon. I tugged my tangled hair into a ponytail and laced up my boots before heading out the window and down the fire escape.

The Compound wasn't awake yet, as labor groups weren't expected to meet until seven and guests usually weren't up and at 'em until around nine or ten, so infecteds with jobs didn't have to be ready until seven thirty. I was the only one out. The sound of my boots crunching against the gravel filled my ears as I made my way to the training building.

The training building was technically open to any infected, should they find the time in their schedules to fit it in, but it was mostly used by those that served as guards or were on call for defense. Most laborers doubled as second line defense if they were needed, so you could sometimes find them here early working out.

There was every kind of exercise equipment out there, plus two gyms, two pools, and two tracks—every exercise junkie's dream. The entire top floor, however, was reserved entirely for Micah. And now for me.

Like usual, I took the back stairs up to avoid running into anyone, if there was anyone crazy enough to be up at five in the morning just to work out.

Micah was there already, boxing a punching bag in the far corner. His training center was huge—the track around the edge was a half mile long—and held any kind of contraption one could dream an assassin in training would need. The middle space was like a boxing ring without the ropes, reserved for hard hand-to-hand combat training, something Micah didn't really need help with, but it was the spot I tended to get wiped out. Directly across from the mat was a giant cast iron gate, which held the more dangerous training equipment.

I walked over to him and leaned against the wall as I watched him pound the punching bag with ferocity, a single line of sweat going down his face. He didn't acknowledge me. He was focused, eyes zeroed in on the bag in front of him. It was training time.

It was only a minute later when our trainers came in—a win because it meant I wasn't late after all, but a loss because now training would really get started.

Many people at the Compound showed an obvious disdain for me, but Roland, the beefy, black head trainer who hated oxygen simply because I breathed it too, was my most common offender. He was a few inches shorter than Micah but about twice as thick and had a presence like nobody I'd ever met. You couldn't catch him in anything besides his navy blue army uniform, which only added to his authoritative aura—he made a great second-in-command for Cyrus. He lived for giving orders and seeing to it that they were followed. Structure. Order. Training. Being the best. That was Roland's game.

Micah was Roland's proudest accomplishment. I only knew that because I'd heard him talking with other officers at Cyrus' fundraisers. Micah had no clue. Part of the assassin training, I guess, was to treat Micah like a hunting dog.

I threw off everything, naturally, since that was the only thing I was good at. I wasn't as fast, or as strong, or as smart as Micah, and I threw off his focus. Apparently, my Micah didn't exist until he met me. Once he'd been completely soulless—the guy that threatened to break my jaw because I didn't torture a man well enough—rather than the kid who sometimes pulled me up after a long plane ride. After he'd spent eight months on a deep cover assignment, in which he spent eight months locked up with me, he was never quite the same, now sliding back and forth between harsh and cruel, much to Roland's frustration. They picked Micah's mental conditioning back up in an effort to reverse my effects, and I was terrified for the day when Roland would try the same awful method on me. He'd always hoped for another Micah, and I was a disappointment on all fronts.

But there was hope, Cyrus would remind Roland, that this training would carry over to when I finally transformed into the true key, when I became the weapon they were waiting for. I would be the best and Roland would get all the credit. I think that's the only reason why he didn't just kill me.

I didn't know what I did to make him hate me so much, but he always complained about my performance. How his team should be better than what I was putting out. How I continually held Micah back.

It was always a great way to start my morning.

"Micah! Nolan!" Roland shouted as he stormed into the training center. "Four laps! Let's go!"

I took off running as Micah was ripping off his boxing gloves—I would take any head start I could get. Despite the constant verbal, and sometimes physical, abuse from Roland pushing me forward, I had only ever outrun Micah once: it was literally by a tenth of a second and I threw up afterward.

This time was no different than usual: Micah finished about fifteen seconds before I did. I crossed the finish line and Roland appeared out of nowhere, clotheslining me while I was still almost at full speed. My body slammed against the ground, knocking the wind out of me as my head took a nasty hit against the floor. I choked for air while the equivalent of cartoon birdies flew around my head.

Roland stood over me, a mountain of a man, a grizzly bear always in a fit of rage.

"Pathetic!" he shouted. He had a slight accent, the inflection you'd hear in the heart of central

Africa, and it always amplified when he shouted. "Pathetic, Nolan!"

I was pretty sure some spit landed on my forehead, but I knew better than to wipe it off in front of him. He blew his whistle again, killing my ears, and ordered us on to our drills that we completed before combat training.

Scottsman, Roland's nearly mute training assistant, ran through the cast iron gate to get Micah's partner of the day. I've only ever heard the scrawny guy speak once—his sole purpose was to do whatever Roland didn't want to do. I don't think he'd ever looked Micah in the eye, but he stared at me in a way that made me want to run, hide, and lock the door behind me.

Micah leapt over the yellow ring around the mat and stood in the center, readying himself for his fight. It was important to find center mat and stay there: step on the yellow ring and you get a nasty electric shock.

Scottsman burst through the gate holding back a ravaging mutt on a leash. Micah bent his knees, eyes focused on the enemy, at the ready.

"Begin!" Roland commanded. Scottsman let the mutt of the leash, and it barreled through the ring and onto the mat. The yellow ring hummed and glowed, letting us know the electricity was on. It was game time.

Mutations were the only things used to train Micah because they were the only things that had a shot at beating him. The first time I'd ever heard of a mutt was way back at the infecteds' club when talking with Daxton—turns out, they're much scarier in person. A mutation occurs when someone doesn't take well to the formula, usually because their body is too mature and the formula feels threatened, so it takes aggressive action. Mutts were nasty, inhuman things that were always out for the kill. They weren't very smart, thank goodness, always taking the obvious approach, but they were insanely strong and nearly impossible to stop.

This mutt used to be a middle-aged man, but its protruding electric blue veins, rabid eyes, and animalistic movements made it look more monstrous than anything. Its wild gaze locked on Micah and it let out a lion-like roar before charging, bent so it moved on all fours.

Micah braced himself, then they clashed. The mutt snarled, trying to claw at Micah's head, neck, and chest. Micah teased it, staying still until the last possible second, then dodging out of the way, increasing the snarls from the frustrated mutt.

I'd watched Micah train for months now and I'd begun noticing patterns to his fighting style. Well, maybe they weren't patterns—that was too predictable. But there was a familiarity that connected each of his bouts in the way he moved and the choices he made. Like there was only a certain amount of programmed strategies in his head. Whatever it was, it was chilling in a way, subtly making him seem less human and more machine.

He was enough of a boy to get cocky though. The mutt screamed in rage, ripping out a fistful of its own hair as it continued to try to get a single swipe on Micah.

I saw it in slow motion: the mutt lunged, and Micah sidestepped out of the way but failed to see the mutt's foot come from the side. The blow caught Micah in the leg, and he fell right onto the yellow ring. Electricity crackled and his body convulsed violently until the mutt grabbed his ankle and dragged him off the ring and onto the mat. Then it attacked.

I gasped in spite of myself and jumped to my feet. "Call it off," I told Roland.

He ignored me, his eyes wide in surprise. "Get back on it, Micah!" he shouted. "Get on it now!"

It was too late. Using claws and teeth, the mutt tore into Micah, stifled moans coming from its victim as arms fought from underneath to get a handle on the monster. Blood splattered. The mutt roared.

"Call it off," I said again, unable to rip my eyes from the scene. "Do it now!"

Roland just shouted louder, as if Micah only needed more motivation. "Get on it! You're losing!" He blew his whistle. "Now!"

The struggle continued, Micah able to get a solid punch across the mutt's face but not much else. He wouldn't tap out. The idiot was going to get eaten alive before he admitted he couldn't take it.

Finally, Roland nodded to Scottsman, who retrieved a gun and loaded it with a tranquilizer the size of my fist. Usually the tranqs were only needed for my rounds—never Micah's. Scottsman shot the weapon and it lodged in the middle of the mutt's back. It shrieked and pulled itself off Micah, thrashing around in an attempt to remove the tranq. Its movements got slower and smaller until it went out cold and fell to the ground. The yellow ring darkened, powering down. It was over.

Several seconds passed in silence as everyone realized what happened. I glanced over at Micah lying on the ground: his shirt was nearly in pieces, his face cut up, a nasty gash on his shoulder but—despite the blood smeared all over him—that seemed to be his only major wound. I breathed a silent sigh of relief when he groaned and pulled himself up.

"Get over here, Micah," Roland ordered, his voice tight.

Micah kept his eyes on the ground as he trudged over to the other side of Roland. Roland turned his back to me, focusing on Micah, and Scottsman backed away to stay out of the line of fire.

"What would you call that, Micah?" Roland asked.

Micah just stared. Roland slapped him across the face.

"What would you call that?" he asked again.

"A failure," Micah answered, his voice resigned.

"A failure?" Roland growled. He hit Micah with every word. "Pathetic! Disgraceful! It was a catastrophe, you wretched swine!"

Micah took it in silence, and I bit my tongue too.

Roland straightened up, making me think he was done. Instead, he whipped around and punched me in the jaw.

"And you!" He grabbed my face in one meaty hand. "Don't you ever, *ever* give me orders again. Your contributions are worthless and out of rank. Understood?"

"Yes, sir," I got through my crushed mouth. He hit me again, then grabbed me by the arm and threw me onto the mat.

"Now let's see if the *girl* can do any better," Roland said, hurling the words at Micah who still hadn't looked up from the ground. "Scottsman!"

Scottsman scrambled back through the gate to get my mutt. Unlike Micah, I'd never been able to beat a mutt—I always ended up needing the tranq before I died—which meant I fought the same one every time. Also unlike Micah, who fought random unfortunate strangers, I had a mutt tailored especially for me.

The gate opened and I readied myself, though even after all this time I was never ready. Scottsman held onto the leash with all his might, holding back my ravaging mutt, a face I knew all too well.

It was Felix.

Felix used to work as second to Sark back when Sark used to work for Alexis. I'd always assumed that Alexis had picked him up after his last fight with Sark—right before we left Chicago for Florida—but I guess Cyrus got to him first. I continued to see that Cyrus had a hold on my life I had yet to really comprehend.

Scottsman let Felix go, the yellow ring glowed, and it began. Felix roared and barreled right at me. Following Micah's lead, I waited until the last moment before sidestepping. There were only so many times I could do that, though, because of all the practice Felix had. Mutts weren't smart enough to think of anything besides the straightforward attack, but Felix and I had been fighting long enough for him to recognize how often I tried to just get out of his way.

He snagged my wrist and yanked me back, then elbowed me in the throat. I ducked down and kicked him in the face. He reeled back then came at me again. Patterns. Like clockwork.

Despite the fact I'd always hated Felix, it was hard to see him like this: nasty blue veins bulging out and disfiguring his skin, animalistic movements and the eyes…the eyes were the worst. There was no light in there. Just mindless bloodlust.

Plus, it was such a sick joke, pitting me against him like this again, as though the tragically cruel aspects of my life were coming full circle. I was living the early days all over again: getting held against my will, pounded by Felix, waiting for the day my secret would ruin everything. Only it was all amplified. Arie's Worst Nightmares: 2.0 Edition. Get it wherever bad luck is sold.

I held up about as long as Micah did. Felix swung at me and I grabbed his wrist, bending his arm behind him and climbing up on his back. Keeping one hand on his, I wrapped my other arm around his neck and choked him. He roared and thrashed but couldn't shake me off.

"Felix," I said in his ear, attempting to be discreet about it. Roland did not approve of me trying to talk through my enemy, but that didn't stop me from trying to awaken Felix every chance I could. He had to be in there somewhere.

"Felix, it's me. It's Arie. You work for Sark, remember? You hate me. We used to do this all the time, remember? Come on, you gotta hear me. I know you're in there."

He stopped thrashing for a moment and I felt a spark of hope—I was getting to him. I saw just in time that he had a different plan.

I jumped off his back right before he slammed me down onto the yellow ring. He caught my ankle, and I fell to the ground, right underneath him.

Oh boy.

"Felix—"

He slammed his fists against my face, then started clawing at me. I kneed him in the gut, threw punches, and wiggled around in an attempt to throw him off, but nothing helped. Once you got under a mutt, there was no getting out.

I trapped a scream in my mouth when I felt his teeth sink into my right shoulder. Somehow I freed my left arm and slapped my hand against his ear. He screamed, rolling halfway off me to reveal the tranq in his back, then went limp. He was out.

I shoved his body off mine and dragged myself up to face my three spectators. Micah stood at ease, his face cold and expressionless; Roland had his whistle in his mouth at the ready, eyes calculating; Scottsman only gazed at me for a moment before coming over to put Felix on the leash and haul him back through the gate.

Keeping my eyes on the ground, I walked back to my spot on Roland's left and waited.

"Well," Roland finally said. "It seems I have two failures on my hands, don't I Nolan?"

"Yes, sir," I said. The movement hurt my jaw.

"Do I deserve failures, Nolan? Can I tolerate failures in my training arena?"

"No, sir. I'll be better, sir."

He bent down to talk in my ear, the scent of new fabric from his suit wafting in my nose.

"Four laps. Now." He blew his whistle, making me jump and nearly blowing my eardrum, and he straightened up. "Both of you! Four laps, now!" He whistled again. I sighed and headed for the track.

Gotta love training, right princess? Vanessa asked. I hated that she made my own voice sound annoying to me.

I didn't have the energy to muster anything smart. *Right. Gotta love it.*

We spent the rest of our training running through our drills. Roland made sure to test every aspect of our physical strength, including our ability to anticipate attacks and make strategies. By the time seven rolled around and I was let go, I was exhausted.

I hadn't even made it out of the building yet when my radio earpiece went off. This time it was a high-pitched beeping, different from the deep blare of the alarm, making me tense up. The beeping served as a pager: Cyrus wanted to talk to me.

He did this all the time and I had no idea why. "I just want to talk, dear," he would say. "I want you to see me as your ally, your friend. After all, you are like a daughter to me."

Our 'talks' just left me more confused than ever, which was a feat because Cyrus often left me very confused. Sometimes we'd talk for about ten minutes and other days I'd be in there for hours, Cyrus rambling on about the universe or his morning or asking me about mine. The first time I was completely unprepared and totally fell for his tactics. Now I knew not to talk about anything personal, as he was a pro at turning it on me and making my whole world baffling, but sometimes I'd slip. It was just so hard to tell what he was after, what to prepare myself for.

I went straight into the single bathroom to clean myself up before the meeting, stopping at my locker to grab a spare black dress before locking the bathroom door behind me and getting to work. The blood from my bite wound washed out nicely, though the flesh was still sore—hopefully it wouldn't be too much of a nuisance during the show tonight.

You've got bags under your eyes, Vanessa noted. *Pretty big ones. And your face is, like, vampire pale.*

I didn't refute her—she was right, after all. Leaning my hands against the sink, I took in my ragged but somewhat presentable appearance, thanks to the basic layer of makeup that was always on my face. Maybe it was just me, but I thought I looked different now than I used to. Not in a bad way, I guess, but I could've sworn I'd aged in the past six months. I looked older.

"Yay for aging," I muttered as I zipped my dress up and made my way out of the training building.

The sun was up now, peeking through the clouds like a shy child underneath the covers. Per usual, I decided to skip breakfast and head home instead, hoping to get in a few hours of sleep before the weekend craziness officially kicked in.

Labor groups were starting to return from breakfast to begin their workday. I passed five of them on the way, setting up their tools and getting instructions from their captains. Rank was the most important thing at the Compound: workers reported to captains, who reported to supervisors, who reported to Roland, who reported to Cyrus. It was all about order and who was in charge of who.

I got into the administration building and took the elevator up, balling my hands into fists to keep them from fidgeting. It was a bad idea to show nerves in front of Cyrus.

Fear is weakness, he would say, *and weakness is death.*

The elevator dinged and opened to an empty white chair. I took a step forward and peeked my head around, finally finding him on the left side of the room, sitting at his desk and leaning over what looked like a touchscreen tablet.

His lifted his head and grinned, gesturing to the empty chair in front of his desk. "Have a seat, dear."

I obeyed, conscious of my posture, crossing my legs and clasping my hands on my knee. As always, the white room was spotless, the smell of cleaner permanently fixed to the air.

Cyrus pushed the tablet a little closer to me. "Now look what I have discovered just today."

I leaned forward to see him playing a game of solitaire. Not even a fancy, smart or science-y kind of solitaire. Just regular solitaire.

Is this a test?

Even Vanessa was stumped. *I have no idea.*

Cyrus waited expectantly, as though he just found the pot of gold at the end of the rainbow and was anticipating my excitement, so I finally answered, "Um, it's solitaire, sir."

He nodded. "Back in my day we had to play with actual cards." He touched a card and it moved across the screen. "Ha! Isn't that astounding?"

"I've been playing solitaire since I was a kid," I said, my voice uncertain. "That's not exactly news."

Cyrus turned off the tablet, letting out a breath of disappointment. "That's one of the problems with your generation, Arie: you were born in a time when remarkable things are commonplace. The true art of discovery has been lost."

He stood and took the tablet in one hand, his silver cane in another, and hobbled over to the bookshelves taking up the far wall. I found it interesting he used the cane in front of me, when he hardly did in the presence of anyone else. "I see you and Roland disagreed today," he commented.

"Is it obvious?" I asked. I started kicking my foot aimlessly. Sitting still was not on my list of talents.

"To me, yes."

"Well, that's not really anything new. Getting along isn't really our strength."

Cyrus stopped at the third shelf and counted down the row of books before sliding the tablet in between two. "No, it's not," he said as he hobbled back and sat down. "Though you tend to forget that he outranks you."

"He's very good at outranking people. Has he…" I tried to find the best words so not to offend. "Did he serve in the military or government or something? He just seems…"

Intense. Cruel.

Psychotic, Vanessa added. *Insane.*

"Like he's had leadership positions before," I finished. That was way too nice for Roland but better safe than sorry.

"Initially, no, though I imagine living in such a war-torn country, military service would seem inevitable." Cyrus gazed at me, but his eyes continued to search everywhere, making me feel exposed. He was about to hit a nerve. "His eldest brother served before he had the thought."

My mouth went dry. I knew where he was headed. I tried not to show my distress, but my voice still shook slightly at the explosion that was always in the back of my mind. "He didn't come home, did he?" My heart ached, the situation all too familiar.

"Oh no, dear, a man came home, it just wasn't his brother."

Cyrus let that sink in for a moment. I pretended like it didn't bother me.

"Oh. Well, that's unfortunate."

He turned his head slightly, staring at a spot next to my head, like a vision that wasn't there. "Be patient, dear. He just wants you to be perfect. We all do." He continued thinking out loud. "If you weren't breached then perhaps we'd be having better success with you by now. Although, I must say your attitude needs adjustment. We aren't going to reach that perfect key if you keep fighting it."

Wait a second. I perked up, my eyebrows creasing. "Wait, what?"

Cyrus moved his attention to me again. "You're mentally blocking the key from taking over—we've discussed this, Arie. You need to just let nature run its course."

"No, no before that." My mind flew back in time to when I ran off to Phoenix for a day, broke into a research facility, and read the file on Philo Castor, the creator of the formula.

If the key has been breached, the file had said, *then extra steps will have to be taken during the peak phase to ensure success.*

"I'm breached?" I asked, my voicing going up an octave on the word.

The animation is Cyrus' face shut down. His eyes went from vibrant to analyzing as he studied me. "Yes. Rather crudely, actually, which makes this process much harder than it has to be. It's a shame your father didn't have a better understanding of what he was really doing. Now we all must deal with the repercussions."

My father?

Cyrus watched me carefully, as though I was the rat in an experiment he was conducting right then.

"I don't...I don't understand." Was this another test? "My father didn't...he didn't breach me, that would...I mean, I would've...I would've known. He did this to me. He infected me."

He raised an eyebrow at me. "You didn't know." I couldn't tell by his inflection if he had actually known that or not.

My hands started vibrating slightly. I clenched them into fists. "Didn't know what?"

"There are different versions of the formula, Arie. Anyone who has done any basic study of the research would know. The versions are nearly identical, but slight variations exist."

I waited for the rest of the explanation, but Cyrus seemed determined to have me piece it together. "So…what? My dad used a different version of the formula on me? Why does that matter? He still infected me."

"Ah, yes, but my situation would be much easier had I been given the option to infect you in a more sophisticated manner at the right time with the right formula, rather than so primitively so many years earlier with the wrong one. However, harder does not mean impossible. I'm sure I still have the capabilities to shape you into what you're meant to be when the time comes."

"You're saying my dad used a different version of the formula on…on *purpose*? Why would he…" I trailed off, starting to connect the impossible dots I saw written in Cyrus' jumpy eyes. I shook my head. "No, that doesn't make sense. It doesn't. You can't know that he—"

"That he was aware you were the key? That he purposely used a slight variation in the formula in an attempt to keep you from your fate?" Cyrus pursed his lips into such a thin line, they almost disappeared. "Yes, I can know that. And I do."

My mouth had fallen open, my jaw hanging uselessly as I tried to comprehend what he was saying. Breaching had always been in the back of my mind since I'd first discovered it in Stephen White's file. Eventually it had seemed too good to be true. I never would've guessed…been able to *imagine* that I was already…that my dad…

"You're wrong," I said. My voice shrunk in on itself, like it knew the truth I couldn't accept. "He was so cruel. I was his lab rat. He…"

"Perhaps he saw the greater good and chose to chase it. One often finds it very difficult to turn against their destiny once it presents itself."

I didn't respond. I stared at the corner of the desk, my mind a blank slate and a chaotic mess at the same time with the major upheaval of thought.

"Now, Arie," Cyrus continued, as though my world wasn't going through a paradigm shift. "I'm getting off-track. I called you up here because I have a job I need done."

"Yeah?" I mumbled, distracted.

"There's an underground structure southwest of the training building. I believe you know the password required to enter. There's a cabinet with rations for the prisoners held there. I need you to deliver them a set so they may eat."

"Um…okay." I jerked to myself to my feet. "Is that all, sir?"

"Yes. You're dismissed."

I turned and walked to the elevator, joints stiff, my fingers tingling.

"Oh, and Arie?" Cyrus called as the elevator dinged. "Pay attention, dear. There may be something you could stand to learn from this experience."

I rode down in the elevator and stepped outside, relieved for the fresh air. The whole conversation had only lasted ten, maybe fifteen minutes, and already I felt the world was different. The sky was a different blue, the sun shone at different angles. Just ten minutes of my life and the whole universe had changed.

Okay, okay. Focus. You have a job to do, remember?

Vanessa rolled her eyes. *Yeah, feeding prisoners. Oh, the joy. Aren't we above stuff like that?*

A pit formed in my stomach as I really thought about what Cyrus had asked me to do. I didn't even know we had prisoners here.

Makes sense, Vanessa said, her voice appreciative. *You don't get to the top without making some enemies.*

I guess so.

Taking a deep breath to clear my head, I followed Cyrus' directions, going back to the training building, then heading farther until I found metal cellar doors sticking two feet out of the ground.

This must be it. I tapped against it with my foot, a stupid way to buy myself time. *Just go in, get the food, drop it, and get out. One minute tops. Piece of cake.*

Heaven forbid you have to try something new, princess, Vanessa commented snidely.

I squatted down and touched the metal. A keyboard touch screen lit up and I typed in one of the many variations of passwords I'd memorized on day one. The metal whirred and clicked, then the double doors popped up. I grabbed the handles and pulled open the doors, having to strain slightly with the weight. Lights flicked on, illuminating a narrow cement staircase.

Here goes nothing.

Cautiously, I tiptoed down the stairs, unsure of what I was walking into. I ended up in a musty cement room: there was only one light on the ceiling, making the space rather dim and adding to the claustrophobic atmosphere. The right wall was lined with vacuum-sealed cabinets as tall as me, and a deadbolted metal door was directly across from me, but that was it.

This is prime horror movie setting, right here.

Vanessa agreed. *Enter stage right, masked murderer.*

I stood there frozen for a minute. Something told me I *really* didn't want to see what was behind that metal door.

Hurry up, Vanessa complained. *You're being a wimp. Just do it.*

Going on the balls of my feet, I crept over to a cabinet and opened it up. There were six shelves, each lined with dozens of red plastic bags that reminded me of dog food. I picked one up and tested its weight—it felt like it was full of gushy oatmeal or something. A sign on the inside of the cabinet door told me I needed to take four bags per shift.

Easy enough. Just four bags in, then get out. No problem.

Though they were fairly heavy, I was able to grasp two in each hand and half drag them to the big metal door. I had to put one hand's worth of bagged food down to tap the door and type in the password. A warning alarm went off three times, then the metal whirred and the door popped. I picked up the bags again and used my foot to nudge it open, revealing a long corridor, the ground wet with an inch of excess water going down a drain in the center of the floor. On either side of the corridor were bars. Prison cells.

Then the smell hit me. I gagged and my eyes watered at the disgusting stench that threatened to kill every living thing it touched. There couldn't actually be anyone in here—who could survive the smell alone for more than five seconds?

The cells were cast in shadows; I couldn't see or hear anyone. Maybe there weren't any prisoners after all.

This is so weird.

There was a white square box drawn next to the drain—I assumed that's where I was supposed to set the food. Trying to keep my feet as dry as possible while holding my breath, I tiptoed farther into the corridor and put the bags down in the square. Still no sign of life.

Huh. Well, I guess that was easy enough.

I straightened up and a hand shot through the bars of the cell next to me and snatched my wrist. My scream got caught in my throat as a bearded prisoner in bright orange grinned at me, four of his top teeth silver.

"You're a new face, aren't you?" he said, clamping harder on my wrist. "They don't send pretties like you down here very often."

I jerked my hand out of his and scrambled backward, running into the bars behind me, where two other hands grabbed my left arm and yanked me against the metal. Like the first, he was wearing an orange jumpsuit, his face scraggly, but he was covered in tattoos—the one on his neck was the same symbol that was on my arms.

"Look here, guys," he called, eyes manic and locked on me. "It's Arie Nolan. Cyrus sent us a key for dinner."

At that the prison suddenly came to life, dozens of emaciated orange jumpsuits howling and beating against the bars, innumerable hands trying to claw their way to me.

My heart was pounding in my chest, but I wanted to stay calm and authoritative, though my voice still kind of shrieked. "Let me go!" I tried to pull away, but the tattooed man yanked me closer, several of his friends helping, pressing me against the bars as though they would pull me through.

He smiled, highlighting the small bird tattoo on his jaw, his nasty breath on my face and dark eyes like black holes. "I've been waiting a very *very* long time to meet you," he said before spitting at me. I turned my head automatically, his spit sliding down my cheek, but he grabbed my jaw and forced me to look into the black holes again. "I've been waiting a very long time to kill you."

"Let me go!" I screamed, thrashing against their grips. "Let me go now!"

Bird Tattooed Man and his cohorts just kept pulling me, sucking me into their cell as I screamed like a maniac.

"Hey!" a voice shouted, commanding the room. Immediately, the yelling and jeering turned to silence. The hands holding me captive released me, and I fell backward into Micah's arms.

I didn't wait. My feet splashed in the water as I bolted out of the corridor, up the stairs, and outside, not stopping until I was on the other side of the training building. I turned to see Micah about ten seconds behind me, having locked the cellar door.

Breathless, I asked, "What was tha—"

"Why were you in there?" he demanded

"Cyrus sent me to drop the food," I explained. "I didn't...I mean..."

Micah's eyebrows shot up. "He sent you in there by yourself?"

I nodded.

"Arie, *I* don't even go in there by myself. And the prisoners know not to mess with me." He shook his head, almost angry but not quite. "What was he thinking?"

My voice trembled slightly, against my permission. "I...I don't know. He said I could learn something from it or something like that." I took a deep shaky breath. "Who are they? Why are they here?"

Micah sighed. "Cyrus keeps tabs on every organization that is at all affiliated with Castor or the formula. If one of them does something he doesn't like, he gives them a warning. If they continue, he kills them or locks them up." He laughed once, a cynical sound. "There are some crazy people out there—people who want you dead. Cyrus wouldn't let any of them find you except—"

"Alexis," I finished. I leaned up against the wall of the building. "But why?"

Micah shrugged. "There must've been something Cyrus wanted to get through Alexis. But then he got it and now…"

"Alexis is dead."

"Now you get it." He looked me in the eyes, serious, almost asking me to believe him. "Cyrus will always end up on top. Always."

Always. The word echoed in my skull. *Always.* I thought of my earlier conversation with Cyrus, how he wanted me to stop mentally fighting the key. *Let nature runs its course.*

I can't. I can't let it win.

Micah chuckled darkly, as though reading my mind. "It's going to happen, Arie. He's invested in you. He'll win. You should just give him what he wants and save yourself all the hell he's putting you through."

I gritted my teeth. "How did you know I was in there?"

He nodded toward the building. "I was coming out of my training when I heard you scream. You're lucky you made that mistake."

"What mistake? Screaming?"

"Leaving the door open behind you." He pointed back toward the cellar. "Wouldn't want any of those guys walking out. That's pretty much common sense." He took a breath. "I'm glad you did it though. I don't know if I would've heard you if the doors were closed."

"What if they got out?"

"As long as you don't go around leaving doors open, they won't."

I wrapped my arms around myself. "But what if they do?"

"They won't."

"But what if they do?"

Bird Tattoo Man's black hole eyes filled my head: *"I've been waiting a very long time to kill you."*

They'd rip me to shreds.

Micah squared his jaw. "I'd kill them all before they touched you."

I nodded, taking several deep breaths. "Thank you. For coming."

He shrugged again. "Don't mention it." Then he turned and walked away.

My gaze wandered to the cellar doors, the ones I'd never noticed before but now wouldn't be able to get out of my mind. I thought of the raging lunatics underneath and shivered.

They knew my name.

Maybe that's what Cyrus meant, Vanessa said, becoming more and more amused with how terrified I was. *Those guys would've found you and murdered you ages ago if it weren't for Cyrus locking them up. You owe him.*

In a crazy way, that made sense. When Vanessa started making sense, I knew it was time to find someone else to talk to. I turned my back on the cellar doors and ran away.

3

In an effort to calm my frayed nerves, I decided to stop by the cafeteria to grab a grilled cheese sandwich, despite having a show tonight. Miss Welch only believed in organic scraps that tasted like cardboard and could sniff out anything fried or buttered from a mile away.

She'll notice for sure, Vanessa told me.

I shrugged. *Unfortunately, my desire for the grilled cheese at this moment outweighs any negative consequence.* Nothing like emotionally eating your problems away. *Maybe if you weren't around, I wouldn't need cheesy bread to keep from insanity.*

She rolled her eyes. *Yeah, keep telling yourself that.*

I didn't actually sit in the cafeteria to eat—I only stayed when Micah was with me, as I had nowhere else to sit among the infecteds. Instead, I chowed down on my sandwich as I walked to the 5-star restaurant on the north side where my only friend worked.

Ellen continued to be an absolute mystery to me. She served as one of the heads of the food department, meaning she had about a million jobs and things she was in charge of, and was almost always working overtime in some way. We met one night months ago—I'd disappointed Miss Welch in a show and she told me to stay after and do the dishes and "consider how my distasteful performances dirty her production." When I got there, Ellen had directed me on where I could help and we just kind of clicked.

I still had no idea why she was my friend. After a few weeks, I just flat-out asked her if she knew who I was. She didn't get what I was talking about, so I finally just ripped off the band-aid and told her I was the key.

She slammed her spoon down on the counter, terrible realization dawning in her eyes. "Holy cannoli, Arie, are you serious?"

It was hard to nod, as I was sure I was condemning the last semi-functional friendship I'd ever have.

"Wow, okay, so I guess that rules out a ton of stuff," she said, eyes wide but pondering, and I could almost see the cogs turning in her head. "Do you sleep hanging upside down?"

Her lack of disdain had floored me. "Uh, no."

"Are you part metal, like a cyborg?"

"No."

It took a few minutes to get through all of the rumors, but then she started asking deeper questions—questions nobody had thought to ask me before.

"So was that a huge strain on your family relationships?" she had asked me. "Does being called a monster really affect your psychology of self?"

I will always remember that moment, that genuine look in her eyes as she tried to understand my life. That's when I decided that maybe humanity had a chance after all, and that maybe I did too.

Ellen just had that effect on me. It was a good effect, which was why I liked to be around her, though Vanessa continued to point out that it couldn't last forever.

I finished my grilled cheese, then made sure to wipe off my dirty feet on the grass before taking the workers' entrance inside the spiffy establishment.

The lunch rush was in full swing, the huge kitchen bustling with chefs and waitresses. I'd hung out here enough that they all had gotten used to me and I knew how to stay out of the way.

Though she could be in number one, Ellen usually worked at station number sixteen because, as she put it, she could survey the kitchen better from the top corner and the sink was bigger. I thought it was because she was great at being a team player, despite being the one telling everyone what to do.

I weaved my way through the dozens of workers to her station. There she was, her white apron stained so much you could hardly tell it was white, her ashy blonde hair pulled up into a lopsided ponytail. It brushed against her shoulder as she leaned over to put something in the oven.

"Hey, Ellen," I said as I slid into her station and plopped myself in my designated spot on the counter.

She turned and put her hand on her hip, flicking her ponytail. "For the millionth time: call me Elle."

Per usual, I just grinned it off. For some reason I felt there was some qualification I didn't have in order to call her by a nickname. My reservations only fueled her mission of finding a nickname for me—a mission that was constantly failing.

She grinned back. "What's up, Arieland?"

I raised a mocking eyebrow. "Arieland?"

"Yeah, yeah, I know. I'll keep working on it." She turned and washed her batter-covered hands in the sink. "So how's your day been?"

I tapped my fingers against the counter as I thought. *Oh, you know, just woke up, fought a mutt, discovered a startling family secret, and was nearly torn to bits by insane prisoners bent on burying me.*

"It's been fine," I said. "Just another day. How about you?"

She dried her hands off on her apron and leaned up against the counter next to me. "Just been cooking—breakfast, now lunch—then I have to make sure dinner is taken care of before I move on over to the production building." She rolled her eyes. "Yay for Friday nights. Are you ready for the show?"

"Nah." I shook my head. "I swear I'm going to give Miss Welch a heart attack."

"Whatever. You say that every time and you always knock it out of the park."

"Yeah, well, we'll see." My gaze wandered around the lively kitchen. I could never understand how Ellen managed the chaos so well. "So what's going on here?" I asked, hoping to get a good story out of her. I needed a major distraction.

She gave a dramatic sigh as she moved to her giant mixer and started throwing ingredients into a bowl. "You would not believe what happened this morning: so, I'm making my morning smoothie in between making guest breakfast, right? No big deal. I do that every morning, right?"

I gave a small smile. "Right."

Her eyes narrowed slightly as she leveled off her cup of flour. "Well this morning Avril overcooked the eggs benedict and somehow the pancakes just didn't get made. Like we can serve burnt plastic and no pancakes."

"Yeah, that's not good."

"No, it's not. So I finally get everything figured out, but now *I'm* behind, so I'm rushing through my smoothie because I need my blender for crepes. And right then Jordan comes over."

"Oooh!" I gave her a knowing grin. "Jordan, huh?"

She rolled her eyes. "I know, it was just not the time. I'm so stressed and trying to get this done and he's talking to me and…I blend my smoothie." She said the words with finality, as though that were the worst possible ending to her story.

I waited for a second. "Okay…why is that so bad?"

Ellen plopped butter in her bowl. "Because I forgot to put the lid on."

I burst out laughing. "Oh no."

She grinned wryly. "Oh yes. Spinach smoothie *everywhere*. Then Jordan laughed at me and walked away."

"He didn't help you clean it up?" I asked.

"Nope."

"Seriously?" I folded my arms across my chest. "Okay, I change my mind. No Jordan. I'm now Team Sam."

She cracked some eggs. "Sam? Really?"

I rolled my eyes. "Oh please. You think he's so cute."

She smiled but didn't say anything, making me smile.

I kicked my legs aimlessly as I watched her add and measure and mix, pots and pans clanking, people chattering and giving orders, the smell of spices and butter and bread all mixed together wafting through the humming kitchen. Hanging out with Ellen was nice, mostly because she was so chill. If I wanted to spend three hours talking, she was for it; if I wanted to spend three hours just sitting in her kitchen and being with her, she was fine. She wasn't afraid of silence, which was great because I didn't always have a ton to say.

Ellen continued baking and putting out fires—literally, on one occasion—while I started working on the mountain of dishes in the sink. Ellen always protested when I did her dishes, but I didn't mind. I liked doing things for her. Plus, any time spent with her was inherently fun. My ten-year-old self would've been utterly shocked to know that I had fun doing the dishes.

We rewarded ourselves afterward by sitting on the counter and eating the leftovers of her creation: the best banana chocolate chip muffins on the face of the planet.

"Hey, I've got a question for you," she said in between gooey bites.

I licked some chocolate off my finger. "I've got an answer."

"I hate to do this, but there's a fundraiser here on Wednesday and my team is also on cafeteria duty—I could really use an extra waitress for the event and—"

"Say no more. I'm there."

"Really?"

"Yeah. Zoe's on lead performance, so I'm free."

She threw her arms around me in a tight hug, a reaction of hers that still caught me off guard. "You're the best!"

I grinned. "I try."

"So what's up with you today? Anything noteworthy?"

Vanessa kindly reminded me of Bird Tattoo Man: *"I've been waiting a very long time to kill you."*

Instantly any solace I'd found with Ellen dried up. My insides felt cold and hollow.

I rubbed my arms, as though to warm me up despite the heat of the ovens. "Uh, well, I talked to Cyrus today."

Ellen stiffened but continued going about her work, trying not to show her distress. "Huh. How was that?"

"Oh, you know." I pulled on the ends of my ponytail. "Just wonderful."

Measuring cups clinked against her bowl as she threw ingredient after ingredient together.

"So what did he say?" she asked.

I brushed my hair behind my ear. "Well...I guess...I didn't know, but I guess I'm...breached."

She glanced at me. "You're peached?"

"No." I leaned forward a bit. "Breached. I learned about it a while ago: if the key is breached then it's harder to make the key into the key."

I braced myself. It always made me nervous to talk about key stuff with her. One of these times I'd cross the line, and she'd walk away from me.

I'm surprised it hasn't happened yet, Vanessa told me. *Nobody just stays friends with the key. It'll come.*

Once again, you are inspiring.

"Wow." She didn't miss a beat. "Okay, so that's a good thing then, right? How'd it happen?"

I cleared my throat. "Well...I guess...there are different kinds of the formula. One of them was created for breaching. For the key. And that's the one that was used on me." I took a breath and dropped my eyes to my hands. "But, uh, that means that my dad probably knew what he was

74

doing. He was, um, trying to protect me, I guess, from being the key.”

Ellen dropped her measuring cup in her bowl and turned to face me, her eyes wide. “Are you sure?”

“It kinda makes sense, now that I think about it. He was so insistent afterwards, like ‘this had to happen’ and stuff with no remorse, plus it explains why he infected his younger and weaker daughter rather than his older and stronger son, *and* why my mom didn’t try to stop him from doing it. I just…” I sighed. “He was just so awful, you know, experimenting and stuff after, and that makes me wonder what he was really thinking. He was always eccentric, but I never thought he could be cruel. But it completely aligns with his obsessive personality. I mean, the guy could barely hold a job just because he was so focused on his new adventures, even when his family’s stability was on the line…” I trailed off and shrugged. “I don’t know.”

Her grey blue eyes were like sponges, soaking in my every word. “How do you feel about it?”

“Well…” I finally just flicked my ponytail behind my shoulder so I’d stop playing with it. “Part of me wants to ask him. But part of me never wants to see him again. And I wonder if it would even matter because I’m already so used to blaming him…” I threw my hands up in the air. “And then I think should just move to Siberia.”

Ellen’s mouth pulled into a half grin. “You’ll need a pretty big coat for that.”

I laughed once, dropping my gaze to the ground. “Yeah.”

She gave me a little squeeze and another muffin.

I smiled. "Thanks." I hoped she knew I meant not just for the food. For some reason, her aura made me feel home, like I could tell her just about anything.

"Anytime, Big A," she said as she turned back toward her bowl, then she stopped and we both burst into laughter. "Okay, I'm definitely not using that one again."

"Good call."

I hung out with her until I had to go get ready for the show. She wished me good luck as I weaved my way out of the kitchen and headed on over to the production building.

Stopping in the girl's locker room, I took a shower, scrubbing off the extra grime and sweat from the past few days, feeling as though I was scrubbing off the memories too. Thinking was a bad idea for me on show nights. If I really thought about what I was doing, I wouldn't be able to make it through and Miss Welch would have my head. In a way, I looked at it much like a production myself—I had to be a different person, or at least act like one. I had to be in the public eye. I had to be entertaining. I had to look like my alarm didn't go off at four thirty this morning just so I could get the tar beat out of me by my bipolar best friend.

It was a lot of pressure for me. But I was sure that's why Cyrus made me do it. Again, his voice from earlier echoed in my head: *You're mentally blocking the key from taking over—we've discussed this, Arie. You need to just let nature run its course.*

I let the water run over my face, washing his voice out of my ears. I'd think about it later.

You know, I'm getting really excited for whenever this 'later' is. Vanessa smirked. *That's going to be an eventful day of reckoning.*

You know, I'm getting really tired of your opinions.

I continued my ritual before the show, heading to my dressing cubicle where a team of four—three girls and one guy—were there waiting for me, standing around a styling chair placed in the center.

The guy motioned for me to sit and I obeyed. He had the perfectly swept up hair, the kind that you see in the magazines. For the next few hours, I was a human Barbie doll, sitting completely still as I was pulled, prodded, brushed, and beautified. I never talked to the Beauty Team while they were working on me and they never talked to me unless vital information needed to be passed along.

Once I was almost done, they left so I could change into my outfit before applying the finishing touches. I stood from my chair and unzipped the bag hanging on my wall to reveal my dress: it was the same style as my favorite black one, which I loved, but it was gold. I might've liked the gold if it weren't for the sequins. Gold sequins. Everywhere.

My stomach clenched with painful nerves. *I don't wear gold sequins.*

You do now, princess. Vanessa just laughed. *That'll stop traffic for sure.*

Lovely.

I didn't have a choice though, so I put on the dress, along with the earrings, shoes, and earpiece that matched. Opening my cubicle door to let them know I was ready, I sat back in my chair and waited for the team. They came in and finished me up. I held my breath to keep from choking on the cloud of hairspray that enveloped me, as my hair was spruced and my face perfected.

The guy took a step back to look at me, then kissed his hand and held it in the air. "Mwah! You're gorgeous."

"Thanks guys," I said as they packed up their supplies and went on to the next performer.

I wandered out of my cubicle and into the common area of the dressing room, people scampering in and out, their hair half done or part of their costume missing. I watched them go twice, once in front of me and once in the giant mirror on the wall across from me. My reflection sparkled thanks to the dress, and I had to get closer to the mirror to get a better look at myself.

The Beauty Team does great work. My face was smooth and clear, despite the colonies of zits I knew were hidden underneath the makeup, and my features were made to look exactly symmetrical, adding to the thought I had earlier that I had aged. It was true that my reflection was beautiful, but I'd bet anyone's would be if they had a Beauty Team on call and four tons of makeup on their face.

"I literally do not care at all whose fault you think it was," Elijah was arguing with another boy as they came into the common room. "Blunders like that will *not* be tolerated on this stage."

The unlucky boy was exasperated. "I told you, Ray—"

Elijah stopped and turned to face him. "You aren't hearing me, so read my lips." He said each word deliberately, like its own shot. "Don't. Let. It. Happen. Again."

The boy pursed his lips. "Fine." Then he stalked away.

Elijah sighed and fixed the cuffs on his gold shirt. Our eyes met in the mirror and he gave me a small grin as he glided over to me.

He rolled his eyes. "Performers—such a prideful group."

My mouth twitched. "Yeah, what a bunch of weirdos."

Taking me by my shoulders, he turned me to face him, and his narrowed eyes went over me again and again, checking me off. Fixing my hair, smoothing my skirt, smudging my blush, and whatever else wasn't up to his par. I didn't usually flinch when Elijah touched me anymore because I'd learned how touchy of a person he was, especially while performing. With everyone. Too many girls had been found crying in the bathroom claiming stories of how he'd horrifically led them on.

"Gorgeous," Elijah told me after I passed inspection. "You dazzle like the North Star."

I tried not to smile too big. "Thanks."

Sadie skipped over to us, violet eyes shining as she asked Elijah to check her off. I bit the inside of my cheek to keep from rolling my eyes and snorting.

I'd already given up any claim I could have to Elijah, since that first month when he'd invited me over after a late rehearsal. I had politely declined, and he just smiled and shrugged, not seeming too upset, but I was sick about it all night until I saw him again the next day, sure he would be bitter about the whole thing—or worse, he would spread some story about how I'd said *yes*, which happened way too much. Elijah did neither. Instead, he complimented my eyeliner and told me my star power had to be heightened for our new chorus. In short, he treated me exactly the same, and my respect for him multiplied by a million.

After sharing a moment with a giggling Sadie, Elijah touched the earpiece in his ear. "Sound check," he said, his voice repeating in my ear. "Sound check, one, two three."

I touched my earpiece. "That's a go."

Miss Welch sauntered into the dressing room, wearing a flowing yellow and pink floral dress that looked like it was made out of my grandma's curtains.

"The director is here," she announced. "Everyone take your places: it's show time."

It's show time.

I followed Elijah up the stairs and onto the darkened stage, grabbing our microphones on the way, several dancers trailing behind us. A sea of partygoers was spread throughout the space, making the once vast and cold room feel crowded and warm with body heat.

Five will turn to six, and then we'll go to seven, and this will be over.

There's a ton of people out there, Vanessa commented, which was very unnecessary.

I fixed my stance, stabilizing myself on my heels. *Shut up.*

They'll all be watching you.

I brushed a rogue piece of hair out of my face. *Shut up.*

Well, I'm just hoping you don't screw up. Especially in front of all those people.

I flipped the switch on my mic, turning it on. *Shut up.*

Who am I kidding? Of course you will. I guess the real question we must ask ourselves is 'how?'

Shut up. Shut up. Shut up.

Elijah gave me a nod and I heard his voice in my ear. "Let's go."

I braced myself. *It's show time.*

I brought the mic to my mouth, transforming into another creature entirely. "Good evening, ladies and gentlemen, boys and girls. Are we ready to have a good time tonight?"

The crowd screamed back at me as the blinding lights illuminated the stage, forcing us out of hiding. The guitar strummed, the drum picked up the beat, and the show began.

For me, starting was always the hardest. As the night went on, it was easier to get caught up in the energy of the party, to immerse myself in the spirit of these young adults whose biggest problems were what drink they should order from the bar and how to get the hot person to dance with them. Despite everything, I still loved music, and I still found solace in it as I lost myself in the blaring notes.

To be fair to the well-dressed kids who turned into senseless idiots on the weekends, they made for a great crowd. They would cheer and dance and sing along, screaming our names, truly making the lively atmosphere what it was. I had to be careful, though, especially when going up and down the runway, because the crowd could get a little *too* excited. We had to have a safety meeting after some guy grabbed Zoe's ankle while she was performing and yanked her off the stage.

Thankfully, I wasn't on stage the entire show—we usually couldn't clear everyone out until one or two in the morning, so we took turns being the main entertainer. I always opened and closed, sometimes doing collaborations with Elijah or Zoe, and would have a block in the middle too. When I wasn't on, Elijah took over, then Zoe, then Ray, then whoever. I was 'off duty' so I usually went down to the kitchen or the bar to find Ellen. If she wasn't around, then I'd hang out in my dressing cubicle until I was needed again.

During my breaks I'd head over to the bar and hang out with Ellen. She'd get me water and I'd take a minute to rest up, then start helping her fill orders. We'd usually have at least a couple incidents in which we'd have to call Andon over to help specific guests—Andon was the saint that would come to our rescue when drunk guys took flirting too far. He had no tolerance for jerks, and since his arms were as thick as my waist, most people tended to back off when he sauntered over. It was nice to have him around, especially on the weekends.

The bar got busy and I helped Ellen's team fill orders, laughing as Ellen broke into a hair-flipping, arms-flying dance routine every chance she got. There was so much going on at once that I didn't notice someone watching me from their seat at the counter until it was too late.

His swept his hand through his crisp bronze hair, held up, I was sure, by the greasy gel it was caked with. "Hey, Arie. What's up?"

My heart sank and I internally groaned, but my face smiled courteously. "Hey, Walker. How's it going?"

"It's going good."

Ellen tapped her foot against mine as she passed—I knew she was smirking, but I couldn't look at her or else I would laugh. I only knew a few things about Walker: he was a frequent partygoer, as his family was one of the more permanent residents, and his name conveniently rhymed with 'stalker' which was the best word to sum up his relationship to me.

His muddy brown eyes stared at me in a way I thought was largely inappropriate. I pretended to be *really* busy cleaning a glass, as though the fate of the Earth depended on my job.

"You know, you do such a great job on stage," he told me for the billionth time since he'd approached me here months ago. "And you're killing it in that dress."

Please, Universe, just let me die. "Thanks, Walker."

Vanessa was disgusted. *Ugh, I'll die with you.*

Since he was a guest, I couldn't tell him to leave me alone, and any sort of nice hint—like me trying to avoid him as though he were a rabid grizzly bear carrying the plague—just went right over his head.

He continued, oblivious to my discomfort. "Really, like, 'sexy' doesn't do you justice at all. You're more than smoking hot."

And you're more than creepy and awkward.

Thankfully, I didn't have to respond to that. A voice came through my earpiece, telling me I needed to prepare backstage.

I tapped my earpiece apologetically. "I'm sorry, I gotta go." I saluted Ellen, who nodded at me with a suppressed grin, and I hoisted myself back over the counter, disappearing before Stalker Walker could say goodbye.

How come Stalker Walkers are the only kind of guys you can attract? Vanessa complained. *I want a hot man all over me. I deserve that.*

You know, anytime you want to get out and try it on your own, I'd support you one hundred percent.

Oh, come on, princess, you don't mean that. She puckered her lips and forced more of her influence on me. *You'd miss me too much.*

I closed my eyes and breathed through my nose, reminding myself I was still in control. I was still here.

Yeah, I said, still managing a sarcastic tone. *You wish.*

~~~

"Left arm please," the boy in the lab coat instructed, his voice monotone but, by the
~~~

animation in his hazel eyes, I sensed that maybe he was flattening his tone on purpose.

I rolled up the black sleeve on my dress, held out my exposed arm, and turned my head as the boy tied a rubber strip around my arm. Even when getting these lab tests done three times a week, I still couldn't watch when my blood was taken. Silly, considering how much blood I'd seen in my time.

The needle pricked me, and I stared at the white wall of the research lab as my blood was forcibly extracted from my body. I hated lab tests. I hated that even when I asked, nobody would tell me what the lab tests were used for, heightening my crushing terror that Cyrus wasn't lying when he said he knew how to bring the key to life.

The boy removed the rubber strip and taped a cotton ball to the inside of my elbow.

"Done," he told me.

I turned my head to see the six vials filled with my blood. "Are you sure you got enough?" I muttered. It was the phrase I used after every blood drawing, hoping I could get some kid in a lab coat to slip up and say, "Oh, well we need six vials because we're using it to create an atomic bomb," or something. Anything. Any clue that would tell me what they were engineering down here.

The boy just shrugged as he gathered the vials. "You're quite the project."

I raised an eyebrow. *Project? Seriously?*

Vanessa was excited. *We went from 'experiment' to 'project.' You know what that means?*

What?

They know what they're doing. Your time's almost up. She smiled. *I'm going to get out of here.*

"Uh, you can go now," the boy said, his face uncertain, bringing me out of my overwrought head.

"Oh. Right." The paper on the examination table crackled as I rolled down my sleeve, slid off the table, and made my way through the automatic door.

The hallway seemed to stretch on forever—I strode past dozens of labs wondering what was going on behind those doors but knowing I couldn't find out. The passwords for the labs were the only ones I wasn't given access to. Of course, the research building was used for medical purposes too, should we need it, but Cyrus didn't get weapons like Micah and the mutations by just guessing.

Right now, behind one of these doors, someone is working to let me out, Vanessa said. *Isn't that exciting?*

I gritted my teeth. *It's not going to happen.*

Oh, princess, the denial is so pitiful. I almost feel bad for you. Almost.

It was cloudy out today. The air wasn't cold, but it wasn't warm either, missing the sun to heat it up. Usually I liked cloudy weather, when it felt the sky was a giant blanket, but today's cloudy was gloomy, like a prison cell. And it wasn't just me who thought that either: I had to stop in on a labor group earlier and break up a brawl two guys had gotten into. Tasks like that made me grateful for my nasty reputation.

Tonight was the fundraiser Ellen had asked me to help with, but I still had some time before she needed me, so I decided to make a much-needed trip to the Dome. It housed what Cyrus considered his future: fourteen infected kids, all under the age of thirteen.

There was a divide in the infected community at the Compound between those like Micah who were raised here, and those like Ellen and I who were brought here. Of course, Ellen was way more adjusted than me: I'd only been here about six months while she'd been here over seven years.

It broke my heart, the thought of these young kids struggling with infection while shut away from the world. Every time I saw them I was reminded of my own favorite infected kids— Hadley and Jacklynn—and I wanted to do whatever I could for them, even if it was just be their friend.

The Dome was on the east side of the Compound, toward the north/south split, a giant white curvature amid the dirt. I typed in the password and stepped into the cavernous space. Fourteen heads turned to look at their visitor.

"Arie!"

Eight kids abandoned what they were doing to come give me hugs and high fives; the other six stayed put. Not every kid was in the Arie Nolan Fan Club. One girl glared at me as though I were steamed broccoli, one girl and one boy were too scared to come within twenty feet of me, and two boys and another girl didn't think I was worth their time. The other eight kids, though, were the best.

Ranger, a ten-year-old with galaxies for eyes scrunched up his face when he saw me, after giving me a high five.

"What happened to your nose?" he asked. "It looks different."

"Yeah," Sharna chirped, flicking her wild blonde hair out of her face. "What happened to your nose?"

I automatically caressed my nose with my fingers—I'd forgotten about my injury. "Oh, uh, I broke it during training this morning." Of course, I didn't know between Micah and Roland who broke it and who re-broke it, but the distinction didn't really matter.

Fozzy's mouth dropped open, releasing his gum, and he quickly retrieved it from the floor and put it back in his mouth. "Did it hurt?"

I shrugged. "Eh, not that bad. How's it going in here?"

Lotti held her hands over her face dramatically. "We're *so* bored!"

"Yeah," Sharna echoed, "we're *so* bored!"

Tai jumped up and down, as though that allowed me to see her better. "I'm so glad you're here! I want to know what happens to the lions!"

I grinned. "All right then, we better get started." We all moved to the sleeping section so they could sit on their cots as I told them stories.

There wasn't much for the kids in The Dome: National Geographic was the only television available, and while there were tons of informative books, blocks, and artistic supplies, the kids often got bored when that was their only entertainment all day every day. They weren't allowed to leave.

They ate, slept, and lived in The Dome, only seeing the three caretakers and any visitors, which was basically just me. The ceiling would open for a few hours every day to allow the kids to get some natural light, but that was about it.

I had wracked my brain trying to think of something I could do to help the kids experience an aspect of growing up that they'd missed out on. It took me a few weeks, but I finally boiled down the epitome of my childhood: I started reenacting every animated movie I'd ever seen. And the kids loved it—even the ones who didn't like me paid attention to the mysterious magical stories.

"We just got to the part where the dad died," JP informed me, his lips unable to contain his oversized teeth.

"Okay." I leaned up against a bed and cleared my throat before continuing the story. "So, the uncle comes over…"

I was a few minutes into it when a little girl came wandering over and sat on my lap, sucking her thumb. She did that every time I came: kept her distance until the story had started, then slowly got closer until she was sitting right in my lap. Her body was teeny—I think she was about six or so— and I'd never heard her speak. She just sucked her thumb. The kids called her Bea, which she responded to, but never with words. Being so young, she was the only kid here that wasn't already infected, though her time was set. The thought broke my heart.

Like her, almost every kid who was raised at the Compound had been donated to Cyrus by their parents in the name of the cause. It still infuriated me that parents had the capacity to just 'donate' their kids. That's what happened to Micah, and I sometimes got the feeling it bothered him more than he let on, despite him swearing on his grave he didn't care to know about his parents or their reasons.

"I'm so sorry," I told him once, after asking how he'd gotten to the Compound. "That's awful."

He'd just smirked. "Don't be. They're dead to me. I have nothing to miss. It's better this way."

I didn't believe that, but he did. Apparently, Cyrus or Roland or someone had sold him on the idea that the Compound was the only place he could belong. That was the very last thing I wanted the kids to think too.

I continued with my story, often interrupted by Ranger asking what color the sky was in a particular scene or Fozzy pulling out an atlas to cross reference landscapes so he could imagine it just right. It was meticulous storytelling.

Because of the constant interruption for details, we didn't get to finish the story by the time my earpiece crackled. Ellen's voice came through, asking if I could come help her out. I let her know I was on my way.

I picked up the thumb-sucking Bea and placed her on the cot next to me. "Okay, guys, I gotta go."

A chorus of 'aw, man' and 'really?' and 'but you didn't finish!' came back at me.

"I know, I'm sorry. We'll finish the story next time, okay?"

"Come back soon!" Elmo crowed.

"Yeah," Sharna said, "come back soon!"

"I will," I promised before I left the Dome and headed for the restaurant.

There was already a crowd at the front door, a long line of chortling and social adults dressed as though they'd missed their prom and were making up for it tonight. Per usual, I took the workers' entrance into the kitchen, finding it half as full as the last time I was here.

Ellen was standing in the middle, surveying her workers, her lopsided ponytail just adding to her stressed demeanor. She perked up when she saw me.

"Oh good," she said, gesturing to me. "I realized I forgot to tell you to wear a dress."

I gave her a thumbs up. "I gotcha covered. Now, what do you need me to do?"

She sighed in defeat. "Everything."

"Come on." I pulled on her arm. "You can do this. Let's get started."

She was right: it was insane. Because of double booking with the cafeteria, Ellen had half the staff, and, because of a special event rather than dinner spread out over a few hours, three times the guests. The kitchen was rampant with semi-organized chaos as everyone rushed to keep up with the demands of the party.

I helped out in the kitchen—mostly just running supplies from one station to another—until the party got started. And, oh what a party. The restaurant was stunning to begin with, but now there were twinkling lights, gold and silver decorative balls, extravagant floral centerpieces on every table, and a small band in the corner playing soft music with Zoe singing along. A banner hung over the sea of people, reminding everyone to donate to the subject of the fundraiser: a Dr. Hammond guy. Whoever he was, he must've been on Cyrus' good side to get such a nice party.

Tying the white apron-like fabric around my waist, I became a waitress for the evening, at the beck and call of the posh and stuck-up guests who laughed at stupid jokes and incessantly bragged about how much money they bathed in that morning.

I hate these people.

Vanessa actually agreed with me. *They're idiots.*

Somehow, I managed to keep the courteous smile on my face, catering to every fork dropped on the floor and returning every slightly burned piece of fish, apologizing for our indecency to avoid getting chewed out or marked down on complaint.

Cyrus even made an appearance, Roland at his side, as they sat at the biggest center table. I made it a point to avoid that table, letting other waitresses with bravery pick it up. Both Cyrus and Roland gave me glances from time to time, but neither actually acknowledged me, which I was grateful for. Getting introduced to their friends was the worst.

By the end of the evening, we were exhausted. After the restaurant was cleaned up, dishes were done, and ingredients put away, Ellen held a celebratory ice cream party on the floor of the kitchen. We all sat around eating out of the cartons.

"To all of us," Ellen announced, holding up a spoonful of strawberry cheesecake ice cream, "for pulling off the greatest fundraiser this world has ever seen."

We ate ourselves into a frozen coma, some people stretching out on the kitchen floor and passing out right there. I sat against the counter, Ellen's head in my lap as she tried to balance her spoon on her nose. My eyes were tired, so I closed them.

"Good job," I said to Ellen, my voice hushed. "Told you you could do it."

"Thanks for your help. You're such a pal, Arimonda." We both burst out in exhausted half laughter.

It took me a long time to fully recognize the sound in the distance. A soft beeping sound. Familiar to me. I ignored it for a minute, then had the feeling I should check it out.

Cracking my eyes open, I was surprised to find myself sprawled on the floor, Ellen's head resting against my legs as she slept. The beeping was coming from my earpiece on the floor next to my face.

I bolted up to see the clock on the oven. It was seven in the morning.

You've got to be kidding me.

Vanessa laughed in disbelief. *Oh man, sucks to be you.*

Gently moving Ellen's head off me and onto my bunched up apron, I snatched my earpiece and hopped across the unconscious bodies on the floor, breaking into a run when I got out the door.

It was cloudy again today. There was no sun to guide me as I sprinted to the training building. I went straight up the stairs and into the bathroom, raiding my locker for extra supplies and changing into combat clothes, lacing up my boots as I half ran into the arena. Straightening up, I saw Micah at the punching bag, Scottsman typing something into a tablet while Roland whistled at Micah to be faster.

The door shut behind me, the sound echoing my damnation throughout the arena. Roland turned, jaw set, glaring lasers at me.

"You're late."

And just like that, those two words became the omen for my entire day.

4

Roland kept me for hours to make up for my tardiness. When the shouting finally ended and I was let go, I stumbled out under the cloudy sky with a dislocated shoulder (kindly set back in place by Micah) and a possibly sprained ankle. I had just taken the first step toward home when a beeping sounded in my ear: Cyrus wanted to talk to me.

I groaned and stopped in my tracks, just standing in the dirt wondering what I should do with my life. Moving to Siberia sounded pretty good.

It was probably a solid three minutes before I ducked back into the training room bathroom, carefully changed into my wrinkled black dress, and half hobbled to the administration building.

Cyrus was sitting at his desk again, but there was no tablet to entertain him this time. His eyes scanned me as I sat down in the chair. I was too tired to tell if my face was giving anything away.

I'm too tired for mind games.

He stared at me. I stared back. He didn't seem to be looking for anything specific. I got increasingly irritated at the thought that he'd dragged me up here for absolutely nothing.

Am I missing something? I was suddenly panicked that I'd forgotten something important. *Let's see, last time we had the solitaire discovery, talked about breaching, he asked me to...*

And then I got it. Teaching moment.

Just get this over with.

I took a deep breath, preparing myself. "Why did you send me into the prison?"

He clasped his hands on his desk. "Well, dear, I'm glad you asked. How was your experience?"

"It was awful," I stated, voice flat.

"I expected as much. Now do you better understand what I've done for you?"

I squared my jaw and just stared at him.

Don't be stubborn, Vanessa told me.

Too late.

Cyrus cleared his throat in disapproval. "I may not look it, Arie, but I am powerful. Do you see that?"

"Yes, sir, I do."

My clipped answer wasn't enough for him. "Do you realize that I control the entire infected world? That people such as the likes of your Alexis only rise to power because I allow them to? They don't have the slightest clue I exist and yet I control them all like puppets until I attain what I need."

"What did you need from Alexis?" I asked because I guess all bets were off for me today.

The normal side of his face pulled into a small grin. "You, among other things."

"Like?"

"Oh, this and that." He motioned with his hands as he rambled. "Certain people in certain places with certain things. Stephen White was a big contributor."

A faint gasp escaped through my teeth, though in hindsight the revelation wasn't surprising. "You were the one who funded White's reversal project."

He grin grew. "Honestly, Arie, did you expect anyone else?"

He's got a point, Vanessa said.

I crossed my legs so I could balance my elbow and rest my head in my hand, leaning forward. I'd only been waiting for this story for years. "Well, what happened? How did he get involved in reversal in the first place?"

Cyrus leaned forward too, his eyes becoming slightly more animated as he got lost in the story. "Naturally, it began with the love of science, the thrill of answering the 'what if' of the ages: what if the formula could be reversed? He worked as a head scientist for Alexis while doubling as a handler in the organization. Eventually, however, White became sympathetic to the infected in his charge. He vowed to help her. They became friends and, later, fell in love. Alexis was enraged when he heard news of the treason."

A single laugh of disbelief escaped me. "Yeah, I bet."

"White fled with his infected lover and a half finished reversal process. I saw the opportunity, approached him, and invited him to come work for me here. His success was monumental, a real accomplishment for our field. Then…" His voice trailed off for a moment, but the silence somehow painted the picture for me.

"You let him get caught, didn't you? By Alexis."

Cyrus sighed. "Tragedies do happen. He was identifying with every infected, and his lover begged him to help reverse them all. I did what was necessary to keep Castor's vision alive."

"Why not just kill him yourself?"

The grin reappeared. "Now, dear, that wouldn't have been nearly as much fun."

My voice lost half its volume. "What about the girl?"

"Once she'd served her purpose, Roland was more than happy to take care of her."

I shuddered in spite of myself. Poor girl.

"Of course, this story does sound familiar to you, doesn't it?" Cyrus' tone was conversational now, anticipating response. "One of Alexis' top men leaving everything he knows simply because he'd grown sympathetic to his infected."

Ding ding. Vanessa smirked. *I believe the answer he's looking for is 'Sark.'*

I couldn't wipe the surprise from my face—I'd never made that connection.

Cyrus chuckled at my expression. "And you thought the comparison between Sark and White didn't mean anything more than matching fates."

I took a deep breath to compose myself. "I was never going to let Sark die like that."

"No, of course not." Cyrus shook his head, almost in appreciation. "Such an ambition, even as a mere adolescent. It's no wonder he survived the challenge he took."

Challenge? "He survived because he's smart and strong," I said, my voice guarded. "He knew what he was doing."

"Well of course he did. I can't imagine being as young as he was and watching what Alexis did to White. That would leave quite the impression, I would say." He stared into space, as if pondering. "Quite the impression."

I folded my arms, not sure where this was headed. "Yeah, it never left him. That's why he had to hide from Alexis."

"Yes, he did. He was quite good at it too, even at your expense."

My eyebrows shot up. "My *expense*? Sark did everything to—"

"I'm aware of the risks he took for you." He nodded in appreciation again. "Quite brave. Quite ambitious. He's always had that about him, hasn't he? The cockiness, in a way. The desire to beat everyone else. Rise to the challenge. Quite interesting. It almost makes me wonder...how much of what he's done was out of his noble heart and how much was out of that cocky ambition?"

I just stared at him, jumbled excuses lodged in my throat.

Cyrus unclasped his hands, leaning back in his chair. "After all, beating the story, the shocking standard set by White—and getting away with it, no less—would be the ultimate ambitious challenge." He paused and looked into my eyes. "Very interesting, isn't it?"

Vanessa was practically squealing with joy. *Oh man, this guy is so good.*

I cleared my throat but the only thing I could think to say was, "That's insane."

"I was only suggesting a possible motive for his actions."

"Well your suggestion is wrong," I said, fighting the desperation creeping into my voice. "Sark and I—"

"I know. You care for one another. A bond forged in the fiery crucible of tribulation doesn't often break easily. Of course, that isn't to say it couldn't."

"I…" I was so confused. "Maybe you just wouldn't understand."

Cyrus nodded at me. "Maybe I wouldn't. But I do find it interesting that this is the second time you've been trapped in a place you didn't want to be and neither Sark nor any other member of your unconventional family has offered any aid. Again."

"That's not fair," I countered. "The first time he thought I was dead. And now…he probably doesn't know I'm here."

"Because you left him nearly dead in a hospital bed in the hands of your adolescent friends and a handful a government agents you barely knew?"

I gritted my teeth. He was twisting everything. "I did that to protect him. To protect all of them."

He raised his good eyebrow. "Protect them from what, dear?"

"From me," I answered automatically, then deflated. My eyes dropped to my hands as I let out a long breath. "Protect them from me."

"It always comes back to that, doesn't it?"

Everything will always come back to that.

Vanessa fake pouted. *Poor Princess Arie doesn't know how to have a healthy relationship because she's a monster. How sad.*

It was quiet as I stared at a hangnail on my finger. It stung. My ankle ached. My insides ached. If it weren't for Cyrus sitting across a desk from me, I would've curled into a ball on the floor.

When did I let him take over this conversation?

Cyrus broke the silence, his voice softer somehow. "Contrary to what you may believe, Arie, I understand the pull of family."

I glanced up at him, but he was staring into space again, lost in another time.

"You have family?" I asked him.

"Had. My family ties forced me to make some hard decisions. There were several wrong choices I made that put me through difficult experiences. Leaving them, being one. Though, one could say returning to see their bodies on the floor of our house was the most difficult experience of my life." His tone hardened. "Pain changes people,

101

Arie. People leave scars that can't heal and then they shun you for appearing so hideous."

A tingle went down my spine, fraying my nerves.

"I'm sorry," I said, not sure why I suddenly felt the need to run.

He ignored me. "Hard choices are coming for you, Arie. And unfortunately I'm not entirely sure you're prepared to make the right ones." He exhaled, as if blowing his troubles away. "Which is why I'm here to help you."

A pit formed in my stomach at his tone. Why did it bother me?

My family ties forced me to make some hard decisions, he'd said. *I'm here to help you.*

"What did you do?" I asked him quietly, my mind racing with the possibilities. "What did you do to them?"

He shifted his jumpy green eyes back to me. "A shipment came in today," he told me, his voice grave. "It's in Roland's possession now, and you know how picky he is with those—especially if he knows it's yours. I hope it gives you some perspective."

A shipment.

I didn't wait for dismissal. I dashed into the elevator, slapping my hand against the door with every second I wasted inside. My ankle screamed at me as I darted out of the elevator and sprinted across the Compound to the warehouse.

I hope they're in pieces, Vanessa told me.

They won't be.

I burst through the door of the warehouse, only stopping to look over the railing and take in the scene one hundred feet below me. A plane had just landed. Nearly twenty armed guards in black uniforms stood in a loose circle around a line of handcuffed people. My heart leapt in my throat when I saw familiar faces: Sark, Hadley, Jacklynn, Alaina, Peter, Brennan, Lucy, Kayla and Daxton. My hands clenched when I saw Lennon. I nearly threw up when I saw ragged versions of my parents at the end of the line.

I didn't have time to process anything though. Two guards were arguing—the two in charge, I assumed—one dark haired and the other blond.

"Did you hear what she did to that guy Linkin last week?" the blond kid was saying, the echoes from his strained voice traveling up to me. "They couldn't even identify him by his *dental records*."

The dark-haired kid was having none of it. "These are our orders. We carry them out."

I didn't have to ask to know what their orders were.

"Hey!" I shouted, my feet taking me down the winding metal staircase two at a time, making the edges of my skirt seem to float in the air.

I felt the room freeze, everyone's heart stopping, my slapping footsteps on the metal stairs the only sound in the silence. Like the blond kid reaffirmed, they were terrified of me—never had I been more grateful for that reputation.

"What do you think you're doing?" I yelled, stalking right up to the two guards.

Blondie's eyes widened and he took a step away from me. Dark Haired held his ground. I kept my eyes on the two in front of me, letting my insane fear overtake what I was doing.

Dark Haired boy met my glare evenly. "We have orders to terminate the new shipment."

"You have new orders now." I gestured to my family but couldn't bring myself to look at their reactions. "I'll take care of it."

He didn't even flinch. "Our orders come from Roland."

"Does it look like Roland's here?"

A few guards shifted on their feet, waiting for the order of dismissal Dark Haired wasn't going to give.

"What's your name?" I demanded, jerking my chin out at Blondie and making him flinch. "Both of you."

Dark Haired gritted his teeth. "Koa. Captain of Labor Group zero-one-nine and the third strike unit."

Poor Blondie could barely keep his voice from trembling. "Cameron. Koa's First Auxiliary."

"Well, *Captain*, your services are no longer required. Get your strike team together and get out."

Cameron started to agree but Koa shook his head. "Our orders are from Roland."

I narrowed my eyes, internally cursing that I was about to sound like Micah. "Captain, do you know who I am?"

Koa shifted his weight uncertainly. "Yes."

"And do you understand my rank?"

"Yes."

"Yes, what?"

Koa scowled. "Yes, ma'am."

"Then why are you still here?"

Cameron tapped Koa on the shoulder with the side of his gun. "C'mon, Koa," he muttered, alarmed eyes still locked on me.

My earpiece beeped in my air, nearly making me jump, and I almost cried. I was late for rehearsal.

Please, please, please buy it. Please just do what I say. I was thirty seconds away from a nervous breakdown.

Koa took a breath. "I'm not sure you're at liberty to command this situation," he said, his voice almost wavering but not quite. "Roland made it clear—"

"Roland's not here and I outrank you," I reminded him, hoping my leaked desperation sounded like animosity. "Now, for the last time, Captain: get your team together and get out." I took a step closer and glared into his eyes as though I could reach into his soul and crush it. "That's an order."

We had a stare-off for the ten longest seconds of my life. Finally, Koa sighed in defeat and dropped his eyes. He made a hand signal in the air and turned to march out of the warehouse, his team following suit.

Breathing hard, I didn't move until I saw the last black uniform disappear behind the door.

Okay, crisis one has been averted, I tried to tell myself calmly. *Now on to the next one.* Unfortunately, I was still in dangerous nervous breakdown territory.

"Come with me," I ordered, beginning to head for the stairs that went down. I took two steps and realized nobody was following.

Bracing myself, I turned to see my line of familiar spectators all staring at me, eyes huge, shocked into silence. I almost laughed at their dazed expressions—I felt so crazy—but instead I just spoke louder.

"I'll explain everything later but *we have to go!*"

Peter took a step toward me, and I decided that was good enough. I turned and scampered past the plane, through a metal door, down more stairs, then slid open the door to the largest storage room. My hands were harsher than I meant to be as I ushered them all inside.

"Stay here and don't leave and I'll be back later," I instructed the floor before seizing the metal door and beginning to slide it back into place. I froze when I saw Hadley curled in a ball on the floor, mouth agape, his eyes locked on me with only one emotion: fear. Hadley was scared of me.

He probably just got an earful from Cameron about how awful you are, Vanessa chimed in cheerfully.

The world stopped turning. Life stopped existing. Everything melted away. It was just me and this little boy. This little boy who stole my heart the bleak night when I promised his parents I'd protect him. This little boy who loved flying paper airplanes and collecting rocks. This little boy who wasn't so little anymore.

Hadley is scared of me.

My earpiece crackled, Elijah's anxious voice coming through. "Arie, where are you? Miss Welch is heading into a frenzy."

Hadley is scared of me. I wrapped an arm around my waist and crumpled to my knees in front of him. *He's scared of me.*

My ear crackled. "Arie? Where are you?"

Slowly, I raised my hand to my ear, pressing the button. "I'm coming," I breathed before turning it off.

Hadley is scared of me. His blue eyes continued to stare at me, fear melting into cautious confusion.

"Don't…" My voice was so quiet that I had to clear my throat and start again, though it didn't help much. "Don't be scared. I'm still…I'm still me."

His voice shook but I heard it crystal clear. "You are?"

My head bounced up and down a hundred times. "Yeah. Yeah, I am. And I…I'm going to come back and protect you, I promise. I just have to go figure some things out first, okay?" I took a shaky breath. "I promise."

Hadley studied me for a moment, then nodded. I nodded to myself before standing up and sliding the door into place.

My body wouldn't move—I gaped at the closed door, on the verge of hyperventilating.

What am I going to do? I bit my lip and pulled on my ponytail. *What am I going to do?*

Well, get your family killed, for one, Vanessa answered. *That'll be fun.*

I gritted my teeth and wrapped my arms around myself, tuning out her excessive comments with the facts I knew were true. It helped calm me to start at the basics and work up.

Your name is Arie, I told myself. *Your name is Arie, you are eighteen years old, and you are infected. You live in the Compound. Your family is here and in danger. There is nothing you can do about that right now. You're late for rehearsal. If you miss rehearsal, suspicions could arise, more people will get involved, and everyone would get in trouble, including your family.*

I took a deep breath. *You're going to go to rehearsal, act like everything is fine, and come back later.*

Another deep breath. I straightened up. Another deep breath. Take one step. Take another. Deep breath. Go to rehearsal.

By the time I got to the production building, I had a better handle on myself. Unfortunately, I then had to deal with Miss Welch. She yelled at me for almost twenty minutes, bringing me in dangerous proximity to the nervous breakdown zone again. I stared at a spot on the wall as she ridiculed my tardiness, my appearance, my wrinkled dress, questioning how much this production team meant to me and if I even cared about my life in general. I don't think she would've appreciated the answers had I been in a position to give them.

Rehearsal was cruel. Thankfully my body had some sort of muscle memory thing going on, allowing me to appease Miss Welch while my mind was thinking about everything but how pointing my toe out changed the ambiance of the number.

What am I going to do? Hadley's fearful face was seared into my memory. *How am I going to explain? What can I even say?*

The last time I saw them Sark was unconscious, Alaina was yelling, Kayla was working on bringing down Alexis, and Peter had witnessed me ugly cry. I left them all without telling anyone besides the government agent Keaton, then got them caught by the real madman when they believed I was carrying out a mission to save their lives. That was not the kind of reunion that promoted good relationships.

The lineup in the warehouse was just the tip of my iceberg. What about all the other infecteds from the club? What about Carl and Sasha and Tristan and others? Liam and Mark? Did they not fill a purpose so Cyrus already killed them?

Not to mention the fact that Lennon was here—did he know his leader was dead? Had he already been with my family, inflicting pain and punishment when Cyrus' men showed up? I couldn't find a real purpose for bringing Alaina's handler here other than to unnerve me.

And I couldn't even tackle my parents. Not yet. It'd been, what…two years now? Three? How was I supposed to talk to them after being separated for that long, especially now that I may or may not know my dad's actual intentions?

Maybe worst of all: what were they going to do when they found out I couldn't save them from this?

The questions never ended. Rehearsal was equal parts short and long, passing in the blink of an eye and yet dragging on for eternities. I couldn't decide if my impatience for it to be over outweighed my dread for what would come after.

Miss Welch dismissed us and I was gone, not even realizing Elijah had asked me a question until I was halfway to the warehouse. The sun was setting, darkness beginning to overtake the sky, the light bursting out in sharp orange rays before it was swallowed by the night.

The engineers had left by then—there was nobody in the warehouse, nobody I had to stop and scare so they wouldn't get in my way. I ran down the two sets of stairs and shoved open the sliding metal door.

Empty.

Musty air was the only thing to greet me, and for a second I wondered if I had imagined the whole thing.

Oh no, princess, Vanessa said. *It's real.*

My hands started shaking as my throat closed up. *What happened to them?*

Reason had gone out the window a long time ago. I marched out of the warehouse and to the administration building. Despite the hours that'd passed, he was still seated behind his desk, eyes distant as though he were waiting for something that happened a long time ago.

I stalked up and slammed my hands on the desk. "What did you do?"

Neither my slamming nor my shouting matched Cyrus' serenity. "Calm down, dear."

"Calm down?" I demanded. "You brought them here! Why…*why* would you bring them here?"

"Be careful, or you'll judge the situation before having all the facts." He closed the book he had been writing in and set his pen down. "Perhaps you don't quite understand the circumstances."

"Understand? *Understand*? I understand that they will die here and you…" I shook my head, exasperated. "This wasn't the deal, Cyrus."

"The deal?" he repeated, raising his good eyebrow. "If we're going back to that, dear, I must question whether you've kept your end of it."

"But I have!" My voice almost broke on the last word. "I'm here. I stick with Micah and obey Roland and let Miss Welch target me even though they all treat me like garbage. I respond to every radio transmission no matter what it is. I go through *every* menial, humiliating, and agonizing thing you force in front of me. What else do you want from me?"

The second the question left my mouth I wished I could take it back. He gazed into my eyes as if reaching down into my being and clawing out every nightmarish secret scar I kept hidden, displaying them for us to see like a museum exhibit.

His voice didn't get harder or louder, but it made me cringe. "I believe you know what I want, dear. The rules haven't changed."

The rules haven't changed.

Suddenly, Cyrus relaxed, reverting back to a cordial tone and giving me a misshapen grin. "Now, as I was saying before you flippantly disregarded your respectful place, I don't believe you truly understand these circumstances. While your blonde scientist friend was getting too close to reversal for comfort, I did not interfere like you seem to think." He leaned back in his chair, twisting his fountain pen slowly in his fingers as he studied me.

I closed my eyes for a moment and took three deep breaths. He was right—Cyrus must be in a great mood if my outburst hadn't angered him. I had to be more careful.

Opening my eyes, I straightened my posture and stared back at him evenly. "Fine. What don't I understand, sir?"

"This morning's shipment wasn't special, Arie. Just another voluntary recruitment case. That's all." With that bombshell, he opened up his book and hunched over to start writing again, as though what he said was nothing.

My mouth fell open, a silent gust of wind blowing out of me like I'd been punched in the gut. I stood there, gawking, trying unsuccessfully to wrap my mind around what he just said.

"Volunt…voluntary recruitment case?" I breathed. "You don't…you don't mean that."

Cyrus didn't even look up at me, focusing on his hands as they created perfect calligraphy on the cream page. "Well, Arie, you know as well as I do how advanced our society is here—the kind of refinement that attracts people. We have infecteds petitioning to be granted access into the Compound all the time, and your family was no different. After a few months of consideration, I decided to grant their request and let them in."

I mulled that over in silence, trying to gauge if he was telling the truth or not. There was no way.

"They weren't aware of your involvement here, of course," Cyrus went on. "Imagine their surprise when they were finally admitted into a safe haven only to find their friend who abandoned them to the wolves. Strange day, indeed."

Unable to find my voice, I did an about-face and took Micah-sized steps to the elevator. Cyrus' voice stopped me halfway.

"I met them, Arie. Wonderful people. Hadley's grown so much, hasn't he?"

I kept walking.

My whole body was shaking when I burst through the door and into the night, nearly crashing into Micah.

I opened my mouth, but he beat me before I could ask. "Yeah." He took on a sarcastic tone. "I just finished giving them the complete Compound tour. They *loved* it. The Q&A at the end was especially satisfying."

A tour? With Micah, of all people? I felt heavier, only imagining how they took that and what idiotic things escaped his mouth. We were back in nervous breakdown zone.

"What's going to happen to them?" I asked, my voice still gone, though I don't know where it went. Probably on a cruise to the Bahamas with my sanity.

"They'll be assigned to a job just like everyone else."

That's lucky, Vanessa muttered. *I thought they'd be sent straight to the mutt house for sure. Too bad.*

She had a point. Their lives were spared, for tonight at least.

What's the endgame, Cyrus? What could you possibly hope to gain from this besides more mouths to feed?

Suddenly Micah exploded, as though something I'd said had angered him, though I'd been really talking to Vanessa—or myself. My skin prickled uncomfortably when I realized I wasn't sure which.

"Look at you, Arie!" he exclaimed. "What is *wrong* with you, huh?"

I recoiled slightly, though he'd said much worse to me in the past.

"Why do you think Cyrus does what he does to you, huh?" Micah went on when I froze. "Why do you think he makes you sing in front of hundreds of people, or have an impossible schedule that leaves you sleep deprived, or train with someone you can't compete with?"

I just stared at him, unsure what move to make. This kind of outburst was unprecedented.

"He's breaking you down," Micah answered for me, "in every single way he knows would be effective for you. Cyrus is patient; he knows how to wait. Having the misfit crew here is just going to make everything worse for you. You're going to lose, and there's nothing you can do about it."

"I have to get them out," I said, my voice hollow. "They can't stay here. They're gonna get hurt, somehow they'll..."

Micah shook his head, giving a scornful laugh, like he couldn't believe what I was saying. "There *is* no way out. You know that better than anyone. You just can't stand the idea of them seeing what you really are."

My hands clenched into fists. "You have no idea what you're talking about."

He opened his mouth as if to argue, but then he stopped himself—very unlike him. Instead, he shook his head and sighed. "Just give Cyrus what he wants before he takes it to the next step."

I snapped my teeth together. "I. Can't."

"Would it really be so bad, Arie? Is becoming the key really the worst thing that could happen?"

"Yes!" I had to hold myself back to keep from hitting him. "And the fact that you can't understand that just proves the kind of monster you are!"

A line like that would've pulled me under, but he just chuckled, a derisive sound. "Well at least I don't pretend to be something I'm not." Then he walked into the building, leaving me with a tongue like sandpaper and a heart that weighed tons.

5

Contrary to my firm belief, the world didn't explode. Maybe it was just my natural pessimism kicking in, but I'd come to learn to expect the absolute worst-case scenario in every situation.

I had to brave the first level of the administration building to access the records and find out where everyone had been placed, though I could guess most of them. Sark, Peter and Brennan were in labor group zero-one-nineteen; Alaina and Lucy were in the kitchen as waitresses; Kayla and Daxton were assigned to the research labs; Hadley and Jacklynn got dumped in the Dome with the rest of the kids while Candace Nolan was added to a cleaning crew.

That's perfect for her, I thought, then stopped, since that was the most normal thought I'd had about my mom in a long time.

There was a mention of Liam Harrison, Alaina's brother, and his 'various associates' being placed in one of the labor camps offsite of the main Compound. It didn't say, though, how many survivors there were or even where exactly the camp was located.

I scanned through the rest, but there was no mention of Lennon or Kurt Nolan. Now I couldn't prepare myself for the location in which I might run into either of them.

This is insane. Cyrus was keeping everything the same. He was going to force the universe to act like nothing was different, knowing that everything had completely changed for me.

I hate him.

The night the new arrivals got there, I didn't sleep a wink, basically lying in semi-conscious anticipation on the cold floor for when my alarm went off and I headed to training, which flew by. I realized that I dreaded any sort of free time or traveling throughout the Compound, terrified I would run into somebody. But that was ridiculous. I loved those people. Why was I so afraid of seeing them after our months of heart wrenching separation?

I didn't know. All I knew was that I only felt my calmest when safely ensnared in an activity.

The Friday show started early that night thanks to some parents paying a fortune for us to host their daughter's twenty-first birthday party. Because of the time change, I had to be at the production building earlier, which I was just fine with.

Unfortunately, Miss Welch still wasn't over my tardiness from yesterday. I spent the time in the beauty chair as a trapped audience to her complaining, moaning and groaning, painting me pictures of the golden days when she was the one on stage rather than being forced to rely on pathetic teenagers who were lucky to have a scrap of talent. It was fun.

To make matters worse, Ellen was on cafeteria duty and wasn't in the building for most of the show, making me a complete loner. Stalker Walker tracked me down and I made the accidental slip that Ellen wasn't there—he was happy to keep me company instead. I sat and somewhat listened as he told me all about his older sister's wedding last month and the online classes he enrolled in because his dad said he had to get a college degree. It made me feel kind of bad, just because he really was a nice guy, in his own twisted way. He just took ten miles when I gave him a centimeter. It made me wish I'd never smiled back politely that night months ago and asked him how he was doing.

Curse being nice. It's no wonder why the bad guys never do it—you just get the short end of the stick.

I put up with it until Walker tried to pull a move on me. Suddenly I was desperately needed back in the dressing room where I hid for the rest of the show.

Despite the birthday girl seeking me out personally at the end to tell me I did a great job, Miss Welch still felt I hadn't learned my lesson: I was on dishes.

There were three others in the kitchen working on cleaning up, but I told them that I'd finish it. They were more than happy to take me up on the offer and I ended up in the dimmed kitchen, alone at the giant dishwashing sink, scrubbing plates at three in the morning.

I was taking out my aggression on some sort of sauce that seemed to have cemented itself on the plate when I heard footsteps—not the steady footsteps of someone walking but the irregular ones of someone attempting to be quiet and quick at the same time.

I stopped my work and strained my ears, but the footsteps stopped too. The thought I was crazy crossed my mind until I sensed someone behind me. We both knew I knew they were there, so I figured there wasn't much else to do but turn around and see what new obstacle awaited me.

I turned and saw Sark. He was thinner and paler than when I last saw him, his cheekbones sticking out more than usual. Dark circles underneath his blue eyes highlighted the wariness in his expression.

We stared at each other. I braced myself for the worst, not sure what that actually entailed. After a few seconds, he closed the space between us in four steps and wrapped me in a crushing hug. I'd never felt so relieved in my life. I dropped my plate in the sudsy water and flung my arms around him, sinking into the sensation of one of his hugs. I felt warm. I felt safe. I felt stupid too. Of course we were okay. It was Sark.

"You're okay," he murmured, more to himself.

"Are you?" I asked with a hollow voice.

"Yeah." He hugged me tighter. "I'm fine."

We broke away, but his gaze surveyed me over and over, as if rememorizing a new face he'd forgotten. I wondered how different I looked since he'd last seen me.

"How'd you find me?" I finally asked.

"I asked around. I'm glad you stayed late—it took me forever to sneak out and get here."

I gave a small grin. "Of course you did."

"So," he said, taking a deep breath and rubbed his hands together, as if ready to hash out a brilliant escape plan. "Not everyone will come, but first thing's first: how are we getting out of here?"

My heart sank. I stepped away from him and clasped my hands. There was no easy way to do this.

A drip of relief fell out of his eyes, guarded suspicion taking its place. "Arie?"

"Um, well…" I trailed off. I had no idea what to say. I should have planned something to say.

Too late now.

He tried to keep his tone light. "You know, usually when you don't answer it means something's going on. Makes me nervous."

Me too.

You should be, Vanessa told me. *He's going to be mad.*

No he won't.

But part of me was afraid he really would.

His eyes shifted again: less relief, more suspicion. "You aren't leaving."

"Sark...I can't."

I was expecting a more surprised reaction, but he didn't miss a beat. "Can't or won't?"

My forehead creased. "What's that supposed to mean?"

Sark chuckled darkly, shaking his head. "You know, I didn't buy it at first. I really wanted to give you the benefit of the doubt but..."

"What are you talking about?"

Relief was gone now. His eyes were all suspicion as he took a stiff half step away from me. "Arie, have you even *tried* to get out of here?"

I recoiled at the furious accusation in his tone. "I can't," I whispered.

"Really? You have access to every part of this place, nearly everyone under your command, and you're telling me you can't get out despite the fact they plan to use you as a weapon?"

I quickly blocked the memory as it came, but parts still pushed through: the conversation. The explosion. The body. The screaming. My screaming.

I shuddered. "I just can't, okay? I'm sorry. I wish I had a better answer. I just...I don't..."

Sark narrowed his eyes. It was a test, I realized. Him coming over here, finding me, talking to me was him testing me. And I had failed.

Told you, Vanessa taunted.

"No," I said, urgently trying to fix the situation. I didn't want it to end up like this. "Let's...let's just talk about something else."

It's been so long.

Wrong thing to say—he ran a hand through his hair, the anger bubbling up from where he had hidden it under the surface. "You want to talk about something else? All right, let's talk about how I was in the hospital—

I wrapped my arms around myself. "Sark—"

"Woke up and asked for you, and they told me *you were gone.*"

A lumped formed in my throat. "I'm sorry," I managed to choke out.

Sark aimed the words at me like javelins. "You didn't warn me. You didn't tell me anything."

"You wouldn't have let me go."

"I had to find out from Lindsey—the government agent we barely knew—that she couldn't find you. Alaina finally fessed up that she knew you left." He shook his head, squaring his jaw in an attempt to distract from his eyes breaking. "I tried to fight my way out to go after you and the doctor finally had to sedate me again."

That hurt. The image chiseled at what was left of my heart and I almost crumbled. My feet were timid as I stepped toward him, my hand half outstretched for his arm as I waited for permission.

Please don't let this happen, I begged myself or Sark or the universe. I wasn't sure which. *It can't end this way.*

Sark hung his head, letting me hug his arm but just standing there, rigid, fully displaying the feelings of betrayal he had been trying to fight.

And I saw it now without knowing what Micah or Cyrus said to Sark and the rest of them. I saw the master plan: paint me as a traitor, now loyal to a different body, only enhanced by the way I act and am received at the Compound, and my resolve to never leave despite the danger. Cutting off my family, my last tie, my last coal in the fire that kept me fighting the fate I was doomed to. Cyrus betting on the fact I was too hopeless to build up the relationships again knowing my future was insecure at best.

Sark's voice was low and rough as he whispered, "When will you get it in your head that people care about you? And what you do—how you handle yourself—affects them too."

"I'm sorry," I whispered again, both for what I did to him and what I now wouldn't. He just pulled his arm out of my hold to turn and stalk out.

My body didn't know how to work. I stayed rooted in place, my head swimming in tears that wouldn't come out, as I considered the new situation.

I didn't know how much time had passed when I jerked myself back over to the sink, picked up the plate and started washing again. Like a robot. Is that what I was now? An unfeeling robot that went through the stupid motions again and again?

My hand raised and dropped forcefully. A crashing sounded as the plate smashed into a million pieces. I crouched down and sat on the floor among the fragmented shards, shards that were broken in a way that just couldn't be fixed. They'd never be whole again.

I wanted to give you the benefit of the doubt, he'd said.

Me too, Sark. Me too.

<div style="text-align:center">~~~</div>

The next person I ran into was in the lab the next afternoon. I was in for my tests again, sitting on the paper covered exam table and picking the nail polish off my fingers while I waited for one of the scientists to come in and get on with it.

The door slid open and a blonde in a lab coat walked in carrying a tablet. Kayla's eyes mirrored the shock that must've been found in mine. She cleared her throat, then turned her attention back to her tablet and began gathering the supplies she needed.

She kept her eyes focused on her tablet. My fingernails got a whole lot more interesting. I could almost see the gray gel of awkwardness in the air.

"Put your finger in this," she ordered, her voice bland, holding out a small box with a hole in it. I obeyed. She still wouldn't look at me.

Do I say anything? I wondered. *But what would I even say?*

As always, Vanessa put in her two cents. *She obviously hates you. If you talk to her, she'll just get even angrier. If you don't, you'll come off a bigger brat than you are.*

I guess with those odds I didn't have much to lose. Thankfully, Kayla made the choice for me.

"Tell me it's not true," she said as she typed into her tablet.

I thought for a moment but came up with nothing good. "I guess it depends on what you think is true."

She sighed, taking the cube off my finger. "Back at the hospital…you gave me Jefferson's flash drive. The next day, you were gone. Nobody had any ideas, which, I assume, was your point."

I nodded though she wasn't looking at me. She wrapped the cuff around my arm to take my blood pressure.

"But Lindsey Carter was keeping what tabs she could on Alexis, anticipating their counterattack. Weeks had passed when she got word that one of his locations had gone down. We deduced that it must've been you."

The cuff tightened on my arm, and she met my eyes.

I cleared my throat. "Yeah. It was me."

Kayla nodded, looking down at her tablet again.

"Will you just…" I sighed. "Will you just tell me what this looks like? From you guys?"

She was quick to respond, her tone edgy. "It looks like you abandoned us for a safe haven."

I almost laughed. The Compound a safe haven? Especially for me?

Kayla didn't notice my reaction. "It looks like you chose your killer friend Micah over us, justifying your leaving by giving me the information you did to take down Alexis. As if that could keep us safe."

"It didn't?" My heart ached.

"Not as much as I'm sure you hoped." She ripped the cuff off my arm and typed in her tablet again.

"Would you believe me if I told you it's not exactly what you think?" I asked.

"I would really want to, Arie." She met my eyes again. "Really. I don't want to think you're the monster they paint you to be. Especially after all the time we spent trying to figure out a way to reverse you…of course I would want to believe you."

I knew Kayla would stick with her facts. She was a scientist, after all.

"So you won't."

"They're just words," she answered. "Yours against the unnerving short man—Cyrus. If you want to prove something then you have to back it up with action."

I winced, thinking of my conversation with Sark last night. "Do you ever see each other?"

"Right now we all sleep in the same quarters." Kayla knew exactly what I was getting at. "Sark was rather colorful last night after talking to you."

"What did he say?" I asked, not sure if I really wanted to know.

"What did he say or what did he shout while storming around the room punching things?"

I couldn't answer that. I just waited. Her eyes softened when she saw mine.

"He said Cyrus was right: it's too late for you. You're established here. You belong here." Her voice nearly broke, surprising me by showing how much she cared for me. She half smiled sadly. "You're the key."

I dropped my eyes and took a shaky breath. "I'm sorry," I mumbled.

Kayla sighed. "It's just—"

The door slid open and another lab coat entered, giving Kayla a disapproving look.

"We aren't supposed to talk," he instructed, gathering the supplies on a silver cart to draw my blood.

Kayla's eyebrows creased in confusion and she adjusted her glasses. "I talked to the other patients."

The guy glared at me but still addressed her. "Yeah, well she's not a patient: she's an experiment."

Ouch. I stared at the ground as Kayla and the guy finished my labs in silence.

"You're done," he told me after taping a cotton ball on my arm. He was only halfway through the second word when I ducked out of the lab.

Later I decided to stop in and see Ellen before the show. I sat in my spot on the counter, popping chocolate chips as though they were painkillers as I listened to her cafeteria duty stories.

"Oh," she said, sautéing vegetables in a pan. "You know what else happened? We got two more waitresses added. They're on Lanny's team, not mine, but I heard they're total newbies—not even transfers. Isn't that crazy that we got two of them at the same time?"

I was about to agree when I saw them enter from the restaurant, both in waitress uniforms. Lucy's brown ringlets were pulled into a bun, leaving her face clear, but she didn't see me. She walked differently somehow, curled inward as if trying to protect herself. Trailing behind her was a head of vibrant fire, and in the half second Alaina and I met eyes, she gave me a glare to match.

"Arie?" Ellen asked, waving a wooden spoon in my face. "Are you there?"

"Uh, yeah." I shook my head to clear it. "Sorry, I just remembered something. I'll see you later, okay?"

"Yeah. Okay." Her tone was passive, shifting her full attention to the frying pan.

I ended up at the cafeteria even though I wasn't very hungry. It was crowded with infecteds coming in for dinner—I just grabbed a roll and wandered through the vast space of people and tables before finding the almost empty one in the back corner. Micah was sitting alone in our spot, chowing down on chicken fried steak, barely giving me an acknowledging glance in between bites of meat.

Sitting across from him, I pulled apart my roll into pieces and ate them one at a time, listening to the loud buzzing of infecteds eating and talking. I was grateful for the noise: Micah was astoundingly stealthy on his feet, but you could hear him chewing from a mile away.

After he'd finished his meal, he tossed me his bag of three mini carrots. I caught it reflexively. I couldn't really remember why, but him giving me his carrots was just one of our things—almost like a peace offering. I think the first time he ever did it was after he nearly beat the life out of me in training. Roland issued me a red card for my incompetence, which banned me from eating for a day, a common punishment at the Compound. And thanks to the brilliance of the chefs in charge, it really was a punishment to miss out on the food. That afternoon, Micah and I were sitting in the cafeteria and he slipped me his carrots in secret. It'd been our thing ever since, when he was in the right mood. I liked it. It was something my friend Micah would do.

I nibbled on the end of a carrot, staring blankly into the sea of people, letting my mind wander. It was then I saw three familiar faces stray into my vision, taking their seats at a table four rows up and one across from mine. Peter started shoveling food into his mouth the second he sat down; Sark was more civilized as he cut into his meat with his plastic silverware; Brennan used his utensils to pick at his food. None of them noticed me, the girl with the half eaten carrot hanging out of her mouth.

They were tired—that was easy to see. Their white t-shirts were already stained with dirt after just one day of work. And though it would've been easy to mistake the few faint dark marks on their faces as more dirt, I could tell the marks were something more painful.

"What happened to them?" I asked Micah, keeping my eyes on the three boys as though that would keep them safe from any more harm.

"Their labor group got a new supervising officer," Micah answered, his voice indifferent, though the fact that he even knew that told me something else entirely. "Maybe he likes to be in charge."

I knew that was a bad sign. "Who?"

"That Lennon guy, or whatever his name is."

I jerked my head to look at Micah. "What?"

He took a long drink of water before responding. "You heard me."

"Lennon is their supervisor?" Even in question the sentence was so many levels of wrong.

"Yeah."

"You've got to be kidding me." I rested my head in my hands, stifling a groan. That was the worst possible thing I didn't even consider. I could only imagine the petty rules Lennon came up with, using his new power to exact revenge on the people he hated most. Especially Sark. Talk about opportune payback.

This is a disaster.

"You can't do anything about it," Micah added, still showing no sign of caring about my new problem. "Just let it go."

Right. Just let it go.

I didn't have any more time to sit and stew about it—my earpiece went off and I was called into production. Keeping my gaze ahead, I made my way out of the cafeteria, about ninety-two percent sure the three boys saw me and a hundred and forty percent sure my stress had exceeded the amount allotted for a healthy life.

The next morning, after much deliberation and almost tears, I decided to bite the bullet and go to the Dome. Despite my reservations, I couldn't live with the idea that the last time I saw Hadley, he saw me as a threat. I didn't know if I could fix anything, but I had to try.

Turned out, all I needed was for him and Jacklynn to go hang out with the other infected kids for a bit. Once I entered, my mini fan club ran up to greet me, per usual, with Hadley and Jacklynn right behind them.

Jacklynn gave me a huge hug, wrapping her arms around my waist. "I missed you so much," she told me in her timid voice.

Hadley jumped up and down next to her. "I did too! I did too! Even more than she did."

And I couldn't help but smile. "I missed you guys too. I can't even tell you how much."

Ranger stepped forward with a serious expression. "We've been taking good care of them," he told me.

"They told us cool stories about you!" Tai exclaimed. "Why did you never tell us those?"

"Yeah," Sharna crowed. "Why did you never tell us those?"

"But I want to know what happens to the lions," Fozzy said. "I really *really* want to know. I've been waiting!"

And there was Sharna again. "Yeah, I've been waiting!"

Grinning, I took my spot on the floor by one of the beds and answered all of their questions and recounted every story they asked about—Hadley adding commentary with Jacklynn nodding along—and I felt right at home.

6

The next two weeks went on the same way: life was normal besides the occasional awkward run-in with someone and my enlarging stress over what to do for my family. The anxiety kept me up at night, making me more tired than I already was. The helplessness was a vacuum with a broken switch, permanently on, permanently sucking everything out of me, every moment of the day.

Today I was on check for labor groups. Checks were every few weeks, just to make sure the laborers were doing their jobs efficiently and correctly. I always rushed through them as quickly as possible to avoid any more interaction than absolutely necessary.

After training, I walked over to the administration building to pick up my tablet, noting the warm earth under my feet. It was hot out, and it was only going to get hotter. My skin was already getting sticky in my long-sleeved black dress; I stifled a moan at the thought of a day full of checks outside.

Presentation, dear, I could almost hear Cyrus telling me at my silent protest for shorts and a t-shirt. *If you can't truly be the star, then at least play the part.*

I'd have to wear the dress. Although technically, it didn't *have* to be long-sleeved. That was my personal preference, for obvious reasons. Cyrus probably wouldn't mind if I walked around baring my blue arms. In fact, he'd probably love it. He made me wear sleeveless dresses every time he brought in new investors to meet me; the blue marks were always a point of interest at those parties.

Despite the heat, I shivered and decided to get on with the day.

It took me a few hours to get through the workers in the fields and orchards. Thankfully they were all on target and meeting their quota—some were even exceeding it—and I wasn't expected to punish anyone. I got a break from the sun when I went inside the buildings for cleaning checks, but those always went relatively quickly, and soon I was back out again. I dragged my feet through the construction checks, getting slower. More nitpicky.

Making the laborers break out in a sweat (or *more* sweat, I should say) at my attention to the details I didn't really care about. The sun beat down on us, edging ever so slowly up and over to the other side of the sky.

Eventually, though, I knew it was inevitable. I'd have to visit *every* labor group and putting one off wouldn't make it go away. With a degraded sigh, I trudged through the dirt over to the last construction site on my list.

Workers scuttled around like ants on the sand, sweat plastering clothes to skin, as they prepared the site for a new ceiling to be put in. Koa stood a few feet from the outer wall, skin glinting, shielding his eyes from the unforgiving sun as he watched a crane lift a giant silver dome. The light reflected off the surface, making it difficult to look at. I steeled myself before approaching him.

"Koa," I greeted him once I was within earshot over the construction chaos.

His shoulders tensed when he heard my voice, but his face was smooth when he turned to look at me. His eyes betrayed him though—they glowed with disdain. "Nolan."

I gestured to my tablet. "I'm here for your check."

"I know," he said coolly, careful to not show his nerves. Koa had never once failed an inspection, but that didn't mean he wasn't still afraid of the consequences. "Go ahead."

Per usual, I kept to myself, and the workers kept to themselves. Nobody really acknowledged me except to get out of the way or exchange nervous glances when they thought I wasn't looking. I completed the checklist swiftly, barely even looking at what I was supposed to. Instead I focused on avoiding three specific people and pretending to look like I was actually doing my job.

I was about ready to pass them and get out of there, when a burst of shouting rose up over the sounds of machinery. I glanced up just in time to see the dome swaying capriciously and Koa waving his hands in the air shouting, "Who touched it? Who touch—get out of the way!"

It was too late. I heard something snap and people screamed and then dust filled my mouth and the world got a whole lot darker.

A few moments passed before my eyes adjusted, which is when I realized what happened: somebody had messed with the crane, which in turn had dropped the domed ceiling. A new stifling heat wave hit me in the face, just as I glanced around at the battered and frightened group of workers trapped underneath with me, coughing and pulling themselves to their feet. I counted fourteen of them. Fourteen including Sark, Brennan, and Peter, and a lump on the edge of the group that looked like it could be a person.

Suddenly the lump started moaning and half shrieking, making everyone jump. "Help! Help, I can't...I can't...someone help me, please."

Everyone craned their necks in the direction of the sound, but it seemed our feet were frozen in place. I realized it was a worker. A girl. Half of her was stuck underneath what was left of a wall that had fallen in the crash.

Automatically I took a step forward, wanting to help. But someone stuck their hand out at me, stopping me, which is when I really took in the scene. The group had congregated, distrustful eyes all on me.

"Not another step," the worker said, still holding out his gorilla arm. After all this time, I'd never learned his name, but the thick scar on his temple helped remind me who he was. And to stay away.

"I just want to check on her," I said. "She's seriously hurt."

By the looks I was getting, you would've thought I was speaking an ancient language. Scarface and the scrawny blond kid next to him blocked my path while Koa jerked his chin out for Cameron to check on the girl.

"Yeah, I bet you want to help her, don't you?" Scarface sneered at me. "Ain't falling for that one."

I rolled my eyes. "No, not again."

"Again?" the blond beanpole asked, confused, and glanced at Scarface. He just glowered at me.

I couldn't help a smirk. "You didn't tell anyone how you got your scar, huh? Couldn't admit you got beat up by a girl?"

One of the workers behind him snickered, eyes wide and thoroughly entertained. Scarface scowled and started for me.

"Take another step and I'll give you a second scar to match." The authority in my tone stopped him short. I held up my index finger to him and glanced at Koa. "I'm going to call this in."

Without waiting for a response, I turned on my heels to face the other direction, painfully aware of the eyes on my back and the whispered conversations. The heat seemed to dry me up from the inside out; I licked my already cracked lips before pressing the button on my earpiece twice, then holding down.

"Micah? It's Arie."

There was only a moment's hesitation before his voice came through my ear. "No, duh. What do you want?"

I took a deep breath, willing myself to be collected, and kept my voice as quiet as I could. "There's been a construction accident on the south side. Almost an entire labor group is stuck underneath a dome ceiling."

"Doesn't matter," Micah said flippantly, already bored. "They should be more careful. Just leave them and move on."

I counted to three. Then six. Got to ten. "Yeah, about that…"

"Is there a problem?" he asked, daring me to say yes.

I squeezed my eyes shut. "Yeah, I can't do that."

"If your precious little Sa—"

"I'm in here too."

The silence in my ear was deafening. I'd barely counted to four when a burst of static erupted the atmosphere, making everyone jump and turn to look at Koa's brick radio that was almost half buried in the dirt next to his foot.

"Zero-one-nineteen, check in now."

Koa's face was pale and sweaty but collected as he picked up the device and answered. "Koa, here."

"This is Micah." Koa's fingers twitched at the name. "I received a report that you and your team are currently unavailable. Is that true?"

"Uh, ye-yes, sir. We believed someone tamper—"

"Is Nolan in there with you?"

Koa hesitated a fraction of a second, then jumped when Micah lost patience. I almost laughed, despite the tension.

"Is Arie Nolan in there, yes or no?"

"Yes, sir, she is."

Micah's tone hardened; I could imagine him narrowing his eyes. "Prove it."

"Prove it, sir?" Koa asked uncertainly, eyes flicking to me again. After all, why would I ever lie to Micah?

Oh, if you only knew.

I gestured to the radio, and Koa tossed it to me with a scowl. Internally steeling myself, I pressed down on the receiver button and brought the box to my face with a wry grin.

"Yep, still here."

The sound of something shattering came through the speaker. Even I couldn't hold back a wince. I kept my voice from shaking though— thank goodness.

"The metal is too hot to touch," I said, as though he cared rather than had half a mind to let me simmer to death. "And way too heavy for us to try to lift, unless you could somehow reattach it to the crane." Dragging my foot against the ground, I dug my toes into the dirt. "We could maybe try digging our way out, but I don't think we have time for that. It's too hot in here, there's not enough water, and we have someone severely injured that needs medical attention now."

Micah's seething voice came through my earpiece now instead of the radio. "Stop this. You know the rules—they deal with the consequences. Now is *not* the time to play superhero."

"I'm not," I growled back, voice quiet and eyes on the ground. "Now get us out before we melt." My dress was already glued to me, sweat rolling down my neck.

"You really think I'm going to come rescue a bunch of useless workers?"

"I'm in here, remember? You want to tell Cyrus I was too *useless* to save? Too bad I'd be dead for that conversation."

"Shut. Up. Now."

"Get us out and I will."

"Oh, there is no 'us' in this situation," Micah bit back. "I'll come dig through the corpses in a few hours to get our precious key."

I clenched my hand into a fist around the radio I was still holding, digging my toe deeper into the dirt. "We won't last that..." Then I realized what he meant. The injured girl could die within an hour, and the others will go out one by one afterwards from the weakest to the strongest. Who was the most likely to survive when nobody else would?

The key, that's who.

"Called it," someone muttered under their breath, while another sighed in exasperation, "I told you they wouldn't care." I guess just hearing whispered snippets of my dialogue was enough for them to figure it out.

"I hope you've rubbed off some of your annoying survivability on your friends," Micah added. "Enjoy your afternoon."

I gritted my teeth and started pacing in a short line, still keeping my distance from the rumbling workers that knew they were dying and could turn into an angry mob at any moment.

It's not going to go down like this.

"You get down here and dig us all out now."

I could almost feel Micah bristling at my tone, my behavior, but he probably assumed all the witnesses would be dead by tonight anyways.

"I hope he dies first so you can smell his rotting corpse for a few hours before you pass out."

I shook my head, the grisly image new fuel. "Fine. I give up. But if they go, I go too."

Micah rolled his eyes, probably. "Yeah, good luck with that. We all dream about being rid of you, but you tend to stick around. You're like a cockroach."

"Yeah, you're right," I said, mocking. "There's just *no way* I could figure out how to die when I'm trapped under a dome with a bunch of construction equipment and a group of dying people that hate me."

For the first time, he didn't have a response for that. The silence in my ear was as thick and stuffy as the silence that had overtaken our little prison.

"Now wouldn't that be a shame," I went on, loving the new power I'd found. "Sure, I have control of them now, but that's not going to last forever, especially if they know nobody is coming for them. And, really, they wouldn't be hard to provoke either. It's like walking on eggshells in here."

I paused, giving him a chance to rebut my threats. He didn't have anything.

This is so much more fun when I can win.

"By the time you got around to getting me, I'd be in a million pieces, murdered too brutally to risk any chance of survival. And then you'd have to march over to Cyrus and tell him that you lost me. Sure, you could blame it on accidents and carelessness, but they'd check my transmission records and find that I'd radioed you for help, and you didn't come. Imagine what Cyrus would do when he found out you let his precious key die."

Despite the overwhelming heat, I got goosebumps at my own words. The fury would be apocalyptic. For once, I held all the bargaining chips.

Finally, his voice came through, edged with dangerous spikes. "You wouldn't dare."

I found myself smiling. "Oh, we both know I would."

He forced my name through his teeth in frustration—I was so glad there was a giant silver dome in between us. "Arie…"

"Now that we're on the same page," I said, "I imagine you have less than thirty minutes to bring a crane or drill or whatever, get us *all* out, and have medical on standby."

There was a beat of silence before Micah muttered lividly, "I hope their lives are worth what I'm going to put you through when you get out."

My blood went icy despite the scalding heat on my skin. Clearing my throat, I finally tore my gaze from the ground to find Koa, Cameron, and a dozen others staring at me with contempt and distrust, unsure how much of that they'd heard.

On second thought, maybe I should just let them kill me.

I tossed the radio back to Koa. He caught it reflexively, clutching it in his hands like a weapon. Besides that, nobody moved, and I got the feeling peaceful relations needed to happen sooner rather than later.

Taking a small step toward the congregated group, I held up my hands in surrender. "They'll come get us out," I told them, my voice nearly swallowed up in the awkward and tense atmosphere. "Just sit tight for a while."

Scarface shook his head and spat in the dirt. "That'll be the day," he muttered.

"Because you threatened them?" Cameron asked, eyeing me doubtfully. "You actually bartered your own life for us?"

"No." Koa glowered at me. "There's no way. It's some kind of elaborate setup. Xander never would've done this." Motions deliberate, he slowly kneeled down to pick up a hammer, keeping his eyes locked on me. "Tell me what you're really up to."

I didn't know who Xander was, but I didn't want to give him the satisfaction of knowing something I didn't—or of beating my brains out.

"I just want to get out," I said evenly. "Same as you."

Scarface scooped up a hand drill and stepped toward me. "Nah, I say we start hacking her up. Maybe if she screams loud enough we can get someone to bust in here."

I tried not to shiver; confidence was key, even if I had to fake it. "They need me alive. You kill me now and they'll leave you to cook in here without another thought."

Scarface grinned at me, exposing a row of thick teeth that could crush bone, probably. "I didn't say I'd kill you, little princess."

Hearing the nickname out loud broke my control. I flinched and took an unsteady step back, then internally cursed myself for showing weakness when Scarface's smile grew.

This is going to go south really fast.

Vanessa squealed and clapped her hands. *This is going to be fun.*

Scarface's blond friend nodded. "Sounds like a plan to me." My stomach knotted when the girl and guy standing next to them each picked up their own weapon.

"They're not going to care what you do to me," I said through my teeth. "As long as I'm alive."

"Doubt that," a girl with unfortunately big lips and small eyes said. "You're their priceless pet, aren't you?"

"It's not going to matter," I tried again. "I swear. So you don't touch me and I won't touch you, and we'll all get out of here in one piece."

"Likely story," the girl sneered, clutching a nail gun.

"You'd do it to any one of us," a boy behind her added.

Got a point there, Vanessa chimed in.

I scanned the group again, hating the odds as I balled my hands into fists. A few were keeping to themselves in the back, watching the conflict with mild interest, fear, curiosity, or some other expression I couldn't read. I didn't know whether any of them would side against me or just stand and watch—specifically what the three boys in the back would do if this actually broke out. We've had our problems, for sure, and the situation was less than ideal, but surely they wouldn't stand back and let the mob take me, right?

A horrible, horrible image appeared in my mind of Sark, Brennan, and Peter helping to hold me down while Scarface hacked me to pieces.

I shivered and my eyes rested on Koa's. "I don't want a fight," I found myself saying to him. "It doesn't have to come to this. Really."

I could see the conflict in his eyes—the odds of getting his crew out, of keeping me in control, of keeping them pacified, of keeping the peace with me because if we all got out I could drag him across the coals just because he hesitated to follow my orders.

"Get down," he finally told me, his jaw clenching as he shifted the hammer in his hand. "On your knees. Now."

I trapped the consuming waves of disappointment, fear, and panic behind a wall in my brain and focused everything on keeping it up.

"Koa—"

"Now. That's an order."

My instincts screamed at me to fight, but I conceded in the name of peace and the slim odds I had of taking every one of them on alone. Gritting my teeth, I slowly got to my knees one at a time. A flicker of surprise passed in Koa's eyes, but I only saw it for a second before Scarface was standing over me, pressing the drill bit against my temple and forcing me to look at the ground. The simmering energy in the group rose up, boiling and ready to spill over. My tongue turned to sandpaper at the thought of a hole in my head and my brains spilling out everywhere.

"Make sure to scream loud, little princess," Scarface said as the masses converge on me and I felt more metal poking me in my neck, shoulder, side. I couldn't find the words to stop them, the panic leaking in from the wall I'd built in my head.

"Stand down," I heard Koa say, and for a second I wondered if I'd imagined it. "I said *stand down.*"

I hadn't. Slowly, the poking metal receded until the drill against my head was the last one left. Koa took my arms and tied my hands behind my back with a cable, and I had to bite my lip to keep my instincts from fighting back.

Koa answered my question disdainfully before I could ask. "Some of us don't *like* torture," he spat at me, pulling the knot against my wrists tight, "which may be a novel idea for you. But if you earn it then I'll step aside."

"Duly noted," I muttered. After a long moment, Scarface growled in defeat and lowered the drill, and Koa took me roughly by the arm and yanked me over to the far side of the dome, throwing me on the ground next to the injured girl. I hissed when my shoulder touched the hot metal.

"Watch her," Koa ordered Cameron, jerking his chin out at me. "Watch them both." And with that, he turned to his group and started gathering ideas to form a strategy.

I turned my attention to the girl. She had brilliant red-orange hair that tangled together in thick dirt-crusted waves, and the sharp freckles to her face were a stark contrast from her soft seafoam eyes. Her jaw was clenched tight, her face shiny with sweat, as she moaned under her breath. The massive obliterated wall obstructed my view of anything below her waist, and I was afraid to find the damage.

"What's your name?" I whispered to her, hiding my voice underneath Koa's. The sea in her eyes widened when I spoke, her eyebrows pulling down, but she didn't tell me to buzz off like I'd expected.

"Mitzi," she groaned.

"You're tough, Mitzi. I can tell."

She took five long, painful ragged breaths. "I'm scared."

I nodded, nearly wincing at the thought of her legs. "You can be both at the same time."

Mulling that over, she nodded back at me.

"I'm a little tied up at the moment," I told her. She had the presence of mind to roll her eyes at my horrible joke—a good sign. "But tell me if there is anything I can do for you, okay?"

She nodded at me again, faster this time. Cameron was watching me now, and Koa had turned to glare, so I shut my mouth like a good little prisoner and waited.

Koa kept his team mostly pacified, which even I had to admit, was impressive. The heat was draining, baking the life out of us, but the stench soon became a contender for the worst thing ever. I didn't know how long we were in there; I could've tried to use my shoulder to press the button on my earpiece to call Micah again, but ultimately I was too afraid to. Instead, I just stared at the ground and waited like everyone else.

My willingness to be pacified seemed to calm most of the workers, but a few of them—Scarface included, which was shocking—still wanted blood. There were a couple times I got a little nervous, but Koa managed to keep everyone away from me. I'd never imagined I'd ever be grateful to him, though I knew it wasn't for my benefit. Strictly survival. I could respect that.

Cameron looked after Mitzi, but I was the one that asked her quiet questions in an effort to distract her. He went about dripping precious water into her mouth from time to time. He must've noticed the way my mouth had dried up into a desert because after the third time administering to the girl, he held out the bottle to me.

My eyebrows shot up in surprise. He shifted on his knees, clearly uncomfortable, but he didn't drop the offering.

"It's yours," I rasped through a shriveled tongue stuck to the roof of my mouth.

Something shifted in his eyes, like I'd confirmed something for him. It was infuriating to not know what trick I'd just fallen for. Instead of enlightening me, he extended his arm further. "We have to keep you alive. Otherwise they'll kill us."

Okay, that was true. He had to know I would last longer than anyone else here though.

I didn't take another second to think it through—my throat ached for it. The slight burn of embarrassment was nothing compared to the intense heat on my skin as Cameron tipped some water into my mouth. Never had I been so grateful for water.

It took effort to not growl when the water stopped, but I knew I'd had enough. More than I should've been given, or expected to be, for that matter. I was about to thank him when Mitzi's breath caught and she whimpered. Careful not to draw attention to myself, I scooted over just enough so my leg was touching her shoulder. It wasn't much comfort, and I wished I could do more.

Where are you, Micah?

I glanced around the space at the workers, some of which were barely conscious. I caught Cameron's eyes. He'd been not-so-discreetly staring at me for a while, but now that he was so close from giving me water, it was getting too weird. After dropping my gaze to my dirty skirt, I finally just looked up and stared right back.

He studied me. I hated it. I felt the sudden urge to tell him off, to threaten, even though that would only make this all ten times worse. The hard lines to his face seemed to melt away for a second, and he became boyish almost, innocently putting a really difficult puzzle together. I found myself mesmerized by the change in his demeanor. What had happened to this kid to change him from such a sweet little boy?

When he finally spoke, his soft voice matched his expression. "You don't belong here," he stated. Not mean or accusing or hateful. Just stating a fact. "You don't, do you?"

A thunderous creaking sound saved me from answering. Everyone jumped to their feet as thin metal arms stuck themselves underneath the far side of the silver dome and began lifting the side up. Sunlight poured in, and I squinted. Cries and whoops of relief escaped some of the workers as they began congregating toward the opening that was growing bigger by the second.

Koa called everyone to order. Without meeting my eyes, he stalked up to me, grabbed me by my arm and jerked me to my feet.

"You go last," he told me.

I nodded at Mitzi. "And she goes first."

"Deal."

Koa and I watched as three workers gently picked Mitzi up and ducked through the opening to freedom. The rest of the team continued, single file. Most were chomping at the bit to get out, but a few lingered behind: Scarface, Sark, Peter, Brennan, and Cameron. I felt all of their eyes on me; I didn't meet any of them. Instead, I waited patiently next to Koa as everyone escaped the stifling dungeon one by one. Once they were gone, Koa turned me around and untied my wrists. Then he disappeared through the hole without another glance.

Rubbing my sore wrists, I took a deep breath, unsure of what awaited me outside.

Here we go.

The balls of my feet pressed softly into the warm dirt as I took careful steps toward the opening. I had to shield my eyes against the unforgiving sun, which prevented me from seeing the gun until it had already fired.

There wasn't any chaos to work through, but I had a difficult time realizing what happened. The rescued workers were stiff and straight in line, at attention, but somehow my eyes flew over them and landed on Mitzi, who was lying in a pool of red.

I didn't think. I dashed to Mitzi's side, sparse gravel digging into my knees, as I bent over her and clutched her red-stained hand in mine.

"Relax," I told her frantic eyes. "Relax. Look at me. Relax."

Words bubbled on her lips, but they wilted away as her sea green eyes went still. Gone.

My teeth clamped together in fury. I jumped to my feet and turned to see Micah standing there with the gun, trying hard to keep his scowl in check.

I forced the words through my teeth. "I said she needed medical."

Micah met my glare evenly, his tone so full of warning and restrained violence that it put my fire out. "Her legs were ruined. She was useless."

Tense silence settled over the site as Micah stared me down. Realization started making its way into me, as I understood how he saw the situation—how *everyone* saw it. The key had defied orders to save a labor group that had messed up. Big time.

Stupid girl, Vanessa muttered.

"Now," Micah continued, addressing everyone, because we were all too eager to fix the mistakes all of us had made before we got busted for it. "Everyone put this place back together. We're going to clean this up now and nobody will—"

"Micah!" Roland barked from a distance, and both Micah and I flinched in spite of ourselves. We turned to see a smug Lennon trailing behind a furious Roland. "Nolan!"

Oh dear.

I glowered at Lennon—the idiot had no idea what game he was playing. Roland stopped a few feet from Micah, glaring back and forth between us and the labor group. If looks could eradicate existences, nobody would never know that Micah and I had ever walked the face of the earth.

"What is going on?" Roland hissed, brawny hands clenching into fists to keep from hitting us in front of anyone. That would be the only thing that could make this worse.

Micah didn't even have to glare at me to keep me quiet. I knew. Instead, we both straightened up respectfully, and Micah took the lead.

"There was a situation with some construction equipment, sir," Micah reported. "It's been taken care of."

Roland growled under his breath as he took in the disaster zone again. "It doesn't look taken care of to me."

"We're handling it, sir."

Lennon snickered nearly inaudibly. "Clearly."

I'm going to murder you.

Roland looked back and forth between the two of us again, and I wondered if the protruding vein in his forehead would pop. It didn't. "Unfortunately, I have a meeting I have to get to." He gritted his teeth, holding himself back. Honestly, I was impressed he did. "Show you're both more capable than the scum in my toes and clean this up. I'll be sure to check in later."

The second Roland was out of earshot, I stomped up to Lennon and punched him across the jaw, smearing Mitzi's blood on his face.

"What was that?" I demanded, punching him again once he got his bearings. "Why on earth would you do something that idiotic? Do you have *any idea* where you are?"

Lennon was bleeding now too, his expression surprised at my brave attack on him, but he still had the nerve to grin at me. "I was doing my job."

"Get this in your head," I growled at him. "You are *nothing* here! Nothing."

Someone grabbed my arm and jerked me around. Micah, naturally. He scowled at Lennon, effectively scaring him a few yards away, before turning on me.

"Fix this," he ordered coldly. He pressed a lighter into my hand and nodded toward Mitzi. "And get rid of it." Then he turned on his heel and stalked away. I tried to melt Lennon with my eyes before he left too, then the high emotions drained out of me and I felt myself droop.

Nobody helped with Mitzi's body—whether they didn't want to get involved further or were ordered not to, I couldn't tell. I didn't really care. I heaved a sigh before setting to work on dragging

Mitzi a safe distance away from any work site and burning her body. The sun was starting to make its descent for the day just as the embers floated up toward the darkening sky.

The Compound was quieter than usual. Flames did that, since fire was how we sent off the dead. The infecteds here were far from united, but most tended to be somber when a fire was lit, if just for the reminder that any day it could be them.

I made my way back to the trashed work site. Koa, Cameron, and two others were there, but they'd sent home everyone else. Without speaking, I stayed and helped clean up the rest of the damaged supplies, pretending like I was taking inventory in my head when really I just felt empty. More than anything, I stayed to evade Micah.

Once it was dark and Koa had called the workday over, I started for home. The fabric of my dress was stiff from dried sweat, but the slight breeze brought no relief—it held the faint smell of smoke.

Still stuck in my thoughts, I noticed the shadow behind me too late. I whipped around and threw my hand out, but the shadow easily ducked. In one motion, it had me by the neck pinned against the wall.

"Mi—Micah," I choked out, clawing at his hands. "Micah, please."

"Begging will get you nowhere," Micah seethed in my ear. My brain rattled when he slammed me against the wall again. "You should know that by now." He released my neck, and I crumpled to the ground in a heap, oxygen rushing back into me in a whoosh only to be forced right back out by Micah's boot in my gut. A breathless cry escaped my cracked lips when he sent another powerful kick into my back, probably hard enough to permanently bend my spine. Then another. Another.

Please stop.

Gasping, I tensed and waited for the next blow. It didn't come. I didn't dare move, sensing him still standing behind me.

Then I heard the loose ground shift, and Micah grabbed a fistful of my hair, yanking my head up.

"Roland just called me in for a report." Even in whisper, I could hear the dark murder of his voice. "After I tell him what really happened here, I'll be back. I'm not done with you."

I couldn't stop the whimper that came at the thought. Smashing my head into the dirt one last time, he was gone.

I listened to his footsteps fade into the night, breathing a sigh of relief that hurt everywhere. My wounds burned; my insides throbbed. Accepting defeat, I just lied in the dirt, watching blood trickle down my middle finger, thinking if I waited long enough then maybe everything would disappear.

It didn't. The pain was still there five, ten, twenty minutes later—or however long it had been since Micah left.

He's going to come back, I told myself, trying not to shudder. *You have to get up and get lost.*

Before I could figure out where to find the willpower to move, I heard the soft shuffle of footsteps getting closer. They were too irregular to be Micah's practiced ones, so either someone was skipping like a disabled penguin or there was more than one person.

Oh great. I was not in the mood to deal with anyone. Or the shape, really.

"Are you out there, pretty little key?"

The voice froze the blood in my veins to ice.

No, no, no, no, no. Not now. Not now.

I clamped my mouth shut and held my breath, wildly glancing around the darkness. He wasn't close enough to see yet, his voice still yards away, maybe more. Maybe less. If I went quietly enough, I could get away. Crawl away. Anything.

"I heard precious Arie got in trouble," Scarface went on in a low mocking voice. "And she might need some help."

Clenching my fists, I ignored my screaming body and pushed myself up on my arms, silently dragging myself away from his voice.

Where am I going to go?

Then a figure came into view and stopped right in my tracks. I barely had time to register the shadow before Scarface's friend called out, "Found her."

Trying to freeze my panic over, I balled up my fists and shot up, punching his jaw. He doubled over, but my attack was short lived. A hand seized me by my hair and yanked me back.

"Where you goin' so fast, princess?" Scarface asked, his breath a foul mixture of rotten meat and toothpaste deficiency, as he pressed the dirty blade of a jagged knife to my cheek.

Somehow, I was able to make my voice harsh and commanding. "Let me go. Now."

His partner glared daggers at me, blood dripping from his lip. "You wish."

"Nah, we just got here, princess," Scarface added. He toyed with the blade against my face, nearly breaking skin but not quite, and took a strand of my hair in his other hand. "We've got all night."

My heart was pounding erratically, and I fought for control of myself. "Let me go," I ordered, "or I will—"

"You'll what?"

Words left me. I thought I was being intimidating, menacing, throwing my weight around, but nothing was coming out of my mouth.

Scarface chuckled. "Not so tough now, are you?"

"Micah will rip you to shreds." I internally winced, both from the stupid defense and my squeaky voice.

"Doubt that. Word is, you pissed him off pretty bad." The knife moved along my face and paused inside my lips with just enough pressure that blood started dribbling from the corners of my mouth. Dirt fell onto my tongue. I went rigidly still. "Are you done with empty threats yet?"

His comrade bounced a few times and glanced around, as though keeping watch, but we all knew nobody would come by—even if I started screaming my head off.

"What are you waiting for?" he asked Scarface, almost complaining.

Scarface's free hand trailed lazily from my hair to my ear and across my jaw. "I wanna take my time here. She's a real prize." He touched my face, and I jerked my head away, wincing as the knife dug further into me. "Attitude aside, she's still a beauty, even all bruised up."

The other guy made a face at me. "She's ugly—average at best. I'm just in it for her name."

Scarface leaned even closer to talk right in my ear, making me shudder in spite of myself. "More blood for me then."

He shifted on his knees, and I took the opportunity to shove against his restraining arm. Some part of me registered the knife slashing across my cheek, but I hardly noticed. I focused everything on forcing my weight forward.

I fell free of Scarface's grasp, and instantly kicked my leg back, sending my foot right into his face. The other guy was on me in a flash. Taking a half second to notice his somewhat shaky steps, I dove straight for his knees, knocking him right down. An elbow to his face had him rolling away from me. My nails dug into the earth as I started pulling myself up to take off.

A hand snatched my ankle and dragged me back. Scarface flipped me on my back and loomed over me, a massive shadow in the night, curling a big hand around my throat and pressing his knee into my gut. Choking both from his hold and weight, I kicked my legs and clawed at his vise of a hand. Nothing gave.

"Now we can play." Scarface grinned at me as he lifted his free hand, still holding the knife, and leaned down close to my face. I swatted him away and he laughed, but his mouth twisted with resentment. "Do you have blue skin too, princess?" I felt the tip of the knife at my collarbone. He slowly dragged it to the right, edging the fabric of my dress farther down my shoulder. "I'd really like to see it."

Using everything I had, I shoved myself upward, trying to force and squirm my way out. Scarface just slammed me down to the ground again, and a mangled cry escaped me.

"Aw, now come on, don't be like that. I just want to carve your blue skin off." He glanced up to grin at his friend. "Think of how much that'll go for."

My skin crawled at the image. In a new burst of panic, I abandoned my futile mission to free my throat from his hand, and reached my arm up, as if going for the knife. Scarface automatically leaned just enough to keep it out of my grasp, and I used the slight shift in balance. Something nasty tore in my left leg as I wrapped myself around his burly body and flipped us around. I half screamed with the effort. But then I was out. I was free.

Both Scarface and his pal jumped me at the same time. Everything went into a blur as survival instinct took over. It ended with me screaming and Scarface gasping in pain on the ground and his knife lodged into his partner's knee. Blood and dirt squished in between my toes as I dragged myself to my feet and took off, knowing I had only bought myself seconds. If that.

With a limp to slow me down, I ran blindly away toward the residence buildings, ducking in between them and weaving in and out. Quickly, though, I found myself lost. I was never over here, and the stupid buildings all looked exactly the same.

Not able to go any farther, I ducked around a corner and pressed myself against the wall, trying to quietly catch my breath.

They're going to find you, Vanessa commented.

I ignored her. *Stay calm. Stay calm. Think. Focus.*

But panic and pain were everywhere, and I didn't have any options. I heard footsteps appear, heading for me, and I steeled myself for the worst.

Someone rounded the corner in a flash, restraining me against the wall and slapping a hand over my mouth, as if they could sense my built-up scream. My terror melted into surprise when I realized it was Peter.

His eyebrows shot up and he let me go. "What are you doing? It's too dangerous to be out here now." Like I didn't know that.

A plea for help was on my tongue, but a different word shoved itself out first. "Leave."

I could almost see his eyes adjusting to the dark as he looked over me, really seeing me and the state I was in. "What happ—"

"Get back here, princess," Scarface shouted, still at least three buildings down, I guessed. "You know you can't hide from us. Not tonight."

I stiffened, and Peter narrowed his eyes, a cold kind of hatred hardening his face until he looked like he was carved out of stone. He started to pull on my wrist, but I hung back.

"You have to leave," I whispered urgently, "before they—"

"They aren't looking for me," he said, his tone livid yet controlled. "But I know what they'll do to you."

I felt bile rise in my throat as I shrunk into the wall. "You do?"

"I wouldn't even repeat half the stuff they say about you, and I'm a jerk."

"But I—"

"Come on, princess!" He was closer now. Much closer. Even with their injuries, if he and his buddy were patrolling together, each taking a side of the building, I wouldn't be able to get out without one of them seeing me. And outrunning them was out of the question, even if I had somewhere safe they couldn't follow, even if I could really fight back…

My hands started shaking with desperation; my legs wobbled underneath me. To my surprise, Peter met my eyes evenly, his grip tightening on my wrist.

"Can you trust me?"

I opened my mouth, but I was stunned to silence. Trust him? I hadn't been able to trust anyone in a long time.

They're coming, Vanessa reminded me, getting antsy with anticipation. *You've got seconds, maybe.*

The last thing I remembered about Peter was him holding me back at the hospital when I wanted to see Sark. When he risked his own life to follow me into Alexis' trap. When he made sure I didn't have to fight alone, and I made it home at the end of the day.

Vanessa wasn't impressed with that round up. *Peter hates you, remember?*

I watched his urgent eyes for a second. *Can you trust me?*

Hesitating, I nodded. Instantly he leaned down to scoop me up and take off. Despite the pain, I wrapped my arms tight around his neck and squeezed my eyes shut, letting him take over.

Peter only ran for less than a minute. Suddenly the wind stopped, I heard a door slide open, and then he stepped inside. It took me a moment to be brave enough to look and see where he'd brought me.

We were inside a residency building—first problem. Two long lines of cots facing each other took up the majority of the space, Sark, Kayla, Brennan, Lucy each occupying one. Two down from Sark, my mom was sitting on the edge of hers, and in the far corner was Lennon, minding his own business. All conversation stopped when they saw Peter carrying me.

Both my mom and Lucy gasped in horror, and Kayla and Sark jumped to their feet. As if reading my mind, Peter waved them off, marching down the middle of the cots. He stopped at the third one on the right—next to Kayla and across from Sark—and gently set me down on it before sitting on the one next to me. Every wide eye was trained on me.

Wow, they really do hate you, don't they? Vanessa observed as the claustrophobia started getting to me.

"I'm not supposed to be in here," I finally blurted hoarsely, just for something to say. At least it was true.

"Why not?" Peter asked, capturing my attention. "You'd rather be hanging out in your penthouse?" He glanced at my shaking hands—which I promptly stuffed underneath my legs—and his voice softened slightly. "You look like crap. I figured you didn't care much where I took you, as long as it was somewhere."

I met his eyes, hoping I conveyed both my gratitude and my warning to stay quiet. "Thank you."

He pursed his lips into a thin line but nodded. I dropped my gaze to my lap. My skirt was half shredded and encrusted with dirt and blood. Tears suddenly sprang in my eyes, and I fought to keep them in.

Kayla was the one who broke the thick silence. "Do I even ask what happened to you?"

I shook my head. It hurt. Everything hurt. "It's nothing," I muttered. The corners of my mouth burned when I spoke.

Something came at me. I tensed and flinched backward, snapping my eyes back up only to see Peter reaching toward me. He held his hand up as if to say "it's just me" before he softly took my chin in his palm, turning my face to inspect it. Within twelve seconds, he dropped his hand. "Sure doesn't look like nothing."

"Is this because of earlier?" Brennan asked me from behind Peter. "Because you helped us?"

Help is a strong word for what I did, don't you think?

The words tasted like metal in my mouth—the words Cyrus had taught me. "I got myself into trouble. It's my fault. I'll be better."

"No, I get it now." Peter leaned his elbows on his knees. "You're not actually a 'princess' here—you're a lapdog." I flinched at the term again and Vanessa smirked. "A dangerous lapdog, but still…still you."

My gaze fell to my lap again, as if he'd beaten the secrets out of me. "They give me power because they want me separated. I'm not…I'm not what Cyrus wants but he doesn't want everyone to see that. So they don't. Usually."

"Until today."

I sighed. "Nobody was supposed to see that. I…I screwed up. But most of the time, the rumors keep everyone in the dark, or at least guessing and confused. For some reason the infecteds here really believe I'll slit their throats for fun—that I'd like to. Combine that with the price on my head and it causes…mixed reactions."

"Yeah, I've noticed."

"Well these 'mixed reactions' are too violent for my taste," Kayla muttered. She reached underneath her cot and pulled out a big white box. It opened to a first aid kit. She raised a finger at me when she saw my expression, my mouth open with protests. "Don't argue. I don't know how much I can help such a mess, but I'm at least cleaning you up."

I shook my head. "You don't have to. I'm fine."

She rolled her eyes. "I'm getting rather tired of that word. My rule is if you come in injured then I help. I don't care if you're 'fine' or whatnot."

My heart sank at the thought. If she had to make that a rule, then how often did they come back at the end of the day with someone bleeding?

Attempting to ignore Kayla's efforts so I wouldn't freak out, I turned all my attention to Peter, who, oddly, was the only person in the room not stressing me out to the max.

"You all..." I trailed off and swallowed hard, hurting my throat, but I had to keep going. I had to know. "Cyrus said you requested admission. To the Compound. You came voluntarily."

Peter stretched his arms out, rolling his eyes. "'Voluntarily' is a bit of a stretch as far as some of us are concerned. But yeah." He met my gaze. "Essentially, we tried to get in here."

I winced as Kayla pressed a wet cotton ball to my cheek, stinging my cut, and I couldn't curb all the judgment in my tone. "*Why?*"

He shrugged. "It's not what we thought, if that's what you mean. This place is brutal. But at the same time, it's...consistent, I guess. Relatively safe, so long as you're the right person or don't wind up in the wrong place. Constant meals, roof over your head, work to keep you busy—and no one trying to hunt you down. It's a different kind of harsh, but in some ways it's easier than out there."

I blinked, trying to wrap my head around that perspective while Kayla started stitching up behind my ear.

Not everyone is as high maintenance as you, princess, Vanessa told me.

"But," Peter went on, "that's for us useless infecteds. I'm getting it's a little different for the key, right?"

I only nodded.

"I take it you didn't waltz in here to claim what was yours like everyone assumes?"

Goosebumps rose on my skin, along with a deep pull in my gut. A longing for freedom. "No. It was more of a…" A dark chuckle bubbled out of me as I thought of the word Cyrus used to phrase my essential kidnapping. "Compromise."

"Pretty great compromise, if he got the key out of it."

"So far, no, but…he says he's almost got it figured out. He gets closer every day."

Kayla piped up, her voice bland with concentration. "They're definitely doing something in the lab. They won't let Daxton or me too close because we know you, but I know it's something monumental. I believe them when they say they'll weaponize you."

"I do too," I murmured.

"They're frustrated, though," Kayla said, breaking her gaze from her stitching to meet my eyes. "You should know that. Whatever you're doing on the mental side is really hindering their work."

A brief smile twitched on my lips, but it vanished with a reminder from Vanessa. "It's just a temporary solution," I said. "They'll get me eventually."

Peter shook his head in exasperation. "That's what I don't get: they treat you like crap, you're relatively in charge, and they're gonna use you to kill a bunch of people and do who knows what else. So why are you still here? Leave."

Ha! Vanessa laughed. *And go where?*

Dropping my gaze, I shook my head, not able to narrow down the ocean of explanation into a coherent stream of words.

"It's not that simple," I finally said.

Behind Peter, Lucy carefully uncurled herself from under Brennan's arm and leaned forward, as if to speak, but a pounding on the door cut her short.

"Open up!" Micah shouted from the other side. "I know she's in there!"

The silence turned tense and brittle. Everyone glanced at me, and I felt the color drain out of my face. Then, at no signal I could tell, everyone sprang into action. I trapped a cry behind my teeth when Peter grabbed me and shoved me under the cot, while Kayla threw a blanket on top, spilling the fabric over the side to conceal me from the front door. Brennan stood and walked past me, switching places with Kayla, and Lucy watched him with fearful guard. Both of them pretended to be oblivious to me. I accidentally met my mom's distressed gaze, but Peter sat back down on his cot, obstructing my view of her.

And despite my destructive fear and screaming body, I felt a twinge of warmth in me: we were still family. Even when they were unsure which side I was on, they still put themselves in between danger and me. No questions asked.

Maybe this isn't hopeless after all.

Vanessa rolled her eyes. *Hopeless is your middle name.*

The attempt to hide me was sweet, but it was futile. This was Micah.

Clenching my teeth together so I wouldn't whimper with the odd angle of my body on the floor, I closed my eyes, wondering how on earth I was going to get out of this one.

I heard the door slide open and Brennan ask flatly, "What do you want?"

Three of Micah's powerful steps pounded. "Where is she?" he demanded, the edge to his voice making me flinch. I was so dead.

"Arie?" For some reason I winced again when Sark said my name. "Why would she be here?"

"I know her—we haven't beaten the predictability out of her yet."

"Seemed to have beaten everything else," Sark growled.

"You miss doing it yourself?"

My eyes snapped open, the silence in the room thick enough to suffocate someone. Squirming, I spared all caution trying to get out before a fight started that Sark wouldn't walk away from. My body whined, my wounds throbbing, my heart pounding, but I forced myself out from underneath the cot and sat up.

"Calm down," I said, instantly reverting to the cool, unconcerned person I always pretended to be, numbing everything inside me. "I'm right here."

Though his face was murderous, a flicker of humor crossed when he saw me. "Underneath a cot."

I shrugged, forcing down the throbbing that came with it. "It's been a weird day."

Micah did a quick glance around the room, taking inventory just as he'd taught me to. Sark and Brennan were standing loosely at either side, as a first line of defense. I felt Peter tensed and ready behind me. Kayla was with Lucy—neither of which would fight, probably—and while Lennon would stay out of it, my mom was a wildcard. So three...three and a half of us, counting my injuries. Three and a half against Micah.

Those odds still don't look good.

I guess he didn't want to take the chance, right at first anyway. He gestured to the door, glowing green eyes glaring at me. "Roland needs to see you. I'm supposed to take you to him."

Liar.

Hoping he wouldn't call my bluff, I tapped a bloody finger to my ear, where my earpiece should've been. It must've been knocked out at some point. "I haven't been called in."

"Well he asked for you."

I gestured around the strained room. "Well I'm busy right now. I'll meet with him later."

Micah gritted his teeth. "You know, you have to pick a side: do you want the pretenses or not?"

"You know, I thought I've made it pretty clear I hate the pretenses."

His tone went mocking. "Right, I forgot, you're the angelic little martyr that never does anything wrong. From here it looks like you have a lot of blood on your hands."

"Wonder whose fault that is."

"Fine." Micah clenched his hands into fists. "Get out here so I can wring your neck or I'll bring this place down to get to you. Better?"

"Much clearer," I muttered. Bracing my arm on the cot, I tried to pull myself up. Peter helped me to my feet, standing with me, but when I took the first painful step forward, he wouldn't release my wrist. I glanced up at him to see he was staring down Micah.

"She'll come out when she's ready," Peter said coolly.

I couldn't help the slight sense of relief that came, knowing I had someone on my side, even if it was seriously bad news. Micah raised an eyebrow in amusement, gaze flickering around the room again. Then the amusement melted down into fury when something new caught his eye. I followed his glare and found Lennon.

"Micah," I started, my tone a warning, though why I felt the need to defend Lennon was a mystery to me.

There's been too much blood today.

"No, I changed my mind," Micah spat, jade eyes hardening. "I want the idiot who started this whole thing first."

"Micah, no." I lurched into the aisle, dragging Peter along with me, to block just as Micah took a step forward. Sark and Brennan closed in on either side. "Just go. He's not worth it."

Lennon only dug his own grave by being stupid enough to speak up. "You're all the idiots." His voice was strained with fear, but still oozing with arrogance. "Alexis will discover this operation eventually and you'll all meet your end."

Oh. Right. I'd forgotten to mention that very tiny major detail.

My shoulders slumped under my wobbling leg, the memory weighing me down, but Micah just laughed.

"Alexis is dead," he scorned. "You might want to check your facts before you assume you have any authority here."

A collective gasp went through the room, but Lennon's was the loudest. "You're lying."

"No, I'm not." Micah did nothing to hide his enjoyment or pride. "He had a hard shell, but he broke easy. He was a coward. He ended up screaming and begging just like everyone else. You've got nothing here." Then he focused on me again. "So, what, that's it? You're all buddies again? Did you even tell them anything?"

I glared at him. "I hear you said enough for the both of us. Now shut up and get out."

"Just like that huh?" He shifted his glower to Sark now, though he still spoke to me. "I guarantee if they knew a quarter of what you've been up to since you left them in the street, they'd steer clear. You're not one of them anymore." The corners of his mouth twitched into a ghost of a smile. "You're with me now."

The words made me shrink in on myself, but I forced my eyes not to drop from his face, even when I saw Sark's hands ball into fists next to me. "I'll see you tomorrow," I said through my teeth.

Micah nodded at me. "Yeah, you will." And with that, he turned and stalked out.

The sharp silence was draining as relief trickled in. I didn't know whether to leave or stay.

I didn't know whether to explain or let them work it out. I didn't know whether to live or die, keep breathing in and out or hold my breath until I turned blue and passed out, so I didn't have to deal with the next five minutes or five hours or five days.

This'll never be over, you know, Vanessa kindly reminded me. *There is no way out for you, ever. Even if you somehow managed to get out of here, you'll never escape me.*

And with that, my hurt leg gave out and I collapsed on the empty cot. It wasn't until then I realized Peter was still holding my wrist; he let me go and sat back down too. Somehow, my eyes met Lennon's aghast expression.

"He's lying," Lennon muttered, his face pale and full of the dread that needed denial. "He's lying, isn't he? He has to be."

I blew out a strand of hair out of my face. "No. He's not."

Brennan crossed the room to sit again, Kayla scooting over to make room for him and Lucy automatically curling into his lap, as though the two of them were connected by magnets. Sark rubbed the back of his neck and took an unsteady breath before sitting down too, and even my mom's expression was shocked. They all watched me expectantly. I didn't know where to start, so I didn't.

"He must've survived," Lennon told his fidgeting hands. "Alexis...couldn't...he could have survived. I'm sure of it." He didn't sound sure at all.

I shook my head, throat thick. "Not the way Micah does it." I wasn't sure why, but I added, "I'm sorry."

"How long ago?" Peter asked, his voice airy with disbelief.

"Um…," I thought for a moment. "What month is it?"

"November," Brennan answered promptly, before stealing a worried glance at Lucy. "Although it could be December by now." Lucy pursed her thin lips until they were whiter than her pale face.

"Then…" I counted in my head, realizing that I'd missed so much of their lives, and of my own—I'd had a birthday pass. "Wow. Six months almost." I looked at Lennon's ashen face. "You really didn't know?"

"I…" He sighed. I'd never seen him so flustered. "No. No, I didn't." He rested his forehead in his spindly hands. "After the fiasco in Denver, it was chaotic. We lost Jefferson. We lost you. Then locations started going, and Alexis was manic, going away for—" He stopped himself, realization dawning in his eyes, raising a blinding accusation. "That was you."

I just nodded.

"Then you and your friend murdered him." The disgust in his tone was ironic, considering how many innocent people both he and Alexis had murdered in their time. "I'll bet that was a wonderful moment for you."

"It wasn't as great as I thought," I admitted. Horror tainted the memory too much to make it a victory.

"Where was he hiding out?" Lennon asked, his tone suddenly turning to dark anger. "Where did you finally find him?"

"No, I…" I watched my hands fidget in my lap, stunned at the question. "I didn't find him. He...he was brought to me, I guess. Cyrus…" My voice got smaller as the memory came barging in. "Cyrus tracked *me* down, and he had...he had Alexis tied up in the back of a van. Micah tore him apart in an alley in Salt Lake City. They...I mean, they left him there, but...but if even his employees never found out then I guess…" I winced. "I guess he wasn't identifiable. Micah probably lit a match on him on our way out and I didn't see."

"An offer you couldn't refuse," Lucy mumbled. I glanced up to see her face was thoughtful, rather than astonished like those around her.

"What?"

Kayla nodded slowly, as if remembering. "That's right. That's what Cyrus told us about you coming here: he made you an offer you couldn't refuse." She snapped her fingers. "Getting rid of Alexis."

I shrugged with one shoulder. "Something like that, I guess."

"I'd do it," Peter said.

Brennan raised an eyebrow. "Well it sounds a lot different when you put it like that. Cyrus has a way of...I don't know, but…" I thought I saw him shiver. "For such a little guy, he sure knows how to make you feel tiny. And crushable. Like…"

"Like he can see all your nightmares," Lucy finished for him, her voice so delicate that I almost couldn't hear her. "And he can make them all come true."

I cringed and clenched my fists. "Yeah, I know." Then I cleared my throat and smoothed out my ruined skirt. I'd been here too long. "I should go. Thanks for not turning me in."

"You sure?" Peter asked me, his eyebrows furrowed with concern.

"Yeah. Micah may have left but...it's just better if nobody else finds out I'm here."

"If you say so." Peter offered his hand to pull me up, and I took it gratefully.

"What happened to the kids?" Lucy asked me, the reminder striking her with new worry. "They were with us when we landed, but now they're gone."

"Oh, right. They're at the Dome with the other infected kids. Actually, they're probably the safest out of all of us. They'll be taken care of there." That reminded me of the advice I gave Ellen a long time ago. "If for whatever reason there's a crisis, go there. It's got extra security and fortifications— it's the safest place to be."

I stepped into the aisle on my good leg, surprised when Sark took a step toward the door too. His blue eyes were hard to decipher as he looked at me and said, "Let me walk you...home, I guess. Wherever you're going."

Micah had given up for the night—hopefully— and Roland wasn't about wasting his time to stalk me. Scarface and his buddy had probably moved on by now, or at least started looking for me somewhere else when they hadn't found me. If anything, I was worried about walking alone with

Sark, who'd been largely quiet through my whole visit.

"That's a good idea," Peter said, further backing me into the corner.

I waved my hand. "No, it's fine. It's pretty late and—"

Sark said, "Don't be ridiculous," just as Peter scoffed, "Don't be stupid," which just made Brennan chuckle once and Kayla roll her eyes.

"The testosterone is always potent around here," Kayla added, walking back to clean up her supplies. "And somehow that doesn't blend well with your passion for inordinate self-sacrifice. Just let them act on their compulsive evolutionary need to protect us from this brutal world." She paused to glance at Peter. "Which reminds me: isn't Alaina off her shift by now?"

Peter's eyes went wide and he ducked out the door without another thought. I took that oddity as my exit, glancing at Sark. He gestured for me to go first, almost in question, so I nodded and went, mostly because I couldn't think of an excuse.

"Goodnight guys," I said with a half wave behind me.

There was a collective mumbled "Goodnight Arie" as I went out the door, Sark trailing close behind. My steps were hesitant until my eyes adjusted to the dark made spotty by industrial lights on the buildings. I surveyed the area quickly; there were no signs of a threat. Cautious and alert, I started for home. My stomach twisted itself in knots when Sark followed.

It was painful, and not just because my body was so angry at me. It hurt me to see Sark and I like this, walking silently with a murky lake of discomfort between us, and I wanted so badly to reach out and find him, but I just didn't know how. I swear I saw him continue to look over at me, again and again, as though seeing me for the first time over and over.

What does he think of me now?

When he wasn't looking at me, I looked everywhere else, my nerves buzzing painfully with the anticipation of attack. After the third check over my shoulder, Sark broke our quiet.

"Expecting someone?" he asked, a slight edge to his casual tone.

"Uh, no." I faced forward again.

"Looks like it."

"Habit."

"You're not safe here," he observed. "Or anywhere."

"It comes with the job."

"Right."

More silence. Too much. Too thick.

"No shoes, huh?" he asked me.

I stole a glance at my bloody and dirty bare feet, suddenly self-conscious. "No, I don't have a whole lot of those."

"Seems weird."

"Roland is possessive about combat boots, and Miss Welch would kill me if I got any of my show heels muddy—that's all I got. I'm used to it now."

"Hm."

I was vomiting words now, unable to stop myself. "I think it's some sort of reverse psychology thing: I'm the most important person here, but not important enough to have shoes. Cyrus likes to play with people's minds."

"Does it work?"

I tried to shrug. "Depends on what he's going for, I guess."

"Probably wants to keep you on edge," Sark guessed.

Then it's working. Out of habit, I glanced to my right again, scanning the darkness for any threats. In my haste I missed one right in front of me: a slight dip in the dirt. I stumbled into it and caught myself on my bad leg. My one knee buckled as the pain flew up from my calf, and I gasped through my teeth.

"Your leg is hurt, Arie," Sark said, his tone clipped, when he stopped next to me.

Half doubled over, I took a breath. "It's not that bad."

"You've been limping this whole time. Don't think I didn't notice."

Then to my surprise, he bent down in the dirt behind me, gently using one hand to hold me up, then bringing the other to the spot of the injury. His hands were warm and calloused as he softly probed my calf with his fingers.

"What did you do—you know, never mind." His fingers went over my leg again, this time in a different pattern. "It's messed up pretty good. You shouldn't be walking on it, at least until you know what it is."

I realized then that I'd been holding my breath. I let it all out in one gust. "Can't be that bad. It'll be fine."

Suddenly his fingers came down hard, right on the worst spot. I half shrieked at the stab of fire, and my other knee buckled, sending me to the ground. Sark wrapped his arm around my waist and caught me from behind right at the last second.

"See?" he said, holding me up against him. "You need to stay off it."

I huffed, digging my fingernails into my palms at the throbbing in my leg that seemed to be spreading everywhere else, each body part not wanting to let another get away with more attention. "Well, pushing on it doesn't help either."

I expected him to let me go, but he didn't. "I'll take you back to Kayla so she can—"

"No, I'm okay. I just..." I slumped back in exhausted defeat as everything caught up with me. "I just want to go home."

I squeaked in surprise when he picked me up off the ground.

"Where's home?" he asked.

"Oh, no, Sark..." I pushed my hands against his chest, but he just reaffirmed his hold on me. "You don't have to—I'm really fine, I just—"

"Let someone do something for you," he said. "I'm gathering that doesn't happen much anymore."

"Uh, no, um, not really, I guess."

There was a half beat of quiet. "You know I'm not putting you down, so you better just tell me where to go."

I debated for a few moments before wrapping my arms around his neck. "Fine." I pointed a finger. "Head that way."

Sark followed, hanging on to me. It was different, somehow, than when Peter had carried me. Granted we'd been running, making an escape, but...Sark held me tighter, almost. Closer. Like if he gave me an inch to breathe then I'd be gone again. Despite my discomfort at being so close to another human being for so long, it was nice.

It was silent. The deathly stillness of night had come over the Compound, making me aware of every one of Sark's soft footsteps and our quiet breaths. My arms were ticked, but I tried as much as possible to hold myself up. Sark wasn't showing any sign of overexertion, but I still felt bad.

"People like to talk about you though," Sark started out of nowhere, breathing awkward life into our dying conversation.

Sarcasm was itching to get out, so I let it. "Really? I hadn't noticed." I paused, wanting to keep my tone light and hide my fear of what he'd heard about me. "What's the craziest thing you've heard?"

Thankfully, he laughed once. "Oh, I don't know. There are a lot of good ones."

"Like drinking the blood of my victims?"

"That one's my favorite."

My mouth hurt when I smiled. I loosened my arms around his neck, letting him support more of my weight.

"The lists go on and on," he continued. "Number of victims, methods of torture, what you do with the bodies, threats you've made, what you will and won't do, number of lovers, kinds of powers..." He trailed off. "You're quite the interesting person."

I realized I'd gone stiff. "Yeah."

"Not all of it's bad, believe it or not."

"Really?"

"Some people think you're some kind of goddess." He smirked, but I got the sense it was from a joke I didn't know. "The saint sent down to save them."

My stomach flipped. I told myself I would not throw up on Sark.

Sark actually laughed at my sickened silence. I'd missed the sound. "Yeah, I figured you'd like that. Probably take the demon from Hell over that any day, huh?"

"I'm more of a blood and guts kind of girl—if the stories are true, anyways."

"I imagine not many of them are." He glanced down at me. "Unless you actually have a long line of guys at your door every night."

Now it was my turn to laugh. "Wow, I *do* sound exotic, don't I?"

Half his mouth pulled up, but it was forced. "You don't, right?"

I raised an eyebrow when I realized he was completely serious. "It's really that believable?"

"Yeah." When I continued to stare at him, dumbfounded, he went on, his tone obvious. "You're pretty, powerful, and unattainable. Your title alone is a magnet. Makes sense why you're so popular in the male department." He tried to keep his tone light, but there was something hiding underneath. I guess he didn't have to talk to Peter to know what some of the infecteds said about me—Sark worked with them too.

"Huh," was all I said.

"So I can mark that one down as myth?" he asked. "No one here?"

"Would you beat them up if there were? Wait on the front porch with a shotgun?"

He shrugged, a real smile playing on his face now. "Depends. Might have to if they don't know what they have."

"Good thing I'm permanently single then." I pursed my lips to keep from grinning when he seemed pleased by that. We were still a team.

See, Cyrus? Sark and I are just fine. It was stupid I let that little man in my head so much.

It got even darker as we left the safety of the industrial lit buildings, and I had to give Sark relative directions to where we were going since I wanted to take the long, back way—he wouldn't put me down—then he looked up at the night sky. The thick clouds were black and angry; it was going to rain tomorrow. Cyrus must not be happy. I shivered at the thought.

"This place is insane," Sark commented. "Where on the planet are we?"

"I have no idea," I admitted. "The weather is all controlled somehow, so there's not even a climate clue."

Sark glanced at me. "They control the *weather*?"

"Don't ask me how. Cyrus just likes...control. Perfection. It's his own little world." I sighed. "You didn't sign up for this, did you?"

He took a moment to answer. In the end, he decided to be honest, rather than lie to ease my conscience. "No. I didn't."

My throat got thick. "I'm so sorry," I whispered.

"I'm not. It brought me back to you."

I shook my head. "There are much much better things in your life than me."

"Then why do I have such a difficult time finding something that measures up?"

That warmed up my core, even though I knew he was stretching it.

"I'm trying to say I missed you," he clarified, his voice losing a serious tone.

Again, I found myself suppressing a laugh. "Well why didn't you just say so?"

Sark chuckled. "I'll be more forward next time."

Finally, I relaxed enough to rest my head against his shoulder. In the dark, I thought I saw the corners of his mouth pull up. He shifted his arms slightly, only to hold me tighter. I realized I was dreading the moment when we'd arrive and he'd have to put me down. It'd been such a long time since I'd felt this relaxed and safe—at home.

But the shadows in my mind kept nagging at me, and even though I didn't want to break our peace, eventually I sighed.

"What happened?"

"They asked to get in, Arie," he told me, his voice dipping with disapproval. "They have to deal with their own consequences."

"But you didn't."

"Despite my reservations, I would've come with them, if it really…" he trailed off. "I don't know. It seems obvious now that I know you're here, but…"

I waited expectantly. The only recruitments I had details of weren't pretty ones, even if the infecteds were petitioning volunteers and Roland let them live.

"It was slick," Sark admitted. "I'll give them that much. We were moving locations, again, in the middle of the night. Didn't even realize our truck was hijacked until we got to the airstrip. I suspected Alexis had finally caught up until I saw Lennon cuffed up just like the rest of us. And your parents…" He blew out a breath. "That was a surprise."

"Do you have any idea where they've been?" I couldn't help asking.

He shook his head. "No. I haven't seen much of your dad since we've been here, but your mom is around all the time." He hesitated. "I…I understand your reservations of course, especially for your dad, but…"

"But?"

"You've done a really great job of ignoring her," he finished quietly.

That bothered me in a way I didn't understand, a huge wave I couldn't quite grasp. "What do you expect me to do?"

"I don't know." He shrugged, bumping my arm, causing it to start throbbing again. It must've gone numb at some point. "But if it were me, I would gladly take the second chance."

The thought rendered me quiet as I absorbed it. Sark went on when I didn't say anything else.

"Anyway, the plane landed and they lined us up, then you came barging in." He laughed once. "That was shocking, to say the least. Points for entrance. After you left, we were rounded up for 'orientation' at the main building where Cyrus gave us an earful about how lucky we were to be there—no, I think the word he actually used was 'blessed'—and the goals and expectations of the Compound, then all about you. I didn't believe a thing he said. And he must've known that because he sent Micah to talk to me, and that guy…"

I winced when his fists clenched, arms flexing, and the extra compression hurt. Quick as it came though, he loosened up.

"That guy gets on my nerves," he finished.

I tried to imagine that conversation and then decided I didn't want to. "I'm guessing he didn't play fair."

"Hardly." The word came through his teeth. "He doesn't deserve you, Arie. Not at all."

That brought me up short—I hadn't been expecting that. "My Micah is there somewhere," I said, a hint defensive. "He just doesn't come out very often. But he's there."

"He just tells you that to keep you around."

"He's *never* told me that. What did he say to you anyway?"

I felt Sark's neck pull taut with tension. He wasn't going to say anything. Before I could figure out how to get it out of him, I realized we were about to walk past my stop.

"Wait," I said, and Sark stopped walking. A weight sunk in my stomach when I realized he'd have to put me down. "This is it."

We both looked over the box of a building that somehow seemed haunted, silent ghosts sticking to the walls.

"Isn't this the maintenance building?" Sark asked, skeptical.

"My penthouse is on the second floor."

Upon my pestering, Sark finally put me down but insisted on me holding onto his arm for support. I led him around the back of the building and tapped the fire escape, a jolt of surprise going through me when I realized what I had done. I just showed someone where I lived—the only safe spot I had at the Compound because nobody knew I was ever there. And here I was, waltzing over with someone—

Not someone, I told myself firmly. *Sark. It's okay.*

"Thank you for walking me here," I said, leaning against the cool metal ladder. "It was...I really appreciate it."

Sark just looked from my leg to the ladder with a raised eyebrow. "You're going to get up there?"

I folded my arms across my chest. "Yes I am, actually."

He suppressed a smile and gestured to the ladder. "Let's see it then."

"Fine."

It was embarrassing, the way I had to drag myself up the ladder and kind of hop along on one leg. Sark followed close behind to brace my fall if it came and stifled his laughter only after I lovingly kicked him. Mercifully, I finally made it, pushing up the window and ducking into the cavern I called home.

"This is where you live?" Sark asked incredulously, looking around at the giant creepy generators.

"No." I led him past the second row of boxes and gestured to my corner. "That's where I live." For some reason, it was kind of exciting to share this with him—a sacred part of me nobody had seen before. "Cozy, huh?"

"You're...you're not kidding."

"It's not that bad. Really. It's nice to have a place to call my own." I hesitated. "It's also kind of a secret, for safety, you know, so if you...wouldn't mind not telling anyone..." I felt stupid now, though I wasn't sure why. Couldn't I trust him?

That seemed to tear Sark out of whatever world he had found himself in. He glanced at me. "And you brought me here?"

I bit my lip and nodded slowly. He watched me again, that same kind of uncertain searching in his eyes, as though seeing me for the first time again. It made my toes curl and my skin prickle uncomfortably, but I forced myself to keep his gaze.

I'm too different, I thought in a panic. *This is too much, I'm too much, he never wanted to be here.*

After seconds or hours—I wasn't sure—he dropped his calculating gaze and ran a hand through his hair. "Wow...thank you. I didn't know...I mean, I assumed we were still...well I hoped at least..." He took a breath to bring himself together. "I didn't know where we stood. If you still felt you could trust me like that."

I blinked in surprise. *He said thank you.*

Too many things formed on my tongue, too many thoughts I wanted to convey somehow, but thankfully something else caught Sark's attention before I could try and fail. He glanced back at my corner and stiffened. Hesitantly, as though walking on sacred ground, he took two steps forward. Then a third. I stumbled after him, confused, and followed his stormy gaze. My heart sank when I realized he saw my marks on the wall, setting a bleak scene against the ominous shadows of the generator lights. I'd forgotten about them.

"Oh, uh…" I pulled on his arm. He didn't budge. "That's just...they're nothing. I get bored sometimes."

He didn't seem to buy my dumb explanation—not that it was surprising. He just stared at the wall for a long time before closing his eyes and sucking in through his teeth.

"I have a question," he finally said quietly. "Actually, I have two questions, and I really need you to answer them honestly. Please."

I cleared my throat to stall. "Okay."

I counted to six before Sark took another breath, then he opened his eyes and turned them on me, paralyzing me with their depth. "You coming here—Cyrus' deal with Alexis...I don't know, maybe it's highly irrational and conceited of me to even think, but I have to...Arie, please tell me you didn't take that deal for me."

At least thirteen different responses went through my head, thirteen different angles, thirteen different versions. Thirteen different ways to gain control, take advantage, pull the power card, lessen my vulnerability. Confused at my hesitation with what to say, I counted to seven before the actual truth fell out of my mouth.

"I didn't really take the deal—it wasn't much of a deal. They—" My voice caught and I forced it to smooth over. "They found me just to witness the murder. Cyrus would've gotten me anyway eventually, if that's what he wanted."

Some of the tension in Sark's stance relaxed. "You never planned on coming here—whether by yourself or with Micah or...you didn't know about it?"

I shook my head.

"So, were you...when you left us at the hospital...were you ever going to come back?"

Come back. Those two words hit me over the head with a chunk of reality.

The key doesn't ever go back, Vanessa quoted to me from one of Cyrus' many mantras about my life. *You can't ever go back. You feel yourself sliding farther every day and you know as well as I do that you'll never be able to go back to anything.*

I can't leave with you, Sark.

"Sark." I wrapped my arms around myself and looked down at my dirty feet. "I shouldn't...oh I hate it, but I shouldn't be talking to you. I should leave you alone. I've...I never wanted you to know, but I've gotten worse, and I'm...I'm not going to get any better."

I felt my bones would crumble inside me and I forced them to stay together, forced my voice to be strong even though I wanted to fall apart. "I'll do everything I can here for you—all of you—but there's only so far I can go. I can't transfer out from Lennon, but I'll see...if there's anything else you guys need, just ask and I'll try to get it. But..." I finally raised my eyes to his—a mistake, as they were much too full of things I didn't want to deal with. "I can't get you out. It's not possible, and I know...I just can't. I would give anything to, but I can't. I'm so sorry." My voice broke on the last word, to my mortification. "I'm so so sorry."

Whatever was left of the uncomfortable murky restraint between us vanished. My broken voice broke the rest of his composed resolve, and his forehead creased so deep, as though the grief of everything had left permanent marks on his body.

"No, Arie." He surged forward and pulled me into a crushing hug. I hated that my first response was to shy away, but Sark held fast, not letting me isolate myself. "It's okay. It's not your fault. It's okay."

I fought the major conflict between my body's instincts and what I knew in my heart until it all wore me out and I was too tired to keep it up. I gave in. I fell into him, letting him hold me, as I chanted a desperate whisper over and over.

"I'm sorry I'm sorry I'm sorry I'm sorry I'm sorry."

"Arie, it's okay." Sark put his hand on the back of my head, holding me to him and softly stroking my hair, just like he used to all those months ago. "It's okay. I'm here, all right? I'm here and I love you and I'm not going anywhere. Nothing is going to change that. I'll always be with you, Arie, even if you turn blue and want to kill me."

"Promise?" I asked, even though it was childish. The idea of even hoping he was being honest was laughable—and it would kill me later.

"Yes. I promise." He hesitated, his hand stalling on my hair for just a moment, then he went on, his voice lower. "It's been bad, hasn't it?"

I shook my head violently, scraping my forehead along his shoulder. "Sark, it's been awful." My breath caught and tears stung my eyes, and my veins burned with hatred at myself for showing such weakness. "And it's only going to get worse."

"You'll find a way, Arie. I know you will. Somehow—I don't know how—it's going to be okay. You're going to be okay."

I gritted my teeth in frustration. He didn't know what he was talking about. He didn't understand the scope of how bad it already was.

He doesn't know about me, Vanessa added with a new kind of smug interest. *Let's tell him. Please? I'd love to see the look on his face when he finds out you're actually insane.*

"It won't," I whispered back. Thankfully he didn't try to refute me.

I don't know how long we stood there like that, but eventually I pulled myself together enough that he felt okay with letting me go, even though his hands hovered over me for a few lingering seconds after they broke contact with me. I was humiliated at my breakdown in front of him, but he didn't seem to mind much. In fact, he was the normal Sark I missed so much, except he watched me a lot more. He insisted on pulling out the first aid kit I kept behind a generator, cleaning up a few more of my scrapes and wrapping up my leg so it had at least some kind of support. Of course, he flipped out when he found my knife and it took me forever to reassure him that I'd never needed to use it before and he didn't need to stay until I fell asleep.

I walked him to the equivalent of the door—the window—and practiced giving him a hug, since I knew that used to feel normal to me. He hugged me back, long and tight.

"Thank you," I said. "For just about everything. I know...I know it's awful but in some ways I'm really glad you're here. I missed you a lot."

Sark grinned, making me smile too. "I'm happy to say that I'll see you tomorrow." He went to duck out the window, then stopped and looked at me. "I will, right?"

I pretended to think. "Yeah, I *guess* I can squeeze that into my schedule."

He rolled his eyes. "Goodnight."

"Be safe."

"You too."

I watched out the window as he climbed down the fire escape and disappeared out of sight. I didn't realize I was still smiling when I snuggled into my makeshift bed. An actual, genuine smile, rather than my practiced, presentable one.

Oh, stop being so happy, Vanessa complained. *We both know this won't last. He thinks he knows it all but once he finds out the whole story, he'll be gone. Unless you kill him first. That would be fun.*

I actually laughed at her, the first time in forever her nagging didn't get to me.

It's a family thing, I told her, feeling warm even against the cold floor. *You just wouldn't understand.*

7

"Arie!" a chorus of kids shouted as I walked into the Dome carrying a giant covered plastic platter. I had to concentrate to keep from dropping it as mini people bombarded me with greetings.

"What's in that?" JP asked, scrunching his nose at my package.

"Yeah," Sharna repeated, "what's in that?"

"I'll show you," I said. "Are your caretakers here?"

"No," Ranger answered. "But we have some visitors."

It was then I noticed the small group of people sitting around the cots: Sark, Peter, Alaina, Brennan, and Lucy. The past couple weeks had proven to me more and more that we were mostly okay—Alaina and I had even spoken a few times without hostility, though it had been replaced by awkward politeness. It was better than I could've hoped for a month ago.

Children trailed after me, everyone talking at once in a desperate fight for my attention, as I went and sat on the floor near the edge of the group and next to Sark, then set my platter on the cot in front of me. Lotti took off the lid to reveal two-dozen sugar cookies topped with icy blue frosting. A collective gasp went through the group of kids, and even several of the kids who stayed on the opposite side of the room peeked over in interest.

"Where did you get those?" Fozzy asked, his hand half outstretched toward the artificial blue, mesmerized.

"They were left over from a party yesterday," I explained. "I figured you guys would need refreshments for your performance."

"You're right!" Tai started bustling around the arena, pulling kids around with her. "Come on everyone!"

Hadley jumped into my line of sight. "You have to watch for my part, okay? It's really cool." He pointed to the audience next to me. "I already showed them, and they said it was cool."

"All right, I'll be watching."

Peter reached forward and stole a cookie. "These are for public consumption, right?"

I grinned. "Absolutely."

"Oh good." Brennan grabbed two for him and Lucy. "I was breaking into a sugar sweat."

Alaina didn't miss out either. "I watched them frost these and it took all of my willpower to not dip my finger in the bowl when I walked by." She illustrated by smearing her finger along the top of her dessert.

Jacklynn sat next to me, apparently opting out of whatever performance the kids had put together and chose to eat a cookie instead. The rest of the kids scurried around, grabbing flashlights and blankets and even a boom box—I hadn't seen one of those since I was twelve—as Tai ordered them all around to prepare for her directorial debut.

"Have you seen this?" I whispered to Sark, careful not to attract attention from the performers.

"No," he whispered back. "Hadley showed me his flip off the cot but that was the only preview I got."

A flip off the cot? My forehead creased with worry. "Did—"

"Relax. He only fell once and he was fine."

The thumb-sucking Bea appeared from nowhere, watching the kids with wide eyes as she staggered over to me and plopped into my lap.

"Hey, sweetie," I said, brushing my fingers through her mess of thin black hair.

"Does she ever talk?" Jacklynn asked me in between bites of cookie.

I shook my head. "Nobody's ever heard her before."

"Do you think she knows how?"

"Um, I don't know. That's a good question." I took a cookie off the tray and offered it to Bea. "Do you want one? It's a cookie."

Bea pulled her finger out of her mouth, making a loud smacking sound, as she took the circular treat and inspected it. Her slobber covered hand swept through the frosting, turning her fingers blue. A gasp escaped her and she looked up at me and gave a toothy smile.

I smiled back. "It's good frosting, huh?"

She bounced in my lap, her hand exploring the frosting, making gasping sounds that could be laughter, generating the attention of our small group of spectators. She was just so cute.

In her excitement, she reached up and touched my face while she bounced, smearing slobber frosting all over me. I went rigid and wrinkled my nose, while everyone started laughing and her gasping got louder.

"That's a good look for you," Sark told me, generating another round of snickers.

With a wry grin, I swiped off what frosting was left on Bea's cookie and wiped it all over Sark's cheek.

Jacklynn covered her mouth with her hand in delighted shock as she giggled. "Oh my goodness!"

"Looks good on you too," I told him.

Sark tried to be serious, but he couldn't keep a smile off his face. "You better watch yourself, Nolan."

For the rest of the time, I was very conscious of him sitting next to me—probably just anticipating his frosting counterattack.

"We're ready!" Tai announced, standing on top of the furthest cot from us. "Presenting our production: Stories with Arie!"

They then went into a somewhat musical retelling of every story I'd ever told them mashed up together. There were roaring lions, swimming mermaids, dancing princesses, flying children, living toys, magic lamps and everything in between. The only music they had was classical, but they sung along to it in broken stanzas that sometimes rhymed and never flowed. Hadley landed his flip off the cot for the finale and beamed with pride. Then they all struck their last pose.

The audience burst into applause besides Peter, but he joined in after Alaina elbowed him. Ecstatic at their performance—which was probably the most fun and creative project any of them had ever done here—they treated themselves to the cookies I'd brought, gushing over how good the blue stuff tasted.

Bea was trying to shove her slobber frosting coated hand in my mouth when the door to the Dome opened. The kids' excited chattering ceased immediately, and I looked across the room to see Micah walking toward us.

Oh great.

Everyone, including me, stiffened, and the kids all moved to crowd behind me. They knew little of life outside the Dome, but they still knew Micah.

"The guard didn't believe you were in here," Micah said as he walked past the audience and stopped in front of me. He raised a mocking eyebrow when he really saw me. "You look ridiculous."

The drying frosting on my face felt funny on my skin when I spoke. "It's called having fun; you should try it sometime. Why was a guard looking for me?"

He held out a tablet and my stomach knotted. "Delivery. Wheels up in one hour."

I felt my insides prickle painfully as I took the tablet from him.

"He knows we're coming," Micah continued, needlessly, in my opinion. "So we gotta cut him off before he can make a run for it. He's a factory worker—the schematics are in the file. Make sure you know them before we take off."

A mutual understanding passed over the room, touching everyone but the kids. They knew what Micah's 'job' was. It wasn't hard to put the pieces together.

I swallowed hard but thankfully my voice held its own. "Fine. I'll be there."

Micah turned and walked out. "And get that garbage off your face," he called as he went out the door.

Ranger leaned over so I could see him, his lips stained blue. "Does that mean you're going on another trip?" he asked.

"Yeah," Sharna said. "Does that mean you're going on another trip?"

"Yep." I forced a believable light tone. "I'll be back in a day or two, okay?"

They all rushed to grab their maps and atlases, discussing where I might be headed and what animals I would see where. I scooped Bea up and set her on the floor next to Jacklynn, then got on my knees and started to stand up.

Sark grabbed my arm and pulled me back down, leaning his face close so he could whisper. His blue eyes searched mine as he asked, "Is he going to hurt you?"

I was caught off guard by the proximity, how many levels there were to his ocean-deep eyes. He was worried, he was suspicious, he was cautious, he was caring, and so many other things in between.

He gripped my arm harder. "Arie, is he going to hurt you?"

"No," I finally whispered. "No. It's not me I'm worried about. I'll be fine."

Sark gazed at me for another moment before letting go of my arm. "Be careful."

"I will."

Making sure to grab my tablet, I stood and left the building, waving goodbye on my way out.

~~~

The plane ride was quiet. Not that Micah and I were usually bursting with engaging conversation, but I sensed he was still mad at me for the labor group incident. He kept to himself. I spent the travel time silent and compliant, memorizing maps of streets and buildings as I tried not to think about what was ahead.

Our plane dropped us off in the middle of a cornfield, leaving us to our assignment, which was where Micah opted to stay. He sat right on the warm ground in between cornstalks to wait. I paced a few feet away and followed suit. Then we
~~~

settled into waiting until dark when it was opportune to strike.

Unfortunately my tablet wasn't programmed with anything remotely entertaining. I was bored stiff. I took a nap, sleeping on and off for a few hours, but it felt like minutes compared to the time I was awake. I tore apart an ear of corn, kernel by kernel. I picked my fingernails. I tried to see how far I could count but gave up at eight hundred and forty-seven.

Micah stared at nothing. Sometimes he slept. Sometimes he didn't. Several times he went over the building plans with me yet again. The astounding boredom I felt didn't seem to bother him.

When the evening settled in and Micah mercifully gave the go ahead, I stood and stretched my stiff muscles, then followed him through the cornfield and toward the bright city lights. The signs were my first clue we were in a different country: I didn't understand a single word.

Good thing you only took one semester of Spanish in high school, Vanessa said snidely.

The sun was stretching its last rays of the day—we had a limited window. Micah broke into a run and I shadowed him, taking the back route into the city so as to limit the number of people that could see us.

The factory we were looking for stood tall on the outskirts of the city, its imposing and bland walls serving as a warning to all who went by, emanating the struggle and toil the workers must've faced inside.

As planned, the workday was over by the time we arrived. Micah had an access key to get in—when I asked he said Cyrus gave it to him—and our entry was smooth. It was finding this Ravi Chiverez in the dark factory that proved to be the hard part.

Metal arms hung limp from the ceiling, frozen conveyer belts spread across the floor, steam whistling every few minutes and making me jump. The few security lights were the only ones on, casting sinister shadows on the walls.

This place is begging for murder, Vanessa said. *It's creepy and gross.*

"Where's the control room?" Micah whispered, glancing around the place as he formed different strategies.

I looked up and pointed to the walkway system about a hundred feet above us. "Up there, center of the building. We're too far left." Following my mental map, I led the way to the back stairs that took us up to the walkways.

Micah blazed in front of me then, his footsteps silent as he stole down the walkway, and I mimicked him, allowing my senses to come into focus and my body to tingle with anticipation and control. We came upon an octagonal glass enclosure connecting all five walkways and looking over the entire factory. A light was on inside. A shadow of a person moved.

But it was no longer a person. This was an assignment.

Micah motioned for me to go around and block the other side. I pressed myself against the floor as

I slid past the glass structure and positioned myself by the door. It was game time.

The sound of a door being thrown open. A man yelling an exclamation. Crashing and thrashing. Then my door opened. A lanky man with a thin mustache skidded to a stop when he saw me blocking his exit. He backed away as Micah and I closed in on him.

"I paid!" he shouted in a thick Spanish accent. "You tell Cyrus I paid! I did!"

The shouting went ignored. Micah grabbed him by his neck, yanking him back, and I stepped to the side thinking I'd get to sit this one out. Too easy.

Ravi struggled for only a second, then pretended to give up, but Micah wasn't that stupid. He was ready when Ravi lunged to make a break for it. Instead of cutting right toward the door, though, Ravi actually surprised Micah by forcing them both to the left and slamming a button on the wall.

A light flashed, nearly blinding me. I shut my eyes and looked away, glancing back a moment later to find Micah bleeding underneath some sort of metal contraption and Ravi dashing out the door. My automatic response was to help Micah. In the same second my instincts screamed: *he's getting away!* just as Micah glared at me with raging jade eyes and ordered, "Get him."

My feet didn't falter. I ran after Ravi, chasing him down the walkway. It wasn't much of a chase. I tackled him to the ground within six and a half seconds of the bright light flashing. He shrieked in terror and tried to scratch my eyes out. A snarl bubbled on my lips.

Make him pay for it, Vanessa crowed at me. *Don't let him get away.*

I didn't. My grip tightened at her command, the faint taste of metal in my mouth, then I was moving my hands. Fast. Hard. My body seemed to know what to do on its own, and it didn't check with my hazy brain before acting. There was yelling in the distance. Something warm on my skin. Liquid on my sleeves. Red.

"Stop!" It took a few seconds to register that I had screamed the word. "Stop now!"

I froze, then jerked myself backward and off my victim. I only caught a glimpse of a mangled Ravi before a figure pounced on it, obstructing my vision, and loud screams and breaks and squelches ensued.

Then it was over.

Micah kicked the body off the walkway, then straightened up and sauntered over, yanking me to my feet.

"Let's go," he instructed as he passed me.

I stared at the red smudge on the silver metal.

"Arie, let's go!"

I did that.

My hands started to shake.

How could I do that?

A hand clamped down on my shoulder, spinning me around and blurring the world. Then the hand slapped me.

"I said, let's go!" Micah grabbed my wrist and dragged me along.

The next thing I knew, I was sitting in the dreaded cargo plane. My legs burned with exertion but that was the only evidence that I'd gotten myself through the city and back to our transportation.

The flight went by in the blink of an eye. I felt like I'd only been staring at the wall for five minutes when we landed. Micah glared at me as he stood, and I realized I'd better get myself together before he lost patience and murdered me too.

As was customary, we made our way through the sleeping Compound to the administration building, up the elevator and into Cyrus' office. He was waiting in his big leather chair, his eyes jumping to my bloody sleeves for just a second.

"The mission was a success," Micah stated before Cyrus could ask.

Cyrus nodded. "Good. Good. And Arie, dear, how was the trip for you?"

I cleared my throat. "Good, sir."

"Do you find it's coming more naturally to you?"

"Somewhat, sir."

He nodded again. "Good. Now I know you may not understand now, but this preparation is vital to your success. And, I must say, you are promising. I fully expect you will go much farther than past ones. Don't you think, Micah?"

Micah couldn't care less. "Yes, sir."

Cyrus slid his fingers over the arm of his chair, musing to himself. "I'll admit, we took quite a hit after Xander's failure. But you, Arie, provide us with a much brighter future."

A nasty headache was brewing but the name still caught my weak attention—infecteds at the Compound had often compared me to this mysterious Xander. And I got the feeling I should be grateful I didn't know him.

"Xander?" I asked, my eyebrows furrowing.

"He was our last key," Cyrus explained, his tone mournful. "We poured every asset into his success, but we lost him in the end." He perked up. "However, I learned much from his failure that will be used for you. You will be the key, my dear, and it will be wonderful."

My hoarse voice cracked, and I felt I'd just been sucker punched in the gut. "Your last *key*?"

"Well, there's more than one of course. Weren't you aware?"

I was too traumatized to fully take that in, to actually process what he meant.

Cyrus took my stunned silence as a 'no.' "No one is as special as they believe they are, dear. The formula has had many more options than you." He waved his hand. "Now, you're both dismissed."

I couldn't feel my feet as I walked with Micah to the elevator. He took off the second it opened, and I wandered home in a daze, the all too familiar, catastrophic beating on my cranium beginning to really pick up. I only half noticed, though, because the dried blood on my wrist was starting to itch. Ravi's blood.

I did that. How could I have done that?

By the time I climbed through the maintenance building window, I was nearly hyperventilating, my hands shaking so hard that I almost couldn't shut the window. Staggering as though I were drunk, I lurched forward, eager to duck under my blanket and hide from Ravi Chiverez.

A body loomed in my way, and I was sure a zombie had come to deal me my end. The fear turned to instinct. I took down the zombie only to find out it wasn't a zombie after all. It was Sark.

I jerked away from him and crumpled to my knees, pressing on my temples. She was coming. "What are you doing here?"

He rubbed the back of his head as he sat up. "Making sure you came home."

"You need to leave." I knew that. It was bad for him to be here. "You need to leave now."

My gaze met his and I remembered earlier, years ago, sitting in the Dome. Blue eyes. His concern. My cheek stinging.

Is he going to hurt you? he'd asked me.

Then my head practically exploded with raging bloodlust, tainted blue, leaving the taste of rusted metal in my mouth. I nearly doubled over as I half choked on nothing.

Sark reached for me. "Arie—"

I hit his hand and cringed away. "Don't touch me. Don't touch me."

"You aren't going to hurt me," Sark said with sincerity. "I know that. You can touch me."

I'm not going to hurt him. I loosened slightly when I realized that was true, despite Vanessa trying to force an override on my mind and body.

Hesitantly, Sark reached again and brushed his curled fingers against my arm. "See?" I saw when his eyes registered the red dried flakes on my skin. His forehead creased.

"It's not mine, it's his," I blurted through labored breathing. "He's dead. He's dead and I kept him from getting away."

Sark nodded once, his face serious but receptive. "Micah killed him?"

"Yeah, but…" I trailed off, Vanessa's command echoing in my skull. The command that I'd obeyed. I leaned away so Sark wasn't touching me anymore. "I could kill you."

"No, you couldn't. We both know that."

I looked down at my colored hand and slid it closer and closer to the hot generator. My fingers tingled at the heat. Touching the metal would scald my skin, burn me like Ravi Chiverez was burned, distract me, maybe, from what was going to happen.

Sark used his hand to push mine away, the heat fading from my skin, and I glanced up at him.

"You're fighting it," he said, "right now. Walk me through it. What's going on in there?"

"I…I don't…" I shook my head, trying to clear it. It just hurt worse. "I hurt him. I don't even know what happened. I was angry and then there was blood."

"But you didn't actually kill the guy, right?"

"No, but…but I lost control." I focused my eyes on his. "I'm getting worse."

Vanessa gave an animalistic shriek of fury, and I felt her essence inside of me, berating against her confinement as she desperately tried to claw her way out of my mental prison. My fingers were twitching, desperate to squeeze the life out of something. To draw more blood. Even my own. My veins pulsed with blood, and I felt the compulsive need to tear into my skin. I clawed at my arm as hard as I could, and when Sark swatted my hand away my fingertips brushed against a metal handle. I didn't remember I had a gun in my thigh holster until I was clutching it in my hand. I sensed Sark stiffen when he recognized he was in the line of fire.

"Arie," he said quietly, fighting to keep his composure. "Stay with me."

The concentration took everything I had. "Ple—please. Please, she…she wants to hurt you. So bad. I can't…"

"You don't want to hurt me," he said. "I know you don't."

Moaning in pain and frustration, I slammed the gun against the ground twice before successfully throwing it out of sight. Vanessa screamed at me in fury just as Sark moved toward me, and I found my hand gripping his throat. He choked, and the sound was enough to get me to jerk myself away.

My whole body shook as I curled into a ball and grabbed fistfuls of hair, keeping myself in a gridlock, forcing every muscle, joint, bone and ligament into immobility. I didn't even care when I tipped sideways onto the floor.

"You need to leave," I told Sark, my voice trembling and strained with exertion. "Leave. I'm…I'm too unstable. I'm going to hurt you."

"You won't hurt me," he said softly, rubbing the side of his neck, as though trying to convince himself too. "You could, but you won't."

I clenched my teeth together as I shook, feeling sweat dripping down my back. "You…you can't know that. You…" My eyes prickled with tears at the thought of trying to explain what was actually happening. "You don't know."

You have no idea how deep and dark and twisted this is. How bad.

Slowly so he didn't surprise me this time, Sark draped my blanket over my rigid form and put a comforting hand on my shoulder. "I know enough. You're stronger than this."

You're losing! Vanessa snarled. *You are pathetic and weak, and I will crush you. You can't do this. Give up.*

I thought my teeth would shatter from how hard I was clamping them. *Go to hell.*

Princess, we're already here.

I was slipping, the edges of my consciousness getting hazy, opening up my weak points. Vanessa attacked with no mercy and all ferocity. I knew if I blacked out, I would wake up as something else.

My current plan wasn't working, so I decided to just throw caution to the wind and get reinforcements in a last-ditch effort to contain the crisis.

Towing my blanket, I unlocked my muscles and dragged myself forward, going until I was practically curled in Sark's lap and rested my forehead on his shoulder. I felt him stiffen at the new closeness, but I focused on two things: breathing in and out, and the sound of his heart beating.

That's human, I told myself. *That's what you are.*

Vanessa glowered. *You have no idea what you are. You're an it.*

I dug my fingernails into my skull, trying to tune her out. Sark took my hands in each of his and pulled them down.

"Don't hurt yourself." His voice was nearly inaudible now, like he was holding his breath, treading carefully as to not wake another monster. "Please. There's no point to it. You aren't the enemy here."

A half whimper, half moan escaped through my teeth, my brain begging me to just raise the white flag and end the searing war trying to split me in two.

"I don't want to be a monster," I whispered. "I really…I really don't."

Sark gave me a gentle hug. "You don't have to be. Not tonight."

I didn't know how long I stayed there, nearly motionless, painful noises forcing themselves through my teeth, as I waited to self-destruct. It had to have been at least hours, but it could've been days for all I knew. I just concentrated on Sark's heartbeat and the consequences of losing.

Five will turn to six, and seven will come, and we can go on to eight. Five. Six. Seven. Eight. Seven. Eight. Eight. Please, eight. Please make this stop.

Eventually Vanessa gave up. She was ruthless and driven, but there was still only so much she could do. I felt her retreat to her spot in the back of my head, small and weak but still livid—she'd put everything she had into that, exhausting us both. My body was grateful when I slowly loosened the tension.

"That's it," Sark encouraged, breaking the anxious silence. "Relax. You're over the worst of it. Just relax."

I found myself listening to him, my body sinking into the blanket, a winded breath escaping my lips as I deflated.

It's over, I told Vanessa. *You lost.*

Her fury heated up my veins, but she smoothed it over with confidence. *My time will come. One of these nights, Arie, I will get out.*

The problem was, I knew she was right. It was only a matter of time.

"Sark?" I asked, breathless, straining under the weight of what I was about to say.

"Yeah?"

"I need you…I mean, I almost…I could've…"

"No, none of that," he said, hastily shutting me down. "You couldn't have done anything to me."

"But I could've." I squeezed my eyes shut and hoped everything would disappear. It didn't. "Sark, if it really…if it really came down to it, if I…I need to know you'll protect yourself. Protect everyone. I need…I need to trust that you'll do what's necessary if…if I'm too far gone. Before they can use me."

I opened my eyes to watch his reaction. I expected him to turn stone cold, to purse his lips and get conflicted eyes and solemnly promise me because he knew. He knew the stakes. He had a whole life of doing what was necessary because it had to be done—I could trust him to do it, however hard it would be.

The effect of my request was near opposite what I expected and seemed to take hold in slow motion. He looked over me once. Then twice. Three times. I felt his hands curl into fists on my back. A fourth time. His expression pulled tight, then broke open, his wounded blue eyes twisting up in a hurricane.

"I ca—" he choked, so low I barely heard. Then he crushed me against his chest, as though through brute strength he could force my broken pieces to stay together.

"Don't ask me that," he breathed, words ragged. "Please. I can't."

"You have to," I insisted. "You have to, Sark."

"No. You can't ask me that. You just can't."

My voice cracked with his. "Then what am I going to do?"

Sark shook his head in fervent denial before burying his face in my hair. "I don't know."

8

My alarm let out its warning blare, reaching in and gradually dragging me out of unconsciousness. It was cruel. I was so comfortable and warm—more than usual. There was a warmth next to me, a steady coziness from the hearth rather than the scalding burn from the generators. I wrapped my blanket tighter around me and scooted closer to the hearth. I didn't want to get up. I wanted to stay with the hearth, its constant inflation, deflation, comforting, as though it were breathing in and out. Breathing in and out…almost like a person.

My eyes snapped open to see a white t-shirt about two inches from my nose. I glanced up at Sark's face, his eyebrows furrowing in confused irritation as my alarm began to wake him up. Reflexively it seemed, his arms tightened around me, like he could protect me from the hideous noise announcing yet another day, and thankfully my squeak of surprise got caught in my throat and died there, inaudible.

"What is that?" Sark mumbled, rubbing his forehead. He cracked his eyes open and raked them across the unfamiliar room. Then his gaze fell on me and a shooting electric current passed between us, shocking us apart.

Boom. Ten thousand strips of awkward confetti thrown in the air, celebrating our awkward party of awkwardness.

I sat up and shoved myself a few feet away from him, running my fingers through my tangled hair as I felt my face burn up in embarrassment. A thought of gratitude that I rarely blushed was the only thought in my head.

Sark dropped his eyes and sat up, running a hand through his hair. I watched my red-stained hand as I half crawled, half reached over to my corner, found my radio and turned off the alarm. The silence made a deafening pulse in my ears.

Let me die. Please, anyone, let me die.

That can be arranged, Vanessa muttered.

"That thing is loud," Sark finally stated.

I laughed once but it sounded like a dying horse. "Yeah, it is."

I tossed the radio back and forth in my hand, both of us staring at the simple motion as though it were the last play of triple overtime in the Superbowl, and we actually cared about football.

"Why are we up so early?" Sark asked.

"I'm sorry, I have training in the morning."

"Every morning?"

"Pretty much."

"Huh."

Ditching the radio, I meticulously folded up my blanket, then put my earpiece in my ear and grabbed my boots, purposely lacing them up slowly and giving the activity my undivided attention. After all, lacing up combat boots was almost as dangerous as defusing a bomb, probably.

Sark finally put our silence out of its misery. "How are you feeling this morning?" he asked, polite and sincere but still a little too formal.

"Better," I answered. "Thank you."

In my peripheral vision, I saw Sark stretch and stand up.

"Well, I'm, uh…I'm gonna head back," he told me. "Get in a few more hours before roll call."

I nodded and glanced up at him. "Yeah. Okay. Good luck."

Good luck? Are you kidding me?

"Well, I guess you don't really need luck," I said, hoping I'd messed up the bomb defusing and my boots would explode and keep me from saying another word. "'Cause luck would mean…yeah, anyway, that's a good idea. Sorry it's early."

"Don't worry about it. See you later."

"Okay."

I heard the window open and his foot hit the metal. Then again. And again. The sound got quieter with every step as he made his way down the ladder. Once I knew it was safe, I moaned and buried my face in my arms.

Vanessa cackled in my head. *What was that?*

Honestly, I didn't know. I'd fallen asleep next to Sark on the couch tons of times before—back when we had one of those wonderful things called 'houses'—and it had never, ever been like *that*. It was always completely normal and nice and…granted, the way I'd been curled in his arms wasn't exactly as innocent as in the past…but how did that make me guilty?

I'm blowing this way out of proportion, I decided. *It was nothing at all.*

Vanessa was still busting up over the whole thing, having a little too much fun. *Oh man, princess, that was the most awkward interaction between two human beings I've ever seen.*

I rolled my eyes, trying to act like I was over it. *Please. How many interactions have you actually seen?*

You know, you're right: I've only seen yours, which means I've only seen awkward ones. My comparison isn't as complete as it could be.

Thanks.

After I changed my shirt, my feet took me to training while my mind wandered to last night. I didn't remember asking him to stay. To be fair, though, I didn't remember anything besides my episode. I remembered telling Sark to leave. I remembered being scared I would lose control and hurt him or scare him at the very least. I remembered being so grateful I didn't have to fight that night alone, like all the others. But I didn't remember the part where I asked him to shack up next to the generator.

He probably just got too tired to do anything but fall asleep, Vanessa said. *You kept him up forever with your pathetic parade.*

I guess so. That was the only thing that made sense. I just didn't get why I was so hung up over it.

For the first time ever, I beat Micah to the training building, and I even made a stop to wash my hands of bloodstains. His face was priceless when he sauntered into the arena and found me stationed smugly at his punching bag.

"Sleep in?" I asked in between punches.

Micah raised an eyebrow and set his jaw, accepting my challenge. He stood across from me, grabbed hold of the bag, then nodded for me to keep going.

I took a breath and pounded the bag. It didn't move. If Micah hadn't been watching me, I would've fallen to the ground and screamed over my knuckles. But his stupid arrogant face kept me from doing so.

"Weak," Micah scoffed. "This is pathetic."

"You're pathetic," I muttered because I couldn't think of anything else. Of course, in about six hours, the perfect comeback would pop into my head, completely useless.

He ignored me. "I just expected more, I guess, after last night."

I concentrated on my glove connecting with the bag. It stayed put. Micah stood relaxed, like a fly was landing on the bag rather than all my body power.

"You took a step in the right direction," he went on. "It's still just a step though. You aren't even close to where you should be."

More punching. "It's your op, isn't it? I'd hate to infringe on your big boy responsibilities and screw it up."

"Still. You could've had him. He opened the door right to you."

My teeth clenched at the memory. "I still saved your sorry butt. Stopping the guy is the extent of what I'll do."

Not for long, princess, Vanessa told me.

Nobody asked you.

Micah rolled his eyes. "You really think that would be it? Honestly? You're afraid of killing someone and, what, never getting over it?"

"No. I'm afraid of killing someone and not feeling a thing." I slammed my fists against the bag with everything I had. The force actually knocked Micah back a step. Our eyes met, both wide with shock. I gave him a brilliant smile. He narrowed his eyes and opened his mouth to speak.

A whistle stopped him. "Four laps!" Roland shouted, entering the arena. "Four laps! Both of you, get moving!"

I took off my gloves and tossed them at Micah before turning around and sprinting down the track.

We were neck and neck—Micah finished first, of course, but I finished right after, faster than I had maybe ever. I gave Micah another smile as I passed him to grab a drink. If his eyes were lasers, I'd be a puddle of Arie wax.

I paid for all of the smug smiles later. After going with the mutts a few rounds, Roland had me take a turn in the ring with Micah. I think I bruised a rib but wasn't sure, though my left wrist was definitely broken. He almost dislocated my jaw, but I was able to twist it on him and dislocate his instead. For that, he was about to snap my neck, but Roland called us on to the next drill. Another win for Arie.

The second Roland dismissed us, I was out, evading any revenge Micah might feel entitled to. Having only gotten two hours of sleep the night before, I went back home to take a nap. Dwindling embarrassment prickled my skin when I saw my blanket folded in the corner rather than sprawled out like usual, and I remembered why I'd taken the time to fold it in the first place.

My earpiece went off all too soon, calling me to rehearsal. I cradled my left wrist as I made my way to the surprisingly busy production building. The second I walked into the dressing room, I was whisked away by a beauty team and ushered into the shower and then my chair, and the long process of putting me together began.

"What's going on?" I asked the girl plucking my eyebrows, watching people bustle past the opening of my cubicle every few seconds. "It's just rehearsal. I don't need to be all dolled up, just presentable."

"There's been a change of plans," she told me, her tongue sticking out as she concentrated on my face. "I don't know details. I just know you need to be perfect."

Coming from the training I'd had, I was forced to forewarn about my wrist, my rib, my beaten body. They took it in without questioning, using the information only to adjust my look. They were used to scraping rogue makeup off me and finding all sorts of scars and bruises underneath. Somehow, they found a way to cover them up. To make me perfect.

It's all about the show.

Today's hairstyle consisted of a curly ponytail—my personal favorite—that highlighted my gold earrings that accented my long-sleeved white lace dress. It was simple yet elegant and, though I wouldn't admit it to the beauty team, I kind of loved it.

My left wrist was confined to a white brace that seamlessly blended into the sleeves of my dress. A needle was mercilessly poked into my side, numbing the area so I'd be able to sing and jump around despite the bruised rib. My face was padded and brushed and smeared until you'd never guess I had been beat up that morning. I wasn't always a fan of the beauty teams, but I had to admit that they did excellent work.

After I was deemed ready, I walked out of my cubicle and searched for someone who could tell me what was going on. Elijah's cubicle door was closed. Miss Welch was nowhere to be found. I caught a glimpse of Zoe, but she disappeared before I could ask.

I wandered onstage where techies were running through backdrops and lighting and smoke machines. The place was nearly empty, making it seem huge, and I marveled and was sickened by the thought that we filled it up with guests every show.

The door to the kitchen was swinging as though someone had just gone through it, giving me the impression the kitchen was alive as well. I caught sight of Ellen in a mint green party dress heading toward the bar. Careful not to mess up the techies' stuff, I ducked offstage and made my way to her.

"Someone's lookin' good," I called as I reached the bar.

Ellen turned my way with a dazzling smile, her eyes widening when she saw me. "Holy, babe alert!" she exclaimed. "Arie, you look beautiful!"

I grinned and gestured to her. "That green is your color. It makes your eyes look bluer and your hair look brighter."

"Aw, you're always so sweet."

I sat on a stool and watched her wipe off the counters. "So do you know what's going on?"

"I'm putting together bits and pieces," she told me. "I guess one of the guests wanted to throw a thank you party, but it was last minute."

"Huh. Okay. Who are we thanking?"

She shrugged, the ends of her curls going up and down with her shoulders. "That's the part I haven't figured out yet."

I nodded. "Gotcha."

Elijah walked up to us, wearing a crisp black suit jacket with no tie, looking flawless, as always. I pretended not to notice Ellen's face turn three shades of red.

"Do you know what's going on?" I asked him.

He leaned against the bar. "A rich guy is throwing a party—no big news there."

"Do you know who it's for?" Ellen asked, biting her lip.

"Well…" His eyebrows scrunched up as he lowered his voice theatrically, the drama king. "I heard a rumor, but I don't think it's true."

Before we could get him to spill the beans, Miss Welch came parading over in a black silk drapey thing (would one call it a dress?) with a long train. "My leads," she said, throwing her arms up in presentation, "are we ready for this evening?"

"Yes, Miss Welch," Elijah and I answered.

"Good." She nodded once in approval. "I know it will be closed off but I'm positive some of our young adult guests will find a way in. It's exciting, I would assume, especially for them. After all, this is unprecedented. As director of this stage, I'm confident this brand new kind of production will be nothing short of absolutely grand."

"What part of tonight is brand new?" I asked, suddenly terrified I'd completely missed a new number or rehearsal.

Thankfully, Miss Welch smiled graciously, exposing her top row of small creamy teeth, only too happy to enlighten me. "Well, Arie, it's not every day a guest pays to show appreciation for the workers. Tonight will be the first of its kind."

I did a double take, my mouth falling open. "Wait, what?"

Miss Welch nodded in excitement, brimming with pride that she had the scoop. "It's true. Traditionally administration won't allow for any displays of employee appreciation, but a guest was so dismayed that we refused to do what he requested, administration had no choice but to consent. I hear the guest paid an exuberant amount to see this through."

"So he wants to thank the Compound workers?" Elijah asked skeptically, arching a perfect eyebrow, as if to say, "What have they ever done?" I bit my tongue to keep from shattering his ignorance.

"Yes," Miss Welch said, readjusting her floral headband. "Evidently he and his family have had such a wonderful time here that he feels the need to show his appreciation."

My tongue seemed to shrivel up in my mouth at the thought. *Oh no, Mr. Sir, we really really don't need your appreciation.*

"That would explain why they're going so easy in the kitchen," Ellen chimed in. She was never afraid to talk to Miss Welch, which was a trait I admired. "They're having us make whatever out of leftover ingredients, leave them out on the back table, and take the rest of the night off."

Miss Welch gestured to Ellen. "Of course, not every employee could get the whole night off—the Compound has to keep running, after all—but it is an interesting turn of events." She looked to Elijah and my gaping face. "I expect people will start showing up in the next half hour. Show's on in the next forty." Then she sashayed away, Elijah following.

My stomach knotted and flipped at the new prospect. I imagined Koa or Cameron or even any of my family in the audience, watching as I flaunted around in a ridiculous outfit. Arie Nolan, the key, serving as entertainment.

"You nervous now?" Ellen joked to me, already on to washing cups.

"Um…" I cleared my throat, trying to keep a joking tone too but it fell flat. "Yeah. The infecteds aren't really…my biggest fans."

"Don't worry," Ellen said. "Besides, who's to say they'll all show up? Just perform like you always do and you'll knock it out of the park. Even if they're still scared of you, they'll be impressed by your talent, beauty and charm."

The corners of my mouth pulled up. "Did you read that off a fortune cookie or something?"

She winked at me. "I have my ways."

I went back into the dressing room, shutting myself in my cubicle to stress out until show time. About ten minutes before we were supposed to start, Elijah knocked on my door, calling everyone into the common area for a team meeting. I joined the standing circle of our production team, everyone dressed to the nines. Zoe, Sadie, and several other girls were wearing these extravagant blue costumes with giant peacock feathers jutting out from their hair.

"All right, listen up," Elijah said, standing at the head of the circle as though we were about to discuss the fate of humankind as we knew it. "We've got a new audience tonight and we're going to need to tailor to them for this to be considered a success. I've gone out there: a big group from the guesthouses is here. They're our biggest fans and will be our best line of support."

The circle nodded in agreement. Despite my nerves, I bit my lip to keep from laughing at how seriously they were taking this.

"Now here comes the harder part. The majority of our audience members are employees. That means we've got cleaning crews, kitchen staff, and a lot of laborers out there." He made a face, as though disgusted by these 'common folk.' "My bet is half of them will take the opportunity to get drunk and enjoy themselves, but the other half will have no patience for our masterful production." Then, to my surprise, Elijah looked to me. "Arie, you're the only one who's had contact with every group. What do you think?"

I blinked and cleared my throat. "Well…you're right. The laborers especially don't like you guys. They think they have all the hard work and all you have to do is dance around."

There were several hisses, eye rolls, and mumbled complaints. I knew what they were thinking because it's what I thought myself: the laborers had no idea what a rehearsal with Miss Welch was like.

"That being said," I went on, "I think a lot of them will think this is stupid, but a lot of them will relax for a night anyway. We just have to cater to the guests and those employees who enjoy the party and build off their energy. That's the best we can do."

Elijah nodded, his expression full of concentration as though he was trying to commit every word I said to memory. "What about you? Sorry to bring it up, but it's a dilemma."

I was both mortified and grateful he vocalized that problem. "Honestly…most of the people out there hate my guts. There's no way Miss Welch will let me cut down my stage time, so we'll just have to mix it up. Have even more dancers onstage at a time than usual. Perform more collaborations than solos. And I probably shouldn't do the introduction—we need to warm them up to me."

"I'll take the intro," Elijah told me. "Everyone stay in tune with each other through headsets to keep up on the program, as we'll probably change it now. And if you aren't onstage or getting dressed, you need to be out in the audience, meeting people, selling alcohol and showing them that we are just as established and important here as anyone else. Understood?"

There were many nods and mumbled concurrences.

Elijah clapped his hands together. "All right, let's hit it."

We filed onto the darkened stage—Zoe was more than happy to fill my spot in the front next to Elijah while I stayed in the back. Hopefully the three lines of performers in front of me would shield the audience when I threw up everywhere.

The lights were slowly raised, bringing us out of darkness, getting brighter and brighter until we were completely illuminated and blinded for life.

"Good evening, ladies and gentlemen," Elijah announced in his mic, his voice like satin. "Are we ready to have a good time tonight?"

The cheer from the audience was half as loud as it normally was—not much of a confidence booster to start.

As Elijah silently told the rest of us, though, the show must go on. We dove into our opening number. Zoe took my parts and I was a backup vocalist, which worked out fine, until we heard Miss Welch in our ears, demanding to know why we'd switched things up without consulting her.

After that, we just had to go for it. I stepped out front and center into the burning spotlight for my duet with Patrick. The audience was abnormally quiet, but at least nobody booed or threw a tomato at me. Patrick and I sold it as best we could, acting as though it was just another Friday night. Just another monkey performance. No big deal.

It took a few numbers, but eventually Elijah was right: the audience started to loosen up. It wasn't like the craziness that came with guest shows, but it was nice to have at least a little bit of energy to work off of, as the entire production team—myself included—was sweating bullets about how this whole thing would go. We all knew Miss Welch would hold the outcome over our heads for weeks if it ended badly.

It was over an hour before I got a break. Once the beauty team fixed me up, I was shoved out into the audience and told to go be social, as though that was something within my realm of capabilities. I wasn't in my safe hoodie or black dress either—I was in bright white, incapable of blending into the shadows. Nearly paralyzed at the thought, I kept my head down and forced my way through the crowds to the bar where Ellen was, hopping over to the other side.

"Arielicious!" She gave me a high five. "You're doing great."

I sighed. "Really?"

"Yeah. Really. It's been a fantastic run so far, for all of you."

"Thanks." I surveyed the half empty bar while keeping my face turned to Ellen. "Is the bar struggling tonight?"

She waved her hand. "It's been going back and forth. One minute this place is a ghost town and the next the five of us can't keep up with all the orders." She gestured to her team working behind her. "It's been fun though. You can tell what employees have never tried alcohol and which ones remember it wistfully."

Ellen was right: the drinkers came in waves. I got more than enough shocked or otherwise hateful looks, but I was surprised at the sheer number of people who just didn't recognize me. Or were too drunk to look close enough.

I should give the beauty team more credit.

I was so stressed about running into infecteds that I didn't even consider what guests I might run into. After handing orders to a giggly girl and her date, I turned and found Stalker Walker sitting at the bar, smiling at me.

Oh boy.

"How'd you sneak in here?" I asked with a half smile on my face because a half was all I could muster.

He seemed to sit up straighter, sending a wave of his cologne my way. "There are some people that can get into any club, no matter how exclusive."

I bit my tongue and Ellen pretended to sneeze next to me to hide her snort. Poor Walker was not very good at impressing me.

He held me captive for ten minutes, telling me about the yacht his dad just bought, but it was unfair because Walker wasn't allowed to drive the speedboat, or something like that, and how—much to my hidden chagrin—his dad had just struck a new deal with Cyrus so their family would be staying at the Compound for a while longer. Dear Ellen came to my rescue when she could, making up random jobs she needed help with or forcing herself into the conversation Walker clearly just wanted to be between him and me. We pretended not to notice. Unfortunately, sometimes playing dumb was the best defense a girl had.

"Sorry," I told both of them when my earpiece went off. "I'm up again." I gave Ellen a grateful look before I practically ran to the dressing room.

I owe you so much.

Adhering to the demands of Miss Welch, I performed several of my solos before teaming up with Elijah for a few collaborations. He had a different determination about him tonight—I mean, he always made his life about the production, but tonight he had a new resolve to prove something to our increasingly excited audience.

There was a lull at the bar when I got back—thankfully, Walker was nowhere to be found. I hopped over the counter to find Ellen talking to the only three guys sitting up to the counter. In the craziness of the evening, I'd forgotten they'd be here.

Ellen gave me a high five. "Seriously, this show is awesome!"

"You are really great," Brennan told me over the beat of Elijah's song, with Peter and Sark nodding in agreement.

"You've been here this whole time?" I asked. "And you're now coming over to say hi? What have you guys been up to?"

Sark shrugged, almost too quickly. "Just checking everything out."

For some reason, Peter thought that was funny. He snickered and added, "Yeah, literally," which generated snickers from Brennan too. I didn't get the chance to ask what the joke was.

"Anyway," Ellen said, continuing with a telling of another kitchen mishap involving watery soup and blood-spotted bread.

Only half listening, I took a nonchalant step to the left, leaning my arm on the bar, my eyes on the glass half filled with clear liquid. I glanced up to see Sark already looking at me rather than Ellen.

"It's water," he told me before I could find the guts to ask.

"Oh, no, I didn't…" A nervous breath escaped me as I tapped my fingers against the bar, dropping my eyes. "Sorry, it's not my place."

I felt a hand on mine and looked up to find Sark's face devoid of anger or offense—both of which I'd anticipated.

He shrugged. "It's probably your place as much as anyone's."

That made me smile. "Somebody has to keep you in line."

Sark grinned back at me and started to respond, but Peter cleared his throat loudly, reminding me that other people were there. I jerked my arm off the bar and directed my attention to the other part of our small group.

Peter gestured to me with a teasing smirk. "It looks like you've made great friends."

My eyebrows furrowed. "Friends? Do you know me at all?"

"They were asking me about Stalker Walker," Ellen explained, grinning. "Now that's a love story for the ages."

I rolled my eyes. "Don't get me started."

"Miss Nolan," a voice greeted, cutting through the crowd and making me tense up. I glanced over to find one of Cyrus' clients, Malwana Goshen, standing at the counter in front of me, lights glinting off the edges of his crisp new suit. "What a pleasant surprise."

I shut myself down at his voice, reverting to the key he expected of me. Eyes blank and cold, body ready to spring, silent and submissive. He watched me with the same callous gray eyes he had a few days ago when I first met him during a demonstration Micah and I did for some of Cyrus' 'friends.' Cyrus was always all too eager to introduce his new key pet to everyone that stopped by, and they were all too eager to see what Micah and I could do. And too many of them—Goshen being one—liked to watch me with a kind of interest Cyrus actually disapproved of.

But Cyrus wasn't here.

"Sir," I said, nodding, my tone empty.

"My, you *are* busy tonight," he commented, eyeing the three guys sitting with us. "Though, I must say, the dress suits you better than even your training attire did. You're rather stunning."

Ew, Vanessa spat. *Gross. He's way too old. My cutoff's at thirty. Thirty-eight tops.*

I barely even heard her. I just stared at Goshen and waited for our confrontation to end.

Then he made a devastating move: he reached across the counter and grabbed my jaw in one hand. I clenched my fists against the bar, but tried to give no other reaction, letting him handle me like the animal he thought of me as. Out of my peripheral, I saw Sark go to make a move, but I made a tiny gesture with my fist.

Stay out of it.

Goshen turned my head back and forth, as if to inspect my face. After ten painfully long seconds, he let me go.

"Remarkable," he said. "It seems you've healed from our demonstration rather impressively. I'd imagine you're great at everything, aren't you?" He gave a distracted glance to Ellen, then did a double take, and I felt her stiffen next to me when he smiled at her.

No. My teeth clamped together with rage. *Not her.*

My blank stare turned to a glower as I deliberately reached out and seized Ellen's wrist, pulling her so I blocked her with my body, my hateful eyes never leaving Goshen. My voice was vacant but still threatening somehow as I finally responded.

"I know how to hurt a lot of people, in a lot of ways." I gave the slightest nod. "But you know that."

Ellen gasped behind me, nearly inaudibly, but I still heard it. "Arie."

She was afraid for me. But I at least had the protection of Cyrus' words, whether or not they were ignored. She didn't.

Goshen's smile fell into a flat line. "Indeed." He grabbed my free hand—my injured one—and seemed to feel around it. The corners of his mouth pulled up when he felt my invisible brace, as though he just poked a hole through me. I fought to keep from clawing his eyes out. Ellen's hand tightened on mine.

"You put on a good show, Miss Nolan," he told me, gesturing to the crowd. "It's too bad Cyrus keeps you on such a short leash."

Someone hissed under their breath, but I refused to let my eyes leave Goshen's to see who it was. He let go of my hand, then turned and made his way through the crowd, disappearing. I didn't move. I heard Ellen let out a huge breath, like she'd been holding it for years.

"Arie?" she asked me, hesitating.

I didn't move. I watched the spot Goshen disappeared. I had the presence of mind to at least let go of Ellen's wrist, which I realized I was holding way too tight.

"Tell me if he talks to you again." It took me a second to realize I said the words.

Ellen's voice teetered with nerves. "Arie, you shouldn't have talked to him like tha—"

"You tell me, okay?"

"Okay." She paused a moment before adding sincerely, "Thank you."

Slowly, I felt me come back to myself. Shoulders relaxed. Pounding heart slowing down. Eyelids blinking again. I still couldn't tear my gaze away from the spot Goshen had been until Ellen slid in front of me.

"Here." She placed a cup in my hand. "Drink this and come back to me. I hate what all those guys turn you into. It's scary."

Vanessa scoffed. *You don't know the half of it.*

I obeyed without really thinking, tipping the liquid into my mouth, and my mind sharpened with recognition. I didn't drink, but I often found myself needing a buzz to get through the shows—Ellen had created my own alcohol-free drink that I'd learned to love. It was lemon-lime-strawberry something, delicious, and calming. The taste helped me to completely relax.

We got a crowd of customers then, and I abandoned my cup to help fill the orders. By the time it died down, Ellen was ready to pretend the whole encounter didn't happen, and I was more than happy with that. Sark, Peter and Brennan caught on, and, thankfully, nobody brought it back up.

"So, we've heard about Stalker Walker," Ellen said, leaning against the counter and flipping her curled hair. "What about you boys? Any 'special someone's in your life?"

She looked to Brennan first. He gave a small smile. "Yes."

"Is she cute?" Ellen asked. "Paired with a glowing personality?"

The smile grew ever so slightly. "Beautiful."

That gave me warm fuzzies inside—Brennan and Lucy had played around the romantic line for years, though we all knew it was a matter of time before they admitted it.

Ellen went on to Peter. "What about you, big guy?"

He broke into a grin. "Taken."

"What?" I asked. That was news to me. "Who?"

"Alaina."

My mouth fell open. "*What*?"

"Oh, you missed it," Brennan realized. "It happened after you left."

Sark rolled his eyes. "Be grateful."

"Seriously?" I asked Peter. "You and Alaina. A thing."

"If they aren't making out then they're shouting at each other," Brennan said. "It's the worst."

Peter just laughed. "They're both jealous." Then he sighed in frustration. "But sometimes she drives me insane. She'll get all clingy and then give me the silent treatment and then I step the wrong way and she'll start yelling at me for everything I've ever done. It's so freaking annoying." He leaned forward and rested his head on his hand, looking at me. "You know her well, right? Why does she do that?"

I blinked in surprise at the fact. I knew nearly everything about Alaina. It was easy to forget that when I barely spoke to her anymore.

"Well, has she ever told you about her dad?" I asked.

"Yeah, he left or something, right?" he answered like it was old news.

I shook my head at his flippancy. "Yeah, he did, and it totally changed the way she saw the world. She had to watch her mom pick up the pieces and it wasn't pretty."

He didn't get it. "What does her mom have to do with us?"

"Because Alaina doesn't want to end up like her," I said, not able to keep some exasperation out of my voice. "No matter how much Alaina loves you or thinks you love her, she'll always be expecting the day when she wakes up and you tell her you want to leave."

That finally struck a chord—a wave of understanding passed through his eyes. "Oh. Well, that explains a lot."

Ellen laughed and I smiled as I rolled my eyes. "There you go, Romeo." I gestured to all three of them in joking. "Anyone else need relationship advice before I'm up again?"

Peter and Brennan burst into snickers again and Peter elbowed Sark. "I think our buddy Sark here could use some help. Maybe you could set him up."

Sark glared genuine murder at them before looking at me and Ellen. "Don't listen to them. They're idiots."

"Why?" Ellen asked. "Who you got your eye on?"

Sark shook his head. "They make stuff up. They need a life."

Peter slapped him on the back. "Yeah, whatever man."

There was a thin parting in the crowd, then Elijah surged forward to the bar, eyes on me. He pointed back and forth between us. "You. Me." The crowd burst into cheers, and I missed the middle of what he said. "Let's go."

Leaning forward to hear him better, I saw Sark's glare shift to Elijah when the performer grabbed my hand, his chocolate skin smooth and silky. "What? I didn't hear you."

"We're battling it out!" Elijah practically shouted, beaming with excitement. "Let's go, girl."

"Wait, you want to do a verse battle *now*?" I glanced around at the full room, my bubbling nerves threatening to boil over. "I don't think that's a good idea."

"You're right: it's a fabulous idea." He kissed my hand, which I used to think was strange until I realized that's how he communicated with everyone. He knew his power was strong. "Please say yes."

I found myself nodding without permission. "Fine, okay."

"Meet me there in two." Then he was gone.

Ellen snickered. "Dang, he barely even had to try."

I rolled my eyes at her. "Please. You'd jump off a cliff if he asked you to."

"Elijah's looking for you, Arie," a buttermilk voice said. I turned to see Zoe standing there, her long blonde hair flowing behind her like a train of gold, highlighted by her perfect posture and angular face. She really looked like a queen. "Better get up there."

"Yeah, I know. I'm on it." I motioned for the guys to stay put, and they nodded in agreement, which is when they saw Zoe. Brennan jerked his gaze down to the counter; Peter smiled and laughed once before taking another swig of his drink; Sark's eyes widened slightly as they automatically went over her, then he took a deep breath. My teeth snapped together so hard I thought they'd chip.

As I jumped over the counter, Zoe smiled a dazzling smile and placed a manicured hand on Sark's shoulder. "Hey, there, stranger. I've never seen you around before."

My skin felt hot and sticky, more than usual, while I forced myself away from the conversation and to the waiting Elijah backstage. That's when it clicked together: Sark liked Zoe.

It makes sense, Vanessa said. *He waited to come see you because he was watching her and now Peter and Brennan are teasing him about it. Besides, she's gorgeous.*

Unfortunately, she was right. But what did it matter anyway? Pretty much every guy had a crush on Zoe. He was only human.

I had a bad taste in my mouth as the beauty team retouched my hair and makeup before sending me back onstage. Elijah beamed at me, practically glowing, as he announced our singing battle over the mic. That caught the crowd's attention. I couldn't help but wince at the roar of excitement that greeted the news.

My nerves melted away a bit once we started, though, just because Elijah knew how to rile me up and provoke my competitive nature. The world was watching, but I still had to win.

Of course, the audience voted Elijah the winner in the end. Figures. The show went on as usual and I found myself looking for Zoe among the backups in every song I was part of, but never saw her. It didn't really matter. We all deserved breaks, including her. She could do whatever she wanted with her time. I didn't care.

Once I was on break again, I pushed through the sweaty masses to get to the bar again, breathing a silent sigh of relief when I saw all three of them still sitting in their spots with only Ellen keeping them company.

"I didn't know you could sing like that," Peter told me when I caught up. "You get on that stage and you're like a different person. You're all outgoing and likeable. It's weird."

"Gee, thanks," I said, going over to plop on the empty seat next to Sark instead of hopping the counter. Wrapping my arm gingerly around me, I leaned over to one side a bit to help ease the ache in my rib. The numbing must've been wearing off.

"Tired?" Ellen asked me.

I nodded, resting my chin in my free hand. "Yep. I'm ready for bed. Being likeable takes energy."

"Ha, no kidding."

I had to keep myself from rolling my eyes when Zoe walked out on stage and hundreds of male voices yelled in approval. Whatever. I was tired. Everything was annoying when I was tired.

We sat in silence for a while, small talk conversations striking up every now and then over the pounding beat and a sea of partying people. My eyes wandered around and I caught sight of Stalker Walker talking to his buddy several yards away. I stiffened and ducked my head, but I knew he saw me. I was just too tired to deal with him now—my people tank had been all used up.

"Stalker Walker?" Ellen asked, suppressing a grin. I nodded.

Sark jumped to his feet, surveying the area as if anticipating lethal attack. "Where?"

"Don't look for him," I hissed as I held my head in my hand. "He's going to come over here."

"Not if I tell him to get lost."

That's the worst idea ever. "Sark, he's nice. He's just weird and thinks we're in love."

"He's a creep," Sark said through his teeth. "I don't like him near you."

"Yes, okay, that's true, but please don't make a scene. Please."

"Give me thirty seconds and he'll never talk to you again."

I snatched his wrist just as he took a step away, yanking him back. "Yeah, no, that's not happening." Getting to my feet, I took Sark's arm and started dragging him away. "Come with me."

Sark dug his heels in the ground. "Where?"

"To hide from him." I gestured to Walker. "Are you gonna help me or not?"

Sark consented, and I pulled him to the far corner, a distance from the bar and main sea of people. Then I stopped and leaned back against the wall, facing him.

"Okay," I said, folding my arms across my chest and trying to look casual but completely captivated—so much so, that nobody would want to interrupt the *super* important conversation we were having. Hopefully. "Talk to me."

Sark raised an eyebrow. "This is your big idea? He'll still be able to find you out here."

Yeah, but I can't actually hide and leave you alone or else you'll beat the kid up and get in insane amounts of trouble.

"It'll work," I told him. "It's brilliant. Walker's got an inferiority complex, I would bet, and is used to his daddy buying him everything. This'll be perfect." *At least I hope so.* The more I looked at Sark, though, the more confident I felt in my plan.

He stepped closer to me, tipping his head slightly to hear me better over the beat of the music. "Why? What's going to stop him?"

"You."

"I thought you just said you don't *want* me to punch his jaw off."

I gave a wry smile. "Punch it off, huh? How dramatic."

He rolled his eyes, annoyed, but couldn't help a small smile. "I know how you love the drama."

"We won't need it."

"I still don't get it."

"*You're* talking to me," I said as I scanned the crowd around us again. "Believe me, someone like Walker won't try to compete with someone like you."

"Someone like me?" The question snapped my attention back to Sark's face, alight with curiosity amid the blaring strobe lights from the stage.

I blinked, suddenly feeling very self-conscious. "Yeah, you know…just…you…" The back of my neck heated up, so I scratched it for something to do.

The corners of his mouth turned up in a suppressed grin at my discomfort. "I what?"

"You're very…you know. You look…" I gestured to him from head to toe. "Like…" I tried to roll my eyes in annoyance, but it didn't feel like I sold it. "You know what I mean." Forgetting all about Walker, I swayed to my right, prepared to somehow nonchalantly walk away.

He put out his arm to brace his hand against the wall, blocking my exit strategy, and suddenly I felt the whole room had gone up at least twenty degrees. "No, I don't think I do."

"Don't be stupid," I told him, trying *really* hard to ignore my heart, which had decided to start sprinting. Performing made your heart beat faster, right? That was normal.

His eyes danced like sapphire flames, his intense gaze drying me up. "You're the one that's stuttering all over the place."

I narrowed my eyes, willing myself to be cool. He would not win whatever confrontation this was. "Ah, so stuttering girls *do* keep your massive ego alive. Funny it took me this long to figure it out."

"Seems to be working on you."

"Oh, so I'm the last one then, huh? You just can't walk away without getting *every* girl to swoon over you?"

He grinned at me, and I gritted my teeth to keep myself in check. "Is that what you would call what you're doing?"

I glared at him. "I'm not doing a thing, sadly for you. Better hurry and find any other girl in this place that'll fall in your lap before your ego takes a hit. I bet Zoe would be first in line."

"Yeah, I bet she would too." My jaw clenched at the enthusiasm in his voice, and he smirked. "That ticks you off, doesn't it?"

I scowled. "No."

"Does too."

"Look who's talking: you really expect me to believe you wanted to punch Walker's jaw off out of the kindness of your noble heart?"

Sark's expression darkened. "It's different. That guy is an undeserving idiot."

I couldn't help sneaking a glance at Zoe on stage, killing it in a brilliant red sleeveless dress without a blue speck of skin in sight.

And she's perfect.

"The real question is," Sark went on, taking back my sullen attention, "if I could get Zoe or any other beautiful girl in this place to fall in my lap—" He leaned in and lowered his voice, as though telling me a secret. "Then why am I over here with you?"

My shoulders went rigid and my breath caught. Sark smirked again.

Two can play this game, pretty boy.

I leaned into him and held his mouth shut with my fingers, smiling triumphantly when Sark went stone still and his breaths stuttered.

"Why *are* you over here?" I murmured in his ear. "Looking for something?"

He mumbled something incoherent before pulling my hand off his face and used it to somehow twist me closer to him. Winding his other arm around me, his mouth grazed my cheek and along my ear. My mind was hazy and my body should not have been in control and I was surprised I could hear anything over my thudding pulse or even concentrate on the anything besides his stupid mouth.

"Don't hit me," he said softly before pressing his lips to mine.

My brain froze. Halted. Emergency breaks. Shock. Panic. My hands balled into fists, my instincts prepared to get rid of the intrusion immediately. But those instincts were put down by a very different kind of instincts that woke up something inside me.

Sark's mouth barely touched mine and I pitched forward into him, accidentally hitting our teeth together in my haste. I didn't care, and he must've not minded either because he didn't stop. He did the very opposite. The initial surface kiss turned to something deeper. He pressed his hand against the small of my back, holding me against him and burning a hole in my dress, probably, based on the heat I felt emanating from his skin. His sure mouth moved against my clumsy one with purpose and need, sending a new kind of thrill through me.

As quick as it started, it stopped. Suddenly I found myself pressed against his chest, one hand around his neck and the other clutching his. His hand on me. His lips on mine.

Then I realized what happened.

What *happened*?

I froze and Sark stiffened. We glanced at each other, then jumped apart. Mortification sent a new heat wave through me that nearly made me pass out. I slapped my hands over my face as though I could hide. When I peeked my eyes through my fingers a second later, prepared to apologize until my face turned blue—what was I even supposed to do?—I realized I was alone. Sark was gone.

"What...?" I asked no one, trying to pull myself together as I glanced wildly around me at the crazy guests absorbed in themselves. "I just...we just...where...?"

We had just been talking, right? Talking, then competing somehow—but we always competed. We were always...not like that, though. Never had he looked at me like that. Never had he been able to do that to me, to get me to talk that way, *act* that way...we had just been talking. How did...we were...

What happened?

After a few deep, disbelieving breaths, I walked back over to the bar to where Ellen was telling another story to Brennan and Peter.

Be casual, I ordered myself, noticing how I kept looking around. Looking for him.

Stop it.

"Hey," I said coolly when I reached my group. "Have you guys seen Sark? I lost him."

Real smooth, Vanessa commented, picking an odd time to pipe up.

Peter appraised me, expression serious. "Depends—before or after you swapped spit?"

My stomach seemed to shrivel in on itself and I tasted bile. "You saw."

Peter burst out in uncontrollable braying laughter, and I would've socked him sober if

Brennan hadn't spoken up with a coy smile his face.

"Sorry, but we were watching. We figured it was going to happen eventually."

What?

Peter exhaled dramatically and pretended to wipe a tear from his face. "Hey, man, you owe me five bucks. Or Cyrus coins. Whatever the heck will get me potato chips in this joint."

Ellen smirked at my gaping expression. "Brennan thought he'd hold it together, but Peter bet he'd break."

I shook my head slowly, still not understanding. "Break what?"

"Do you really think we would come to this lame party for our own fun?" Peter asked, clearly enjoying himself. "Sark drags us here and then he's so floored by how pretty he thinks you are that it takes an hour for him to come over and say hi. And even then, his only motivation is to come grill Ellen about the guy he saw you talking to."

"You're making that up."

"Please, Arie!" Ellen squealed. "He couldn't take his eyes off you all night! How did you not notice?"

"Seriously," Brennan added, nodding at me. "Ever since he walked into our building at four thirty this morning—"

"And he fessed up where he'd been all night," Peter cut in, winking at me.

"He's been so distracted," Brennan continued. "Koa kept getting mad at him because he couldn't focus."

I rubbed my forehead, my brain aching at the incoming of such foreign information. "How long?"

"I'd say since we first got here," he glanced at Peter, "don't you think?"

"Easy," Peter agreed. "Somethin's in the air here 'cause it flipped a switch on him. He's fought it like crazy. It's been driving *us* crazy."

For some reason, my insides bristled at that. "Fought it?"

Peter rolled his eyes as he took the last swig of his drink. "Oh, you know, the drama: what'll she do, what'll she think, can I risk ruining our relationship, yada yada yada." He wagged his eyebrows at me. "Though from here it looked like you weren't suffering too much."

Brennan and Ellen snickered, and I decided then that I was done. "I have to go," I said, annoyance hardening my voice. "Nice seeing you guys."

Peter waved. "We'll see you tomorrow. At least, I know Sark hopes so. I really hope I'm there for your opening conversation."

At that, I turned and sauntered away, pushing through the crowds to get back to the dressing room. So many things were running through my head, I couldn't place them all, and with each step I got increasingly overwhelmed at everything I couldn't decipher, passing by hundreds of faces but only seeing Sark.

9

The next three days were absolutely slammed: training, rehearsal, investor meetings, sleeping, and other stuff I came up with. I didn't have much time for anything else, including my usual visits to a certain labor group to say hi.

"Are you kidding me?" Ellen exclaimed when she found out, throwing a wooden spoon at me. "Sark kissed you three days ago and you haven't even stopped to see him?"

I took extra time bending down to retrieve her weapon that had clattered to the floor after hitting me. "I've been...busy." Even my voice wasn't convinced of my resolve. "I haven't had time."

"Seriously, girl?" Ellen put her hand on her hip. "A guy like that comes after you and you *make* time for him."

"I know," I said, watching my hands sheepishly.

Okay, so I probably could have cut 'staring at the wall' from my schedule to make the time to talk to Sark. I just didn't know what I would say. It was awful for me to wait—if I were Sark, I'd be freaking out that I had ruined everything. He hadn't. I wasn't angry. I wasn't upset. I wasn't grossed out either. I was just confused. And I really needed to tell him that. It was mean to not ease his surely distraught conscience.

The night it happened, I didn't sleep a second. I watched the ceiling all night. It wasn't until morning came and my cheeks were sore, I realized that I'd been smiling all night too.

But the more I thought about it, the more I couldn't remember exactly how it happened. Details got blurry. Had I been acting in a flirtatious way that night? Probably not, since I was sure I didn't have a flirtatious bone in my body. But had I come off desperate? Now that I realized that actually kissing him wasn't the problem, I wondered if I'd been subconsciously pining for it. After all, I had no clue what to do in that situation. In second grade my crush kissed me on the top of the slide—I didn't count any of the kisses that came from my high school boyfriend, Connor, because it turned out he was paid by Sark's boss to be there. When it came to this kind of stuff, I was about as clueless as a nineteen-year-old girl could be.

By the time three days had passed, I'd had way too much time to replay different versions of the memory in my head, and I couldn't remember if Sark had kissed me out of his own free will or if I'd thrown myself at him like all the other wasted girls at the club. Because of that slight discrepancy in memory, I couldn't bring myself to face him.

Tonight was no different: on my way home I battled with myself, going back and forth, but eventually chickened out. Rather than stop by Sark's labor group, I decided to go home and get in some more staring at the wall before going to bed.

Is this really all you're going to do with your life? Vanessa complained. *It's pathetic. I'm so bored.*

I rolled my eyes. *Well, I haven't quite memorized the wall yet.*

As I approached the maintenance building, I saw a group of people convening at the main door, which I realized must've been a cleaning crew. I was in the middle of my usual plan for this case— ignore and pass—when one of the crew members caught my eye. I didn't realize it was her until we were only three feet apart.

Suddenly Sark's voice echoed in my head: *If it were me, I'd gladly take the second chance.*

I didn't know why but I stopped right there mid-step. She was watching me, her mouth pulled into a small sad grin, her mouth that knew smiles and cries and shouting and consoling like only a mother's could.

"Hi," I said, my fidgety hands clamping down on each other to keep them from moving.

Her grin grew ever so slightly. "Hi."

A current went through me at her voice. It had been so long since I'd heard it.

She turned to her finished crew for a half second and waved them on before darting her eyes back to me, as though I would disappear if she weren't watching me. Her eyes were a darker blue, like the night sky seconds before the last hint of light disappeared behind the horizon. They went over me again and again, committing me to memory.

"You look beautiful," she told me, her soft voice breaking slightly despite her willpower to keep it together. "You're all grown up."

Another current went through me, laced with understanding, her simple phrase unlocking a vision I'd never cared to think about. A mother losing her son, then her daughter, and maybe even her husband somewhere along the way. A mother prepping for her oldest's funeral while conducting the search for her youngest, knowing somewhere in her heart that her daughter wasn't missing but running. A mother pushing through freezing winds to ask strangers on the street if they recognized the picture. A mother crying on my empty bed in anguish that she'd let her children down.

"Thanks," I managed with a squeaky voice. "Are you, um…how are you?"

She nodded once, as if on defense. She felt she was walking on eggshells here. "I'm good."

That couldn't have been completely true: her dirty blonde hair was ridden with grays, the ends frayed, which only made her look pale and sickly. I'd gotten my height from her—she'd always been skinny but now it was too much, like she'd forgotten to eat too many days in a row, almost as if she were making the transition into a ghost. She looked fragile. A ball of stress.

"How are you?" she asked me, eyes widening and chest puffing slightly in anticipation.

I knew she vainly hoped for more than what she was asking—after all, there were years' worth of answers I could give—but the only thing I could come up with was, "I'm good."

She deflated, trying to hide her disappointment, but she bit her lip and that gave her away. "Good. I'm glad."

We looked at each other in silence. I was afraid the silence would make her leave, but I didn't have any words to fill it up.

Why do you want her to stay? Vanessa asked, annoyed. *I thought you were mad at her.*

That was true. I was mad at her. I had been for years. It was easy to villainize a distant thing, to blame it and hate it. But it was so different now, having her standing right in front of me, when the yearning for my old, easier life took ahold of me. I had the sudden urge to just break down and tell her everything about my messed-up world, how I had no clue what to do, and wait for her advice.

Because she's my mom.

Her footsteps broke the silence as she closed the huge small gap between us and wrapped her arms tightly around me, a slight sigh of pain and relief escaping her lips.

Another current, more powerful than the other two: memories. When I fell off my bike and she put a band-aid on my bleeding elbow. When I was convinced there was a monster under my bed and she sang to me until I fell asleep. When I finally got the memo that girls my age wore makeup and panicked that I didn't know what to do, and she took me to the store to buy my own mascara, then showed me how to put it on after I poked myself in the eye. When she first taught me how to play the piano and calmed me down after I screamed in frustration when I hit the wrong key. When she'd be up late doing work and I'd bring my homework in and sit on the office floor and we'd listen to music and laugh and eat ice cream.

"I just wanted to say hi, baby," she whispered in my ear. "That's all." She gave me a squeeze before quickly turning to catch up with her crew.

I watched her go, doing nothing to stop her, but the little girl inside me was crying for her mom to come back and sing the monsters away.

~~~

The next morning's training was a nightmare. Last night they'd reset Micah on his brainwashing cycle—their control over him had begun to run thin after a few weeks since the last cycle. I shuddered at the thought of what they must've put him through last night, but my concern quickly froze into terror when I was pitted against him in the ring. His jade eyes were sharp but distant, vacant but ruthless, and it was like he barely recognized me as we battled it out over and over.
~~~

Somehow I managed to keep myself from getting majorly injured, and finally Roland pulled me out and had Scottsman run me on the track while he coached Micah through focusing on the punching bag. The bag had to be replaced three times.

My skin prickled with discomfort, my eyes glued to ground, as I felt Scottsman's quiet, vigilant gaze on me while I ran my guts out. When I felt my legs were going to fall off, Roland called us up to the roof for tactical drills. I took the stairs two at a time—anything to get away from Scottsman—and broke out onto the roof to find not only Roland and Micah, but Cyrus too, as well as two whole strike units dressed in flexible armor suits.

Oh great.

Roland ran us through every tactical drill we'd been taught, the strike team members standing in as our enemies. They were trained well, but Roland never let us go against fewer than ten of them at a time. Ten against the two of us. I was just grateful I wasn't against Micah again.

Really, he was like a mutt, except he'd listen to Roland's orders, and it scared me to see him like that. I felt Cyrus' beady eyes on my back as I worked, and I knew he was shaping me up to be exactly the same.

The drills were brutal. We went again and again, the sun beating down on us, waves of battered and bloodied strike team members getting traded out for fresh new ones every fifteen minutes. I tried to be careful not to seriously hurt anyone, but with nearly five guys on my back at a time, I found myself going into survival mode, hoping none of my practiced and skillful attacks hit a lethal mark.

Micah didn't worry about that, though. By the end of our training session—which went an hour longer than usual—four strike team members were dead.

Dead.

They were *dead* because of a *training exercise*. And that didn't account for the ones who were seriously injured.

Sweat dripped down my back as I felt the color drain from my face when I saw the beaten corpses on the ground, both Micah and I spotted with their blood. Once we were excused, I dashed to the bathroom, gagged in the sink a few times, then rinsed myself of blood and sunk to the ground, wrapping my arms around myself.

A solid chunk of time had passed when I was summoned back to the training roof again. I felt my face rearrange into a cold mask when I saw that Cyrus wasn't our only audience anymore: about a dozen of his high-profile investor guests were there, Italian shoes shiny and collared shirts crisp, seated on the sidelines and discussing among themselves. I forced myself not to scowl when I saw Goshen next to Cyrus.

Roland barked orders, and I fell into line next to Micah, at ease, coiled and ready to spring when given the word. He gave it, and we surged at the new strike team posed against us. I didn't allow myself to think or panic. I just let my body and instincts take over, letting them do what they were trained for.

The sun was setting when Cyrus mercifully clapped his hands together in applause. His investor friends followed suit, marking the end of our show. They were impressed. At least, that's what I gathered from the bits of conversation that made their way into my ears. I was trying to block all senses as best I could. That made it easier to forget the details of events like these later.

I ached all over as I shuffled to the cafeteria, my stomach yelling at me to give it something before it died of sheer emptiness. My nose wrinkled at the strong smell of fish cooking; I decided to skip the course, grabbing a boiled egg and handful of strawberries instead. I'd just sat down to eat when my earpiece crackled again. I stiffened, my heart stuttering at the thought of facing another demonstration.

Instead, a transmission blared in my ear. "Nolan, do you copy?" a female voice asked.

With a slight sigh of relief, I ate a quick bite of strawberry before holding down the button on my earpiece. "Yeah, I'm here."

"A fight has broken out among two employees—Micah and assisting guards are unavailable. Are you in a position to go down there?"

I made a face at no one in particular, careful to keep my disdain out of my voice. "Yeah, sure. Where is it?"

"South side, thirty-sixth quadrant."

"Copy that. I'll take care of it." I shoved the rest of my boiled egg in my mouth, dusted myself off, and went on my way.

I heard the crowd before I saw it—that was another stupid thing about the fighting. There was a high spirit of competition between all infected groups, especially labor groups, so fellow workers didn't do anything to stop the fight. They cheered it on.

I had to stop for a few seconds, take a deep breath and steel myself before pressing on with the assignment.

"All right, break it up!" I shouted, beginning to push my way through the crowd. I only had to be aggressive for a minute—once people saw it was me, they calmed down and parted, turning back to their jobs before I looked at them again. Among the dispersing wave, I caught a glimpse of Cameron, and at the front of the circle I bumped into Peter and Brennan. I followed their gaze to the brawl in the center of the deforming circle, Scarface rolling in the dirt with Sark.

"Hey!" I ran forward, ignoring my slight sense of satisfaction that Sark seemed to be winning, and grabbed Sark's shoulder, shoving him off and onto the ground. "What's going on?" I demanded, looking between the two of them.

They both slumped in resignation and dropped their eyes, but while Scarface seemed to do so out of infuriated acceptance, Sark emanated shame.

"Do we have a problem here?" I asked.

Silence greeted me. I cleared my throat.

"I said, do we have a problem here?"

"No, ma'am," Scarface finally muttered grudgingly, his gaze slowly traveling up me, as if working up the courage to meet my glare, but he only got halfway before he was staring at the dirt again.

Sark sighed. "No."

"Good." I glanced around, aiming my order to the stragglers too. "Then everyone get lost." They all obeyed. Scarface and Sark dragged themselves to their feet. I put myself in front of Sark, glaring at him. "Except you."

He sighed again but waited next to me. I watched as all the workers left, then stalked away, motioning for Sark to follow me. I stopped on the other side of a residency building, positioning myself so I still had a good vantage point of the darkening Compound should anyone come by, then turned on him.

"What was that?" I demanded, throwing my hands up in the air.

"Nothing," Sark muttered, looking at my feet.

"Nothing? Really? Do you realize how lucky you are that I was the one called down to put that out? If it'd been anyone else, you'd be in *so* much trouble." I actually stomped my foot, rubbing my forehead in frustration. "That was so stupid! Why would you get mixed up in petty crap like that? You're so much better than that, Sark!"

He laughed once, a cynical sound, before glancing up at me. Immediately, all the derisive hostility drained out of his expression, replaced with concern.

"What happened to you?" he asked, brushing my bruised face with his hand. My skin tingled where he touched me, and my breath caught.

I counted to three in my head to keep myself level. "You tell me first. What was the fighting about?" Not that I couldn't guess.

He dropped his hand, and it was like a wall went up in his expression, purposely keeping me out of something. "Nothing. He got on my nerves, I snapped back, and it escalated from there." He nodded at me. "Now you tell me what happened to you."

I folded my arms. "I had training this morning."

He waited but I didn't offer anything else. His eyes narrowed in suspicion. "Did Micah do that to you?"

I hoped I didn't look guilty. Now was not the time to feed that fire. "I'm not giving you details if you won't give me any."

"Look, I..." Sark ran a hand through his hair. "There are things that I..." He shook his head, looking at his knuckles again, his voice getting quieter. "It's stupid. I'll just—"

"It's not stupid. Tell me. Please?"

It took him a minute to answer. "I'm not who I used to be, and you know that." He gave a quick glance up to me, as if waiting for confirmation.

"Of course I do," I said as I nodded. "You've come so far, and I...I don't want to sound stupid, but I really am proud of you."

He winced. "I want to deserve that. I disappoint myself. And you. I was raised to fight, to abuse, to throw the first punch and make sure the other guy doesn't get to walk away." His tone hardened. "I'm not a good person, Arie. I want to be, but I'm too much—"

Scathing outrage overtook me when I realized what he was saying. "Aiden McCoy," I said, my words furious at the universe for putting him where he was, "you are *nothing* like your father."

Sark shrunk at the mention of his dad. I'd never seen him so small, so accepting of his place backed up in a corner just to get pummeled over and over. "I came from him, Arie. I turned out like him. I'll end up like him too." Something in his eyes broke as he looked over me, then took an unsteady step back.

"No," I insisted, stepping forward. "Your mom taught you better than that. Look at us. Look at *me*. You think for one second your dad would treat me the same way you are now if we were alone behind a building?"

He sucked in a sharp breath, like I'd punched him in the gut. "Arie..." Then he shook his head furiously, as if trying to empty it before the contents burned him.

I grabbed him by the shoulders, forcing him to look in my eyes. I was desperate he understood this. "Yeah, Sark, you made awful choices, and so did he. But you're *different* now. That's something he never had. He never changed for you, and he never changed for your mom, but you changed for me. And you know I'm not the only one who thinks you make such a wonderful person when you try." My voice faltered. "You are...Sark, you are the best person I've ever met. Yeah, you have two sides to you, but that's one of the best things about you. You're soft and hard and kind and mean and strong and so gentle. I never feel safer with anyone else, or more respected or valued, than when I'm with you. You see me, as a person, and I can't...I can't tell you how much that means to me."

Somehow throughout me talking, we'd gotten a lot closer to each other than when I started. I wasn't sure who instigated it—though I was afraid of the thought that I wasn't innocent at all—but my arms were inching farther up his shoulders and around his neck, and I felt myself sinking into something the rational side of my brain was screaming at me to avoid.

A burst of sound stole my attention. I turned my head to see a rowdy group of well-dressed young guys quite a distance away, their boisterous yelling indecipherable from where I stood.

I froze, somewhat aware of Sark asking if I was okay, then snatched his hand and pulled him along as I ran away. I didn't stop until we were behind the far residency building, ducking in the space between it and the manufacturing building next to it. Even from here, though, I could still hear the shouting.

Sark was leaning against the wall trying to catch his breath—in my haste I'd forgotten to slow down a bit for him. After a few moments he straightened up and looked at me.

"What was that?" he asked.

I just shook my head like it was no big deal, not wanting to get into it, though it was pretty much impossible he hadn't heard guys talking before. After all, it wasn't just the snobby guests us girls had to hide from when they got a certain way. However, most workers knew it was too dangerous to go for me. Guests, on the other hand, were either too stupid to understand I could kill them with one hand or knew I wasn't allowed to hurt them.

"Nothing," I said, straightening up too. "Sometimes it's just easier to avoid some people."

Avoid the problem: that was my motto. For most girls, that was the only thing to do, besides the ones who sought out that kind of attention from the male species, either just for fun or making a trade. The thought made me sick.

Sark raised an eyebrow, not buying it at all. "Like who?"

Everyone, it seems.

There was something inherently special and alluring about being the key, apparently, because it had become a game among the most disgusting offenders to see who could corner me first. Cyrus has rules protecting only me, but that only heightened the guys' competition, and they went so far as to keep a running bet with gross amounts of money. They'd formed a predatory pack, crossing over the line to our world every once in a while, looking for companionship while keeping an eye out for the one girl Cyrus said they couldn't have.

There was another burst of shouting, jeering and laughter—too far away for me to actually be afraid—but I couldn't help but wince when I heard a whistle, wondering who they were degrading now. Sark heard it too, helping him connect the dots to something I think he already knew, and suddenly I had a pretty good idea of what the brawl in the dirt was about. His eyes instantly exploded with raging fury, his jaw clenching with his fists as he scowled, and the murderous hatred rolled off him in waves.

I automatically took a terrified step away from him, knowing anything in his path would be sorry. But then he went to leave, and I scrambled forward, pushing him back into the alley and straining to keep him there.

"I'll kill them," he threatened quietly, as he was so livid he couldn't speak at normal volume. Somehow that was scarier. "I'll skin alive every last one of them that even *thought* about touching you."

I held my braced arms against his shoulders as he tried to push past me. "Please don't, Sark. You can't."

He tried to shake me off, a flash of surprise registering across his face when he found he couldn't even budge me. "Why? You think any one of those low lives stand a chance?"

"No, but you'll get in so much trouble. We can't fight back against any of the guests, ever, no matter…" I hesitated. "No matter what they're doing. Or how much they deserve it. Roland would torture you for days, then publicly execute you. It's not worth it."

He stopped fighting against me, but he hadn't cooled off a bit. "It's not *worth it*? So, you're just expected to take it? Ignore the fact that every man here is actively trying to take advantage of you, that they think of you and treat you as nothing more than a thing that they can play with whenever they want?"

"You don't," I blurted, then my gaze and arms dropped from him when the two words froze his anger in place. "Well, not that I...I just mean that you...you don't scare me that way—or at all. In any way, really, I just...know I don't have to worry. About that. You know, with you. Ever."

I cringed. That was the most idiotic thing I'd ever said. I swayed on my feet, fighting the urge to just take off running right there and never see him again.

"You seem pretty scared right now," Sark said, his voice soft with a slight teasing edge. I glanced back up at him to see his eyes still blazing with anger, but the rest of him had relaxed, a tiny smile playing in the corners of his mouth.

I laughed once. "I know. You're making me nervous."

Some of the fire in his eyes went out, somberness taking its place. "That's my fault." He took a breath. "I'm sorry I kissed you. That was...that was way out of line in so many ways. It was inappropriate and uncalled for, and I swear I'll never put you through it again."

I opened my mouth, then shut it when I recognized what he said, sinking slightly in what I realized was disappointment. "Oh. Right."

Stop it. You need to get out of this situation now.

He misread my reaction completely, his words speeding up slightly with nerves. He thought he'd blown it. "I really don't have an excuse. I don't want you thinking I can't control myself. I can. And if it's okay with you, I'd really like things between us to go back to how they were—I can't stand you ignoring me." He met my eyes seriously. "I promise I'll be normal. We can pretend this didn't happen. I won't..." He sighed, tipping his head in the direction of the guys I was hiding from. "I just can't have you thinking I'm like them."

That struck a chord, bringing me out of my shell-shocked state. My eyebrows furrowed. "No. No, of course not. You never could be. That's what I was telling you, just a minute ago when..."

When I almost kissed you.

Then I knew why I'd been avoiding him the last few days—I wanted him to kiss me again. I wanted it so badly, but I knew I couldn't have it. I couldn't chase it. That would be breaking a major rule of mine I hadn't dealt with in a long time.

I ached for him, and I realized I was going to blow everything, in that moment. I had to get out of there before I did something irreversible to the both of us. Teetering on the balls of my feet, I leaned backward to bolt.

Sark snatched me back faster than I could blink. Holding my arms to trap me against the wall, his eyes bore into mine, a new kind of desperation in them. Desperate hope. He knew I was trying to run. He knew me well enough to know what that probably meant.

I'm so predictable.

"Arie," he breathed, "you—"

"Don't do this," I pleaded. "It's not...this is bad."

"No, you have to tell me. Please, Arie, you have to. Please."

I shook my head fiercely, tears stinging my eyes, as whispered words came spilling out faster than I could keep track of what I was saying. "I'm like your sister, Sark, and you're my brother, and I can't…I can't feel this way. It's bad. It's bad for me and for you, and you can't…you can't be with me like this…it's not…we can't cross that line. I can't cross that line. I'm never supposed to cross that line. Ever."

"What if we cross that line together?"

I wish I could.

Racking my brain, I tried to grasp anything I could say that would be valid. The idea sent sharp spokes into my chest, but I spit it out anyways. "What about Erika?" I asked, which was a good point because it was true. "How am I supposed to do that to her?"

That brought him to a halt. He watched me for a moment, his face way too close to mine, then he sighed. "I've thought a lot about that, since I realized I…" He dropped his eyes and relaxed his hold on me.

He's thought about her. That made my stomach churn in horror and excitement. Because if he was thinking about Erika and this situation, then he was taking this situation very seriously. And I couldn't afford that.

"I was angry with myself," Sark finally said. "For a lot of different reasons. And maybe I'll tell you more about her and me someday, but…the point is…" He met my eyes again. "I made peace with it."

Curiosity got the better of me. My eyebrows pulled down in confusion. "How? You two were *married.* And I'm just…"

"You're not 'just' anyone," Sark said, a slight growl to his voice. "And she would tell me that. She would tell me to move on and only settle for the best. She'd want both of us to be happy, in whatever way that was. She'd hope for that. And we…things have changed so much since she was here—*we've* changed so much."

I found myself nodding. That was true. I couldn't imagine feeling this way about the Sark that was with Erika, and I was sure the feeling was mutual.

"I feel like you got older," he said with a small grin. "Kind of caught me off guard when I saw you again. Not quite a little sister anymore."

"You got younger." I felt the corners of my mouth twitch. "And not quite as airheaded."

He laughed. I loved the sound of it, and I wanted to hear it again. He was right: things were so different, even if we were just using that to justify what we wanted.

But not different enough.

I tried to pull away, but Sark held fast. "Don't I get a chance to plead my case?"

Shaking my head, I pulled on his shirtsleeves in frustration. This train was derailing fast. "You don't have a case. You can't—"

"Love you?"

I winced. "You don't love me. You might think you do, but you don't."

"Arie, that makes no sen—"

"You've always been there for me," I said, word vomit coming out again. "Since you decided to turn it around, you've *always* been there, and you've always adapted to what you thought I needed: my brother or my dad or my best friend or some crazy mix of all of them. And now you think I need someone to love me, so you've convinced yourself you do." I stopped to take a breath, since I was nearly hyperventilating at that point. "But you really don't."

Sark blinked, stunned to sad silence as he tried to formulate a response. "That's…really intelligent, actually." He cleared his throat. "But it's not true. And I think you know that."

"I don't." My voice cracked again, weakening my resolve. The tears were threatening to come back. "I don't know anything."

He closed the last of the distance between us with one step. I could sense his body heat, feel him breathing, almost hear his heart beating. When he spoke, his voice was low and soft but rough at the same time.

"How can I prove it to you?"

We were gravitating. I couldn't help it. My very being wanted to be with him, and I was having a hard time controlling it. My eyes closed, our noses brushing, our lips just whispers apart.

I was going to lose this battle.

"Please don't," I whispered.

"Please tell me why. If it feels wrong, then tell me, and I swear I'll leave you alone. I promise on my life I'll do anything to make this right."

You can't let him blame himself. You have to be honest this time.

"I…" I shook my head, grabbing my own wrist out of habit, feeling the heat of the blue underneath, and held it to my chest. "I can't."

He glanced at my hands and understanding crossed his face. "Arie." He said my name like it was the most beautiful thing he'd ever heard, but it was glass. And if he wasn't careful, it would cut us both.

"You know what I am," I said, shaking my head again. "You know what I'm going to be. I can't…I can't do that to you. Or to me."

"Arie—"

"You can't love a monster, Sark." My voice caught. "This isn't some story where the girl falls in love and gets her prince. I'm not the princess. I'm the monster. I'm the awful dragon, the thing that you *kill*. I'm a freak—"

I didn't get to finish. He grabbed my head, fingers in my hair, and crushed his lips against mine, cutting me off. No hesitation this time, no small peck like in the club a few nights ago. He channeled everything he had into me. I took his shirt in my fists and started to push him away, but I wasn't fast enough. I melted into him. I forgot about everything wrong in my life, everything I was afraid of, everything that loomed over me, and instead I focused on him.

On us.

It was like he was an extension of me on my fingertips: the fabric of his shirt, the tight muscles in his shoulders, the softness of his neck and cheek and hair. His lips on mine, slow and deep and searching and finding. His strong arm around my waist, his other hand tracing up my back and neck, his fingers tugging softly on the strands of my hair as they intertwined themselves in me.

"You can't believe them," he told me after an eternity, breathing the words into my mouth. "They say those things about you to hurt you. It's not true. You have to know that."

"It is true." My rational brain was too far away to come up with anything smarter than that. "It just is."

Sark shook his head, shaking mine along with it, and he was kissing me again with a new kind of ferocity, as though through sheer willpower he could get me to believe him. I let him. I let him kiss my mouth like I was the one keeping him alive. I let him press me against the wall and hold me like he would never let me go again. I didn't want him to. I let my hands run up his chest and over his shoulders, my fingers run through his hair, my arms pull him closer when we were already as close as possible. I almost found myself believing him. I loved the feeling that he loved me back, and that was a very dangerous thing to love.

Eventually, though, he gave up. I felt it when he did. Part of me wanted to cry out for him not to stop—that I didn't mean it, that I loved him, that I would be his no matter what until the day I died. That argument was rather compelling, so I bit my tongue to keep from following through. I tasted blood just as Sark broke away from me. We clung to each other while we struggled to catch our breaths, both of us wired and defeated at the same time.

What the heck are you doing? This couldn't end well. Nothing here could end well, not with me, not like this, not here.

"You must hate me," he said after a minute, raising his head to look at me, shame in his eyes.

My insides seemed to sharpen, automatically engaging in the protocol my new instincts thought was necessary. "That would be easier, wouldn't it?"

He shook his head, his mouth twisting with something like annoyance and hurt, or maybe regret. I couldn't figure it out. "Will you talk to me? Please?"

"No." My voice was cold. Even I was shocked I could force that much cruelty in my tone after all the warmth and love he'd just shared with me. I pulled my arms off of him. "I don't have anything to say to you. Now get away from me."

Sark recoiled like I'd slapped him—it hurt my wrecked heart, but I couldn't care at that moment. I had to snip away the attachments I'd thoughtlessly made to him. I had to not care. I wasn't *supposed* to care.

Instead of calling me a bad name and backing away like I'd been aiming for, he hugged me. That's when I realized I was shaking.

"They've got you so hardened up," he whispered in my ear, his voice so soft and kind that I almost started sobbing right there. "I hate it. Let it down for a second, Arie. You've got to be tired of it. This isn't you. Put it down and let me in, just for a minute. Please?"

I could barely hear myself. "You don't want to come in. It's a mess."

"Try me."

I moaned in frustration at everything. "I'm so tired, Sark." The words trembled with me. "I'm so tired, and it's so heavy, and I don't know how much longer I can take it. Sometimes I don't even know who I am anymore. I lose myself. I can't find myself. And I…most days I have a hard time finding any point in all of it. Most days I come way too close to quitting. And that scares me because I don't even care."

My confession hung in the cooling air around us. The night settled in, the sun completely gone now. He hugged me for a long time. When he spoke again, I had a better sense of the world around me, and I was hoping to keep it in check.

"What can I do?" Sark asked me. "What do you need, right now?"

"There's not…I mean…"

"There's got to be something. Anything. Even if it's small."

I thought for a moment before I pulled away from him to watch his face. "Act normal."

He stifled a laugh of disbelief. "Act normal? What part of this is normal?"

"Act like you would in this situation if I hadn't ruined it."

His expression darkened. "You didn't ruin—"

"Please, Sark?" I asked. "You'd be light and funny and making careful jokes within reason because you don't want to push me. You'd be all swelled up in pride but trying not to act too triumphant because you know I'm competitive." I took a breath. "I need *you*. Even if I keep breaking down, I need you to be you."

He nodded, absorbing that. "Okay. Okay, I see what you mean." He let go of me fully, stepping away so I could have room to breathe. "Do I get a chance to warm up first?"

I actually rolled my eyes. The familiar action made me feel a little bit better. "And there you are."

"Well, it's a good question," he mused, getting more and more comfortable with himself. "I mean, the girl of my dreams just made out with me—and she's great at it—so now I have to decide what to do with this information."

I gave a small ghost of a smile. He was trying for me.

After looking up at the night sky for a moment, as if realizing how late it was, he gazed at me again. "Can we go back to your room now?"

My body got stiff and tingly, my mind spluttering like an old engine, as I felt my neck get hot, the blush probably rising all the way to my cheeks and making me look like a huge idiot.

Sark leaned closer to my still form with a small smile on his face. "Get your mind out of the gutter, Nolan," he whispered in my ear, teasing me. "I meant you look exhausted." He straightened up. "You need sleep, and I don't want you walking alone at night with those..." He paused, eyes flashing with fury for a second. "*People* wandering around."

After a moment, I nodded. He gestured for me to lead the way, then fell into step next to me while we walked to the maintenance building. Once we passed the last of the residency areas, he reached out and took my hand.

"Am I allowed to do this?" he asked me.

My fingers curled around his, and I found myself nodding without permission.

"Yes," I said as another thought occurred to me. "But only when it's just us."

Some of the light in his tone darkened, though I could tell he tried to hide it. "You don't want people knowing?"

There shouldn't be anything to know.

"The wrong people can't know." My hand squeezed his at the thought. "They'd do awful things to you. Use you. Torture you and kill you and make me…make me…" I couldn't even finish. I was feeling lightheaded.

This is such a bad idea.

"Hey, it's okay," Sark told me. "I'll be careful. I promise. Not a soul will find out, if that's what you want."

I nodded, but I still felt I was going to pass out.

"I care about you," I found myself whispering, my voice cracking with panic and desperation at the truth of the words. "I care about you a lot."

He squeezed my hand back. "I know you do."

"I can't lose you. Especially not now."

"You won't."

"You might leave me."

"I don't think I could."

"You might."

"If I did, I'd come back. Crawling and begging."

"You might hate me one day."

"Why?"

"Because I did something bad. Or because you get sick of me."

"There's nothing you can do that I can judge you for." He pointed at himself. "Wanted criminal, remember? And I'll never get sick of you. You're my favorite person."

"I'll never measure up to you. I'll just pull you down."

For the first time, he hesitated. "You make me the best person I've ever been."

We stopped at the base of the ladder on the wall of the maintenance building. I touched the cool, smooth metal as Sark gave me a look that was all parts amused, confused, and pained.

"You done yet?"

I watched him for a second, then let out a long breath that seemed to deflate every part of me. "For now, I guess. I'm tired."

He glanced up at the window. "Can I come up?"

My heart fluttered and my stomach turned to a rock. "Why?"

One corner of his mouth pulled up into a half sad smile. "Because I'm worried—you look like you're unraveling at the seams. I think I did too much damage." Ever so slowly, he barely brushed his fingers against my cheek. "What's going to happen when I leave you alone tonight?"

I shrugged. *Probably something bad.* I gave his hand a gentle tug before letting go of it and climbing up the ladder, hoping he got the message that—against all my reason and better judgment— he could come up.

The air was musty upstairs. Thick. It added to the disorienting blackness, interrupted every few feet by a generator backlight. The shadows were creepy, a fact I'd always tried to avoid but it seemed too obvious now. Stumbling through the eerie dark, my skin prickled when I heard the window shut behind me.

Get a grip, I told myself as I sat down next to a light on the wall, across from the dark corner my pillow resided in. *You're going to just embarrass yourself more.*

Sark appeared through the black. Steps deliberate, he made his way over and sat next to me, keeping a few feet in between us. Neither of us said anything. He'd been in my room before, so I didn't know why I was so self-conscious that he was sitting there.

Get a grip.

"You didn't do any damage," I finally told him, like an afterthought, keeping my gaze forward. "If anything, you're way too patient with me."

He shifted next to me, stretching his legs out. "I feel like I scarred you for life." His tone had that hint of teasing again, but only a hint. The rest of it was completely guilty.

"You didn't." My voice sounded more like myself. I was getting a grip. "I promise. I'm just really messed up. Some situations highlight it more than others. Sorry you had to see it. I think I've burned through most of it now."

I've got scars everywhere, Sark. Do you understand that?

That thought sent me on a different thought train, one that I'd never had to consider before. I really was covered in scars. The blue arms were obvious, but there was a reason Miss Welch didn't let me go anywhere without spending time in the makeup chair.

My scars didn't bother me. I kept them covered. Nobody saw them, even me. That had always been the end of it.

Until now. Because what if there *was* a situation where they'd be uncovered? A situation with someone whose opinion I cared about. A situation where the fabric would be peeled back and the makeup smudged and the real me out and exposed.

I shivered and wrapped my arms around my legs.

"You okay?" Sark asked softly.

Resting my chin on my knees, I closed my eyes. "I've got scars all over me. You can't always tell, but they're there. My arms are bright blue, for crying out loud. I'm not a pretty person, Sark, on any level." A scornful laugh bubbled out of my lips as I thought of the men that tripped over their own feet chasing me. "I'd disappoint them. I'll disappoint you eventually." I opened my eyes and turned to look at him. "Have I talked you out of this yet?"

Sark's face was unreadable, the shadows from the generator lights casting an odd glow over his features. He sat still for a moment, looking at his hand, before sticking it out to me and under the generator light we were next to. Confused, I opened my mouth to ask what he was doing, but then I saw the angry pinkish red line that ran jagged down the inside edge of his pinky finger.

"What happened?" I asked.

"Peter dropped a nail gun. Luckily it wasn't loaded." He offered his hand again, as if granting permission, and I took it in both of mine, running the tip of my index finger along the healing wound as gently as possible.

Keeping his injured hand in mine, he bent his knee and pulled up the edge of his pants, revealing a long scar along the top of his ankle. It looked faded—the injury must've been years ago—but it left a mark that said it went deep.

"It was a bike accident," Sark told me. "I was ten, I think, or twelve. I was racing these four older kids on a bet when I crashed. My mom was so mad. I didn't care, though, because I still won the money."

I smiled fondly at the image of little Sark taking on the big kids in a bike race. I wished so badly I could see it in real life.

Sark laughed quietly. "They beat me up a few days later. Didn't like some kid stealing their thunder, I guess." He let his pant leg fall down, hiding his ankle. "I've been in a lot of fights. Had a lot of injuries. These ones aren't the worst I've got, by a long shot. They're the most innocent though, probably. What's funny is you're so concerned about being good enough for me, you haven't even considered the idea that I don't deserve you in the slightest."

I shook my head but stopped the cynical remark from leaving my mouth. The truth was, I liked this conversation. I liked the intimacy of him talking to me this way. I liked being with him. Underneath all of my fears, the thought of being with him like this calmed me in ways I couldn't describe and couldn't get anywhere else.

"Do you have a lot of scars?" I asked. It was a silly question, really, considering the history of Sark's life. I'd just never thought about it before.

"More than I'd like to admit." He shrugged. "But it's better than being dead. Some days I'm actually proud, in a weird way. They mean something, you know? I showed up. I came, I fought, and, yeah, maybe I lost, but I'm still here."

"Yeah." I brushed his pinky scar again, then glanced back up at him. "Will you show me?"

He went to move, then stopped himself. Suddenly he was trying very hard not to smile. "Now? Or later?"

I shook my head, confused. "Why not now?"

"Because," he said, failing to keep the smile away, "I'd have to start removing clothing and I'm not sure that's what you want right now."

I dropped my eyes to my hands, commanding myself not to imagine anything because—even though I didn't know for sure—he probably wasn't *ugly*, despite the scars, and the emotions rushing through me felt so foreign I knew I wouldn't be able to trust myself to be rational in that situation.

What is happening to me?

"Oh," I told my hands, hoping I wasn't blushing again. "Right. Later then."

Sark burst out laughing and nudged me with his shoulder. "You're cute."

Cute? I studied him for a moment, trying to see if I could detect a hint of impatience or annoyance or negativity toward what was just the beginning of my conservative tendencies. There was nothing. He just smiled at me. A tension inside me relaxed when I realized he really didn't expect anything from me. I smiled back. Then I yawned.

"Go to sleep," Sark told me. His comfortable confidence seemed to falter just a bit. "I'll, um, leave so you can…"

I ignored him, grabbing my t-shirt and leggings before pulling myself up. "Close your eyes," I said, teasing, as I walked away from him and stowed myself behind a generator. It was probably my fastest clothes change ever. When I came back, I was happy to find him still there, sitting against the wall, shoulders nearly hunched as he concentrated his whole being on watching a spot on the floor. His concentration broke when I tossed my dirty clothes in my corner.

"You look tired too," I said as I sat down by my pillow and pulled my blanket over me. "Is Lennon just killing you?"

Sark shook his head—not a denial but a dismissal. He didn't want to talk about it. That made my panic at the situation spike, but he shook his head again when he saw the change in my expression.

"No, Arie, it's fine. I just get too tired to talk about bad things sometimes, you know?"

I bit my lip as I took that in. I did know. I nodded. "Okay. But we'll talk about it later, right?"

He sighed. "If you want to. But now you should get some rest. I'll stay until you're asleep." He stopped, as if realizing what he said. "Only if you need me to. Because you're scared, I mean."

We both knew hiding out in the secret space of the maintenance building was the safest place to be—I really didn't need to be scared. I wasn't.

I pursed my lips, willing myself not to succumb to the smile I was feeling. "Maybe just for a minute. Thank you." Burrowing down, I rested my head on my pillow, turning my body so my back was to him, my face to blackness.

His voice was bland. "You're welcome."

A few minutes passed in darkness. I couldn't relax. I closed my eyes. I tried to force myself asleep, but all I could focus on was the quiet sound of Sark's breathing just a few feet from me. The corners of my mouth turned up. I couldn't bring them back down.

More minutes passed. I realized I was too still and not comfortable, my arm falling asleep under me. I tried to loosen up. Really, my ears just strained to hear a break in his rhythm, as if I could sense the moment he would leave. I didn't know what I would do when it came.

Get yourself together, I ordered myself. *This is absolutely crazy.*

But I was still halfway smiling. I couldn't help it. Not that Sark was ever less than totally respectful and considerate toward me, but I was surprised at how warmed I was at the thought of him sitting there, watching over me. I knew he was exhausted, and I could feel his discomfort from here at the hazy situation we'd found ourselves in. And he was still here. Not only here, but here for me. Not to criticize or complain or change my behavior or demand things from me I didn't want to give or make me feel stupid or inferior—like everyone else seemed to these days.

Maybe I was just used to being treated like dirt around the Compound, but the sweetness of Sark's patience and waiting made my mouth smile and my insides swell. I couldn't ignore that. I was having a hard time ignoring it. I decided if I was going to be crazy and break my own rules, then I should jump in with both feet, try something maybe a little less responsible for a change. Plus, I owed it to Sark to pick a side and stick to it honestly.

Plus, I really wanted this.

My eyes opened. "Sark?" I asked, my soft voice breaking through the silent darkness.

"Yeah?"

"Come here."

Rustling sounded, fabric against the floor, as he scooted over until he was sitting next to me. He leaned over to look at my face, his eyes concerned. "What's wrong?"

I reached up and grabbed a fistful of his shirt, then pulled him down to me and kissed him, my mouth moving with a new kind of sureness now that I was giving it what it wanted. Sark froze in surprise, barely having the presence of mind to catch himself before he fell.

"Please stay," I whispered to him.

Part of me was still afraid I was dreaming the whole thing up, and this would be the part where he laughed derisively or spat at me or pushed me away in disgust and walked out.

Instead he suppressed a smile. "I thought you'd never ask." Shuffling around my setup, he stretched out next to me, wrapped me up in his arms and let me nestle myself into his chest, as his fingers went through the ends of my hair over and over. I sensed my soul sigh in contentment. And I knew that if there was one thing on Earth I wanted more than anything else, it was to freeze that moment forever.

After his fingers were done with my hair and had moved on to tracing around my ear, he gently touched his lips to my forehead. "Are you doing any better? You had me worried there for a while."

I nodded. "A lot better, actually. You were right after all."

"I usually am." He tilted my head up to look at him, and I could barely make out his grin in the dim light. "What was I right about this time?"

I clasped my hand around the back of his neck and pulled my face closer to his, finding myself grinning too. "This was a pretty great idea. Sorry it took me a moment."

He pressed his face against mine. "Better late than never."

Biting the inside of my cheek, I searched myself for the courage to act like I wanted, but I was coming up empty. I let out a frustrated breath. "I just might need some help sometimes. Like now."

Nodding, he edged himself forward just enough for our lips to touch, igniting some confidence in me, then we kissed again, and again, three or four or five times—I lost count—before I fell asleep in his arms.

When I woke up to my blaring alarm in the morning, he was gone. Probably had a check in or something. I was sad and somewhat unsure of myself and life in general until I turned and realized his smell was stuck to my blanket. Then I smiled, replaying last night over and over again in my head, memorizing every word and touch and feeling, and locking it all away.

In the days that followed, I relied on those locked away memories and feelings to keep me going, and Sark gave me many more to add to the pile. When we snuck around to be together, even when it was just for a few minutes so I could ask him about his day, I felt better. A little stronger.

Vanessa attacked him with ferocity. Sark had to remind me constantly that his feelings were genuine, he didn't actually hate me, I wasn't an insecure mess that just wasted his time. When I was with him, it was easier to believe him. When I was alone, it was harder to keep Vanessa at bay. She'd whisper and shout at me, and I'd try to shut her out, but it didn't always work. Some ideas stuck. And she never let up, knowing that every time she tainted an aspect of my life, she was one step closer to being free.

10

Micah rolled the apple across the table to me. I caught it and rolled it back. He caught it and rolled it back. Over and over. Again and again. The game was simple and mind numbing, but it was the only positive interaction I'd had with Micah all day.

It was late—dinner was pretty much over in the cafeteria. There were a few half empty tables scattered around, the last wave of employees grabbing their food before the place shut down for the night. It was quieter than usual, as if someone had turned down the volume of buzzing conversations a few notches. Rain tapped against the ceiling, creating its own furious music.

I tried to ignore the scarlet that splattered my hands, arms, dress, and hair. If I looked at my red-stained finger too long, I would start hyperventilating, so I didn't. I focused on the bruised apple, allowing the last hour to melt into the back of my brain where hopefully it would stay a muddled mess. That was usually at least a little effective, especially since I'd been at the Compound so long, but the power wasn't as potent tonight. Maybe if they hadn't seen me, I wouldn't care as much.

But they had seen. Because there was a senseless guest staying here named Andy Sinclair who decided to not only screw up but get caught. Andy and his buddies were hanging out in the production building, which doubled as a lounge on most weekdays. Of course, while Andy was there, several labor groups were also there working on upgrades, as there was always something Miss Welch wanted bigger and better. I'd even seen Sark and Peter and Brennan and Cameron and others working from time to time before.

The problem wasn't that they were there. The problem was Andy was there at the same time.

I didn't want to do it. I tried to refuse, but Micah wouldn't take no for an answer, and I was too terrified of his stone-cold death glare to stay strong. So, in my glittering navy cocktail dress, I made my way through the half filled lounge, glancing through so many faces to find the one I was looking for: a twenty-six-year-old with clean cut golden honey hair, bronze eyes, and a thumb-sized brown birthmark on the right side of his jaw.

It took me two minutes to find him, leaning back easily against the bar with arms sprawled on the counter as he listened to one of his seven friends tell a story. My heels made a soft clacking sound as I paced over to him, feeling my insides morph into something else to complete the task at hand. When Brennan waved at me from across the room after putting up a beam next to Sark, I ignored him. I steeled myself and kept going. And when I reached Andy and forced the prettiest practiced smile I could muster, I knew by the way his eyes widened with a lazy grin that I already had him.

It took me sixteen and a half minutes to pry him away. Sixteen and a half minutes of me feigning interest in a naïve kid, of laughing at lame jokes, of suffering through the humiliating comments, jokes, and complaints from Andy's entourage that he was the lucky one. Sixteen and half tortuous minutes of invading his personal space and my own, letting him twist his arm around me so I could twist him around my finger. My charade only broke for a second when he put his hand on my neck, using his fingers to tilt my chin up as his lips grazed against my ear to whisper what he thought was his grand idea. Because when he tilted my head, somehow— maybe by habit—my eyes landed right on Sark's. And the look he gave me scorched everything I had left inside.

I felt like ash when the sixteen and a half minutes ended, when I finally convinced Andy to follow me across the lounge, me trying to ignore the attention we received while he seemed to feed off of it. We went past the construction zone and into a back supply room filled with discarded costumes and extra lights, where we could be alone.

We weren't alone, though, because Micah was there waiting. Micah was there waiting because Andy Sinclair and his buddies had betrayed Cyrus, foolishly betting with money that wasn't theirs. Our orders weren't to kill, but to send a message, and sometimes that was even worse.

I walked out of that closet an hour and twenty-seven minutes later. My dress had been ripped on one side halfway up my thigh, the navy ends glittering purple now, and my hair was a mess. Though he could no longer speak, see out of one eye, use his right hand, or walk normally, if at all, Micah and I left Andy behind to fend for himself. Based on the way every single one of the workers scattered at our exit, I knew they all must've heard the screaming.

For fear of what Micah would do if I broke his rank, I followed him out of the production building, surprised when we ended up at our table in the cafeteria. I wasn't planning on eating; he didn't either. But we sat there in vacant silence, rolling an apple we found on the floor back to each other over and over again as the rain began to pound an angry song against the roof.

I didn't know how long we stayed like that. The dinner rush started petering out. I was used to feeling that people were watching me, but I still jumped in surprise when I decided to glance up and saw Lucy staring at me from the cafeteria line. Her thin brown ringlets framed her face twisted up in some mix of fear and disbelief. When she quickly turned and darted out of the building, I knew she must've talked to Brennan.

Micah hissed under his breath when my distraction caused me to catch the apple late, breaking our rhythm. I dropped my gaze back to our table and refocused on our activity. Micah's gaze never broke from the apple, his jade eyes calculating and hateful but unstable, as if planning the apple's slow and painful demise. I was just glad he wasn't planning mine. He was using the apple as a means to focus his energy on something—I didn't think he'd tore into Andy as much as he'd wanted to. I felt a painful hollow pang in my chest as I wished I could talk to him about what happened. Wished for my friend to come back.

I wrapped my free arm around my waist, holding myself, though it felt there was nothing inside to even hold. I was empty. Numb. So cold and frosted over that I didn't dare stand in case I shattered into shards of ice. The loneliness made me feel so tightly twisted and contorted, yet so vastly hollow: I couldn't even find it in me to be afraid of the thought I didn't care about Andy at all. I just rolled the apple, ignored my red fingers, and waited to collapse in on myself.

We'd been playing for quite a while when I caught sight of Roland entering from the front of the cafeteria and heading towards us. I was surprised to see him here, but then remembered that tonight's dish had been lemon-roasted chicken—his favorite. He probably showed up at the end of the day just to snag all the leftovers.

Micah and I both straightened up when Roland stopped at our table, having to walk halfway down the length of the empty rectangle bench to reach us stuffed in the corner. He placed two tablets on the table.

"New assignment," he told us. "Needs to be carried out this evening. Understood?"

"Yes, sir," we responded.

"Good." He nodded, then headed back to the front where the dwindling line was.

We both grabbed the tablets and used our fingerprints to bring them to life. I shivered at the thought of another assignment already, but then realized that the last one had been almost two weeks ago.

The details popped up on the screen and I scanned through them. My eyes widened in horror when I got the gist of what was supposed to happen: an entire guesthouse here at the Compound needed to be terminated. We were to wait until dark then activate the building's security measures, locking everyone inside, then go through and kill everyone living in that building. Thirty-six people would be dead by morning.

"Micah, we can't do this," I whispered, going back over the information hoping that I'd missed something.

He scoffed. "Last time I checked, *you* don't do anything."

I looked up at him. "There are kids in there. We can't just herd them like sheep and then slaughter them all."

Faster than I could blink, he stood and wrapped a hand behind my neck, slamming my face onto my tablet and holding me there. "Whose op is this?" he demanded, spitting into my ear.

"Yours," I gasped, my fear nearly taking my voice from me. Shards from the tablet screen dug into my chin.

"And who makes the decisions? Whose judgment do we trust here?"

"Yours."

"And who needs to learn to shut up when she doesn't know what she's talking about?"

I didn't have the words to answer. Suddenly, I felt the apple had a better chance of survival than I did.

"That's what I thought," he said, his tone sharp enough to cut me. "I've never needed your help before, and I don't need it now. I'll do this myself."

Slamming my head again before releasing me, Micah got up from the table and headed for the back door. Acting on reckless impulse, or maybe just pure desperation, I stood up and took a step toward him, hiding my shaking hands behind my back.

"I want to talk to Micah," I told him.

He stopped in his tracks and turned around, an eyebrow raised mockingly. "I'm right here."

"No." I shook my head. "I want to talk to *my* Micah. I know it's almost like there's two of you in there. I want to talk to him."

Micah just narrowed his jade eyes at me, jaw locked, anticipating attack. Talking through that wall would be pretty much impossible.

"I know they make you feel crazy," I went on, somehow able to keep my voice from trembling. "They make you feel like you're insane and that you have to depend on them to be whole. But you're not crazy, Micah. You're trying to deal with an immense amount of awful and horrible things. You never wanted to be this. I know it."

Something like a growl went through his teeth. His body went rigid, his muscles locking. He was preparing himself. My odds were not looking good.

My earpiece crackled and I heard Roland's warning voice on the other end. "Nolan do not antagonize him. He's wired for the kill; he will attack you."

Roland must've still been in the cafeteria. He was watching this unfold right now and warning me that I didn't have a chance.

"Remember when I first met you?" I asked Micah. I had to be careful though. This was dangerous territory for both of us, as we'd swore to each other we'd never bring up that time period again. "Remember when we were locked up together and you pretty much saved me? You'd talk to me and take my drugs for me and tell me everything would be okay." I took a deep breath. "I want to talk to that kid. He had a soul. He had a heart. And I know he's in there."

"Acting," Micah said through his teeth. "You were an assignment. That was it."

I shook my head. "I don't believe that. You can pretend to just be an errand boy, but I see past it. Micah, a person, is in there. I've seen him. You can't hide him from me."

Out of my peripheral vision, I saw employees getting up from their table and leaving. My earpiece crackled again. "Nolan, I'm evacuating the building," Roland told me. "Micah is unstable, and he will wipe out this whole place, including you, if you don't let him go. I order you to walk away now."

Micah somehow relaxed and stiffened at the same time. Then he sent a chill down my spine by smiling at me, the kind of smile the monsters under your bed gave you before they dragged you underneath and sucked you away forever.

"I have wanted to snap your neck for so long," he told me, taking a step toward me.

I forced myself to hold my ground, though my voice was higher than usual. "Why is that?"

"We had a system. It worked. We worked hard and, thanks to me, we got our jobs done." He gritted his teeth. "Then he met you and you ruined everything. You messed with his head."

His head? My heart ached at the use of third person. I knew he was messed up, but this was worse than I thought.

Micah took another step toward me, his eyes glinting with hatred. "Micah couldn't handle this job. He was too pathetically weak to see the job through. He created me to take the brunt, to do the dirty work and be done with it. Then he shacked up with you for eight months and suddenly he cares again." He rolled his eyes. "Cyrus sent us to kill you as a test for all of us—Micah couldn't go through with it and gave you an out. And if that wasn't enough, he broke protocol time and time again to come to his pal Arie's aid. And just like that—" He snapped his fingers. "Little Micah is weak again. All because of a stupid little key who doesn't understand her place in this world."

Crackle. "Nolan, back down now!"

I shook my head. "You're not weak, Micah. Caring isn't weakness—it's one of the bravest things you can do. Make your own choice. Fight this. You don't have to be what they tell you."

He scoffed. "That's rich, coming from you. You let your whole life crumble over one label."

Ouch. That one hurt. "Fight him, Micah." My hands shook harder. "There are kids in that building. They don't deserve to die. Their parents don't either. You don't get to make the choice of whether or not they live."

"Why do you even care?" he demanded. "Their money funds this hellhole. You should be happy to kill them."

My throat closed up, but I still forced words through it. "I'm not."

Another step to me. Another warning in my ear. One last stride to close the distance.

Micah grabbed my throat in his hand, holding me with just enough pressure to keep me rooted in place. I held my breath and stayed perfectly still as he pressed his cheek against mine to whisper in my ear.

"Despite the orders they gave me to keep you alive, I would snap your neck right now." He brushed his thumb against my collarbone to prove his point, making me shiver in spite of myself. "And you know I could. I could make your last breath the most excruciating of your life. But I won't. Instead, I will go to that building and round all thirty-six of them up and lock them in one room. Then I'll make them watch as I tear each and every one of them apart, slowly, enough so they know their own scream well before their corpse finally hits the ground. One by one. All because of you."

He waited a few seconds to let that gruesome image sear itself into my brain before releasing me and stalking out the back door.

Roland was in my ear again. "Nolan, you stand down. You stand down or he will kill you."

I didn't count on Roland much, but we both knew I couldn't last in a fight against Micah, especially one where he didn't hold back. Where he attacked to kill. I wouldn't stand a chance.

But I thought of those poor people trapped with the monster I'd just witnessed. If they died tonight, I would never sleep again.

I felt like it was a crossroads—not for me as the key, a soldier, or an experiment. Me as a person. Me as Arie. Whose side was I really on?

Ripping my earpiece out of my ear, I ran to the back door, hearing Roland shouting my name from across the room. I only paused to smash the glass box on the wall and slam my fist on the button twice, enacting security protocols, then slipped out into the rain seconds before the protocols were activated. Now every building in the Compound was on lockdown. Nobody could get out, and, if I'd done it in time, Micah wouldn't be able to enter any building, even with his clearance.

I ran through the pounding rain in the night, my bare feet sloshing in water and throwing my balance, as I fought to catch up with Micah. I stopped when I saw his frozen figure in the blackness, a few yards in front of me.

He knows I activated security. My stomach knotted but I was too hyped up on adrenaline to care. *He knows I blew his chance.*

I didn't have to announce myself. Slowly, he turned around to face me, the fury rolling off of him in giant waves, nearly drowning me. His jade eyes seemed to glow in the dark. Stone. Rigid. Unfeeling. A monster.

"I warned you, Arie," he said through his teeth. Then he lunged at me.

11

The administration building had a basement—a giant marble assembly hall with a fifty-foot-long stage at the front. Should they be summoned, employees were to abandon whatever they were doing, meet with their group, and have their leader guide them to their designated space in the assembly hall. Then they were to stand, wait, and listen. It was a rare occasion when an announcement was important enough for Cyrus to give himself; public punishment was much more common. Even then, the assembly hall was rarely used.

A guard had me by the arm and dragged me to the assembly hall, down the middle aisle between hundreds of gathered employees standing at attention. My bare legs squeaked against the marble floor, leaving behind a trail of mud, rainwater and blood, all of which were flowing from my soaked body. An open gash the size of my palm on the back of my left calf prevented me from walking on my own, though the guard would've had to drag me no matter what to get me to come here.

By the time Roland finally disengaged the security protocols, Micah and I were in full swing, rapidly approaching my certain death. To keep their precious key alive, they ended up having to shoot Micah with a paralyzer dart because there was no way to stop the rabid ferocity he had ripped me apart with. Honestly, I think Roland was pleasantly surprised that I held up so well—he thought he'd lost me for sure.

My right eye was swollen shut, but I could still half watch the hundreds of shoes pass by my line of sight or catch a glimpse of Micah being dragged in front of me. When the guard dumped my body onstage and my good eye found Cyrus, I wished that Roland had been too late. Cyrus stared fire into my soul, standing in between the crumpled messes that were Micah and me, and in front of Roland, Scottsman, Miss Welch, and every other administrator at the Compound.

Cyrus turned his attention to the masses. "My children," his voice echoed out into the deathly silent space. "I extend my sincere apologies that your tasks this evening were interrupted. However, this meeting is vital to the wellbeing of our community. It has come to my attention that we are not the united utopia we had the potential of becoming—that potential has been lost in a muddled lake of misconception. Let me make this abundantly clear."

Roland stepped forward as Cyrus spread his arms wide over Micah and me. "Here we have two individuals that represent the strongest and most powerful that you have to offer. Despite their knowledge of and dedication to our cause, they disobeyed direct orders."

As if an extension of Cyrus' body, Roland stomped his heavy boot on my mangled leg. They must've done something to Micah too because there were two stifled screams of pain that ricocheted in the silence.

I was panting as I closed my eye and tried to curl tighter into a ball without jostling my broken collarbone. Everything hurt so badly. Why didn't Roland just let Micah kill me?

"They stand as an example," Cyrus went on, his tone sharpening. "No one here is exempt from the rules. If we wish to attain the highest level, we must be completely united as one with no discord. For their dreadful actions, Micah will be confined to the Chair and Arie in the Box. Five days will suffice, effective immediately."

A slight grumble went through the crowd, and I almost cried. They were sending me to the Box. I'd worked so hard to keep myself from those walls of perdition because I knew I couldn't handle another second in them, let alone five days. A pang of guilt went through me too at the thought of Micah strapped to his most hated chair.

"Let this be a lesson to all: any weakness will be terminated, as weakness is death," Cyrus warned before closing with his standard. "We can be better than this. We must be better than this. You are dismissed."

I heard the slow shuffling of feet as everyone filed out. I was jealous. The least they could do was take me with them.

Minutes passed before the shuffling was gone and silence settled. I braced myself for impending doom.

Cyrus' voice reflected murder. "Get. Up."

I winced in spite of myself before opening my eye, trapping moans behind my teeth as I pulled myself up, putting most of my weight on my right leg. The paralyzing drug must've worn off because Micah stood up next to me. I didn't dare even glance at him.

It was Cyrus, Roland and about twenty armed guards now—everyone else had left.

"Do you think I'm stupid, Arie?" Cyrus asked me. For once, his eyes stayed still, staring down into the chasm of my being.

"No, sir," I answered, the words distorted by my swollen lip. "I don't."

"Do you think I'm stupid?" he shouted, making me cringe. It was rare he raised his voice like that. "Tell me, honestly."

I shook my head softly. "No, sir."

"Did you really actually think that you could fool me? That I truly believed your sweet little lie for months?"

I stayed very quiet.

Cyrus nodded and Roland stepped up to me, kicking my good leg out from under me and seizing me by my hair as I crumpled to the ground. Two guards closed in on me, one of them holding a long metal rod with claws on one end and some sort of cylinder contraption on the other. She stood the rod on the floor and the metal claws dug into the marble, securing it there, and it stood a little higher than eye level with me on the stage. Roland then grabbed my right arm and forced it through the horizontal metal cylinder, my hand popping out on the other side. The other guard pressed a button on a remote and the cylinder clamped down on my arm. I had to hold back a cry. The metal cut through my dress and into my skin, securing my arm in place from above my elbow to my palm.

"Do you really think I didn't know?" Cyrus asked from behind me. "I've known you were lying to me from day one. I've known that—despite both of your supposed accounts—you have never aided in assignments the way you were intended to. Rather, you actually have spent your time actively fighting against them."

He stepped closer to me. Because of my spot on the ground, he was several inches taller, and he hunched down to whisper in my ear. "That ends now."

One of the guards went out the door and returned dragging a gagged man bound at hands and feet. I'd guess he was mid-thirties though that's all I could gather—his black clothing gave me little to go on in way of profiling, which I assumed was the point.

The guard dropped the wide-eyed man on the ground several yards in front of me. It wasn't until Roland loaded a gun and forced it into my captive arm's fist that I realized what was going on. The barrel of the gun was aimed directly at the man.

"Arie Nolan," Cyrus said in my ear. "Your new assignment is to shoot and kill this man. Now."

"No," I whispered. I could feel Vanessa rising up in me, extending herself to encompass all parts of me, anticipating an opportunity to attack. I tried to drop the gun but the metal dug into my muscles so I couldn't unclench my hand. "No, no. I won't."

"You will, dear." Cyrus brushed his hand against my face, and I recoiled. "You are a murderer. You will follow orders, you will pull the trigger, and you will kill him."

The poor man must've been given a paralyzer himself. High-pitched sounds came from his subdued mouth like he was thrashing around, though he stayed still. The terror in his eyes. His eyes on me. Me with the gun. Me the murderer. Arie the key.

Don't do it, I commanded myself, concentrating on the man's eyes, his most human feature. *You can't do this. You won't do this. You aren't a murderer.*

But I could feel it. I could feel the bloodlust coursing through my veins, the all-consuming desire to rip something apart piece by piece and watch it die. Vanessa fed the savagery. Embraced it. Brought it to the forefront so it was all I could see or taste or smell. The monster inside me wanted to kill this man.

My finger twitched on the trigger and the man cowered.

"Do it," a voice hissed. I couldn't tell if it was Cyrus or Vanessa or me. "Do it. Spill the blood. Watch in flow. Bask in its warmth. You're a killer."

I'm a killer. My finger twitched again, and my heart jumped with it. What was I doing?

I gritted my teeth, whispering to myself. "Your name is Arie Nolan. You are nineteen years old now. You are not a murderer."

"Do it. Do it now."

I was reaching for any humanity I could find, knowing once I went down this road I'd never be able to come back. "Your name is Arie Nolan. You have family. You don't like it when they die. You had a brother and he died when he wasn't supposed to." That hit a sensitive nerve, so I chased it. "Your brother didn't deserve to die. This man doesn't either."

Cyrus grabbed a fistful of my hair and yanked my head closer to him. "Realize who you are, Arie. We all think of ourselves as crusaders in one way or another. That's not you. You've never been good enough to be the person you wanted to be. Abandon that ideal. Embrace your future. You are the key. You will do what I say." Grabbing my free arm, he found a tear in the fabric and yanked, a tearing sound pulling at my ears as my blue flesh was exposed, and Cyrus put my wrist in my face. "You're branded. You belong to me. You are my key."

I am the key. I couldn't tell the difference between my thoughts and Vanessa's, though I guess at this point it didn't matter. *I am the key and I will kill him.* The fire rose in me, burning me up from the core, and I didn't know how to fight it. My finger twitched, pulling the trigger enough to move it but not enough to shoot.

"My name is Arie Nolan. I am not a murderer."

Something pricked my neck, sending a scalding electric current through my body and I half screamed, tears beginning to fall down my face. My finger shook. My body shook. The fire, the darkness, the bloodlust was overwhelming me.

I was going to lose this battle.

"Your name is irrelevant," Cyrus told me, voice sharp with waning patience, "just as this man is. Just as you are. Perfection requires obedience. Perfection will give you power, a future. Seek it out. Obey. Kill this man."

No, I cried to myself. *Please don't.* But I heard the command from my brain travel down my nerves to my hand. The command to pull the trigger.

I pulled right as Micah stepped forward and forced the gun out of my hand—probably breaking a finger or two—then aimed it at the victim and put three bullets in his chest. The man slumped forward. Scarlet dripped onto the white marble. The only sound in the silence was my tortured gasping.

I glanced at Micah, my mouth hanging open. He wasn't looking at me. He tossed the gun on the ground, his face cold and expressionless as blood seeped from the gash on his head, then held his hands up in surrender. The guards handcuffed him immediately. My gaze went back to the corpse.

"You are both weak," Cyrus spat. "I cannot tolerate weakness. Weakness is fallacy. Weakness is death. Weakness will destroy us all!" He took a deep breath, as though his anger was tiring and he needed to compose himself. "Take them both away. Give her a triple dose. I want her to feel everything."

My arm was released from its prison. Through the tears in fabric I could see the thick bruises on my skin from the shackles, my muscles sighing in relief at their freedom. The relief didn't last long. All at once I was whisked away to meet my punishment.

The Box was exactly that—a box. It was barely tall enough to sit up straight and almost long enough to stretch out your legs. There was enough air to keep you alive. Not a speck of light. No sound but your own scream.

The prospect of being trapped was scary enough in itself, but that wasn't even the worst part. The worst part was the powerful hallucinogen Roland would shoot into your veins seconds before locking you inside. And just like that, you were trapped in total darkness with every one of your worst nightmares brought to life as your only company.

I'd been in the Box four times. After my last breakout attempt, I was thrown in there and it took me three days to recover. I'd never tried to escape since. The hallucinations were too vivid. Too real.

"Please don't," I caught myself whispering to Roland as he readied the syringe. "I can't go back in."

There was no pity from him. "You bring this on yourself, Nolan." Then he shoved the needle in my arm, dumping three times the average amount of drugs into my bloodstream.

The effects were almost instantaneous, faster than they'd ever been before. I tasted metal and blood. Roland got fuzzy around the edges before his face turned bright purple. I was numbed to my body convulsing. The world blurred around me and then I felt myself scrunch, the freezing metal underneath me, and I knew I was inside. Then the world went black.

The darkness was disorienting. You don't know what's real or what's not, or even if *you're* real or not. You can't see yourself. You can't see anything except what the drugs decide to pull from your mind.

I smelled blood. The taste grew stronger in my mouth. My body slowly began to be rocked side to side, as though caught in a slight wave of the ocean. A warm ocean. A red ocean. Blood.

I gasped and struggled against the current until I got to shore. Panting at my exertion, I collapsed onto the sand only to find it was uncomfortable. Grainy. Pointy. It sliced my skin and blood dripped from me. Now the beach was red.

Then I heard it. The slow, deep grumble started off soft. I could feel it in my bones. It grew louder, bigger, more defined.

My eyes glanced around to find a source for the noise, but I only saw the red ocean surrounding me on every side. I was on an island. An island of blood.

They appeared. Slowly at first. The winds combined essences from the atmosphere and they built together, forming a being. Tons of them. Blue. Bent. Wild. Mutts.

But they weren't just any mutts—I knew them. Every person I'd ever killed with Micah was now standing in front of me. Zombie mutts. Vengeful zombie mutts. Running on all fours, they leaped up to me, snarling as they surrounded me. I was on an island. I had nowhere to go.

They forced me down on my back, each of them holding my wrist or ankle or head to keep me secure.

"I'm sorry," I tried to tell them, but I was cut off by louder growling. Taking my eyes off the sunny grey sky, I looked in front of me to see another crowd of ravaging zombie mutts, snapping their teeth at me. I was horrified to find familiar faces: Ellen, Hadley, Jacklynn, my mom, Peter, Lucy and so many others. There were some I knew intimately and some who I walked by from time to time. People who were once a part of my life, now reduced to a pack of mutated monstrosities.

One mutt broke away from the pack, the bulging blue veins deforming his face making him nearly unrecognizable. Nearly. But not quite.

He bounded on all fours to me, leaning over my ensnared body, breathing on my face. It reeked of rotting corpses and decaying flesh. My throat closed up and I fought against the mutt's holds, but they just snarled and held on tighter, digging their broken nails into my skin.

Sark smiled at me, revealing a set of jagged and pointed teeth. His elbows bent as he lowered himself, resting his cheek against mine to whisper in my ear. On the other side of my face, he traced his finger down, slowly, from my temple to my collarbone.

"Hey, sweetheart," he growled before sinking his teeth into my neck. I screamed.

12

Getting out of the Box was always difficult. The door is opened and you're free to walk out, but sometimes it takes hours—or days, on a few occasions—before you realize it's open. Then you have to make yourself get out. After spending an eternity locked in limbo, it takes a lot of trust to believe there really is a better, safer world on the other side of the confining walls.

Eventually I made myself crawl through the opening, my arms shaking with the weight of my body. It was bright. It hurt my eyes. A hiss escaped me as I crumpled to the ground and squeezed my eyes shut.

I kept them closed as arms picked me up off the ground and set me somewhere else. It wasn't until I felt my body against theirs that I realized I was shaking, quiet dry sobs spilling out of my mouth.

My brain didn't comprehend the meaning of dignity. I didn't panic when my ripped apart dress was torn off me, but I did when I felt liquid underneath me, rising higher and higher until it reached my shoulders. I was in the ocean again. The red ocean.

I started to thrash around, getting even more violent when unknown hands restrained my flailing limbs. Then the liquid was dumped over my head and down my face. It was clean. It was pure. It was water.

I stopped moving. After a few moments, the hands released me. I stayed still as my skin and hair were scrubbed clean of dried mud, blood, vomit and waste. Then the hands left me alone.

I didn't know how long I soaked in the water before I could open my eyes. I was in a tub in a teeny white room. A towel and a pile of clothes were the only items on the square counter next to the door. Surveying my body, I found my left calf and right shoulder wrapped in waterproof bandages, a red rectangle imprinted on my right palm, and numerous bruises and cuts—but no bite marks, no slices, no missing limbs. My brain saved that information as it tried to work through what had been real and what hadn't been.

Half the water sloshed out of the tub as I grabbed the side of the counter and pulled myself up. My body gave a dull ache but that was it. Some doctor must've taken pity on me and gave me painkillers. What an angel.

By some miracle, I was able to keep myself from falling to the ground despite the hazardous way my wet feet kept slipping on the tile. I barely had room in the space to stand up straight and dry off with the towel.

I froze when I saw the blue on my arms. Blue. Mutt. I was a mutt.

I screamed and then the world went black. When I opened my eyes again, I found myself scrunched up on the floor with a nasty headache. My arms were still blue, but I remembered now. I wasn't a mutt. At least, not yet.

Pulling myself up, I went to work on getting dressed. My elbow hit against the wall numerous times as I pulled the clothes on, silently thanking whoever had left me with a grey hoodie.

Bless you.

There weren't any socks or shoes. Not that I really cared. It was just another thing to do before I left the nice, safe washroom.

I didn't know how long I stared at the door before I finally placed my hand on the pad on the wall. The door slid open to the hallway of labs. Part of me wondered how I got all the way from the Box to the research building so fast. Another part was afraid of leaving. Another part knew who I had to find.

It took me awhile to get out of the building, mostly because I got lost once and I walked really slowly. One step at a time. I finally got outside. There wasn't any snow on the ground, but it was cold enough to have some. I squinted my eyes as I wrapped my arms around myself and made my way through the Compound. With bare feet and wet hair, I nearly froze, my teeth chattering highlighting my headache.

Thankfully, I found him in the second place I tried—I didn't think I had the energy to get anywhere else.

It was ironic that we ended up here again. The cafeteria was crowded with the lunch rush. There were too many people. It made my headache worse. I clenched my teeth and forced myself deeper into the building, walking as though the ground was as fragile as I felt, gently caressing the balls of my feet against the surface with each careful step.

I was surprised to find more than one person at our table. Micah was scrunched into his usual corner, his back to the front, while Ellen, Sark, Peter and my mom sat across from him. Ellen was saying something to Micah in exasperation. Sark and Peter just looked guarded and frustrated, while my mom had eyes sick with worry.

I made my way around the table to my spot in the corner across from Micah. Ellen saw me first. She gasped and nearly tripped over the bench as she lurched for me, Sark right after her. I took a step back, rocking on my heels, and they stopped. I gave them each a small nod, hoping they got the idea. I was barely managing the overload of stimulus in the room. Having someone touch me was a bad idea.

Ellen stared at me for a few more seconds before sitting back down, making sure to leave my space open. Sark stayed standing, his eyes a heavy weight on my shoulders, but gave me room to pass. I didn't meet any eyes as I took my slow shuffled steps to my corner and sat down, turning so I could lean against the wall, pull my legs up on the bench and wrap my arms around me knees. Then I glanced at Micah and winced. He was bruised everywhere, but the burn marks stood out, marking his temples, his neck, his wrists. He didn't look good.

"They let you out early too, huh?" he remarked, his tone casual as he poked his steamed vegetables with his fork.

My eyebrows furrowed. Early? What was he talking about?

Like the frustrating guy he was, he purposely avoided looking at my confused expression, forcing me to speak.

"Early?" I asked. My voice was high and cracked, raspy and barely audible. It hurt my throat to talk.

"Yeah." He met my eyes now. "You'll never believe it: when security protocols were activated the other night, several guests saw two people fighting to the death outside their building. They believed someone was coming to attack them and Cyrus' people saved them."

My eyebrows shot up. That was new.

"They donated a bunch of money to say thanks and we got off early, in case they wanted to meet us. Sick appreciation, I guess."

Wow. I cleared my throat, but it just hurt worse and didn't help my voice at all. "How early?"

He gestured to those sitting next to me. "Your crew here tells me it's been three days."

Only three days? It felt like three years, three eons, since I'd been sitting here rolling an apple to him.

I dropped my eyes, taking a minute to muster up the courage before asking, "Are you mad?"

It was a stupid question, really, but I just needed to know.

He let out a long breath. A long one. Too long. How did he have lungs for that? Then he said, "Nobody has ever talked to me like that. Ever." There was nothing menacing about the words. He was just stating a fact.

I glanced up at him. He shrugged.

"You continually ruin my life, but for some reason I'm always really glad I haven't killed you yet."

The corners of my mouth pulled up ever so slightly. Coming from Micah, that was a high compliment.

I rested my chin on my knees and closed my eyes. I didn't realize how bright and colorful the cafeteria was until I was in the dark again. Darkness helped. Less stimulus. But I couldn't block the sound. Voices and walking and clinking. Someone dropped their plate on the floor, and I cringed at the chainsaw that went through my brain.

"Do you want anything to eat?" Ellen finally asked timidly. "You're probably…since they probably didn't…"

"No thanks." I held up my right palm without opening my eyes to show her the red rectangle that would be flagged in the cafeteria line. "I'm on red card."

"At least take these," I heard Micah say. I cracked my eyes open to see him offering his small bag of mini carrots.

With a tiny smile, I took them from him just as he took a chunk out of his chicken leg with his teeth. He flashed to a blue monster, viciously chewing on a piece of flesh. I gasped and dropped the bag of carrots on the table. Then he flashed back to normal Micah.

I rubbed my forehead with my hand, as if I could rub out my headache. "Sorry."

"Did they really give you a triple dose?" Micah asked, his tone quiet.

I gave my best nod and held my legs tighter.

"How's that?"

"Um...I'm not...entirely sure this conversation is happening."

"Yeah, I bet."

We continued in silence. I nibbled on the end of a carrot and stared into space, trying to ignore the colored animals I saw that probably weren't real. Eventually, Micah left, saying that he needed to go train to catch up from three days of doing nothing, though I knew it was more for coping than anything. Shortly after, Ellen turned to me.

"I've got to get back on duty," she said, doing nothing to hide her worry. "What can I do for you?"

It took me a second to focus my eyes on her. "Nothing. I'm okay. Thank you, though."

She didn't buy that. "I'll come visit you after my shift."

"No, really. I'll call you if I need something." I uncurled my legs from myself and sat up straight. "I'll probably just go sleep forever."

"Okay." She reached to give me a hug, then stopped herself when she saw my expression. "Okay, just be careful. Please check in so I know you're alive."

"I will."

My mom stood up with her. Both of them gave me an anxious last glance before leaving. The second Ellen's spot was vacated, Sark slid down next to me, raking his eyes over me again and again. His mouth hung open, but no words came out. After a moment, he shut it and pursed his lips into a thin white line. I didn't have anything to say either.

Both he and Peter pulled me up when I was ready. Without a word, they kept with my painfully slow pace as I made my way out the back door of the cafeteria. My head throbbed with every step, making it hard to concentrate. I stopped to take a break once we were outside, the building hiding us from the rest of the Compound.

"So how big of a security detail do you need?" Peter finally asked. His tone was quietly cautious—not like him at all—and I realized I must've looked worse than I thought. "I can grab Brennan and maybe even Cameron—"

"No," I said once I understood what he was talking about. "You don't have to…escort me anywhere. They let me go. Nobody will be attacking me."

"You sure?"

I gave a small smile. It was nice that they cared so much. "Yeah. Thank you, though. Really. I appreciate it." I wrapped my arms tighter around myself against the cold wind. "Now both of you get back before you're late."

Peter nodded and gave Sark a slap on the back. "I'll cover for you." Then he disappeared around the side of the building.

"You go too," I told Sark. "I don't want you to get in trouble."

A shiver went through my body. It hurt. I winced and doubled over. Sark moved to grab onto me in case I fell, but I stepped away from him and kept myself up.

"Don't shut me out of this," Sark said, his voice full of concern. "You need help."

"I'm fine," I said, then straightened up and faced him. There were his ocean eyes. Not a blood ocean. A real one. I could see the waves, the hurricane, the days spent wondering what happened to me. It had been bad for him too.

I reached out my left pointer finger toward him, my hand shaking slightly, and I nodded at his hand. He was confused at first, but eventually held his hand out with his palm facing up. I counted to three before touching his hand with my finger. It burned. I jumped backward and hissed.

Sark reached for me, but I stopped him and tried it again. Touched his palm. It hurt. I concentrated, telling my brain that the pain was an illusion. It was all in my head. Ever so slowly, I was able to move my finger up his arm and rest my hand on his shoulder. Then I did the same with my other hand. When I had a handle on that, I took a step forward, sinking myself into him, then nuzzled my face against his cheek. I did it.

A short gasp escaped through his teeth. "You're freezing."

I nodded, part of me feeling bad about that fact, but I couldn't act on it. Instead, I soaked up his warmth. He raised his arms and draped them over me, encasing me in a soft hug.

"I'm going to go," I whispered to him. "You get back to work before Koa yells at you."

"I'm taking you home."

"No, you're already late." I decided to take the slightly less noble approach. "Please? I can't spend all day worrying about how much trouble you're in. I'm too tired."

"You need help." I felt his jaw clench. "I'm not just going to send you off alone."

"Walk me halfway. Walk me to your work site and I can go from there."

"I'm taking you home, Arie. And we should really find some extra blankets or something because you'll freeze in there too. Parts of your hair are already frozen, and your skin is like ice."

"I'm just going to go sleep. Walk me halfway and then come over when you're off. I'll be fine."

"No. I'm taking you home. Once I know you're there safely, I'll go back to work just so Koa can see my face. Then I'll come back. Don't argue with me, okay?"

I sighed. "Fine."

Walking made everything worse. I tried to go as fast as I could, but still wouldn't beat a turtle in a race. I teetered from time to time, the chaos in my head making it hard to put one foot in front of the other. My skin tingled like I was standing too close to a fire though there was only a chilly wind. My muscles were knotted, my bones achy. I felt like a walking zombie.

Sark stayed by my side, arm at the ready to catch me just in case. I did okay until we got to the maintenance building—my heart sank, and my knees shook when I saw the ladder.

"I got it," Sark said before I started crying. He wrapped an arm around my waist, securing me against him, then grabbed on to the ladder with his other hand. "Hang on to me, okay?"

I nodded and obeyed, hiding my face in his shoulder and using everything I had left to cling to him. We rose higher. His body tensed under me with each step, and I wondered how he had the strength to pull us both. He did it though. After a few minutes I heard the window slide open and his mumbled apology before he had to shove me inside. I fell to my knees on the floor, but he was there in a second to help me up and over to my corner. Curling into a ball, I huddled close to a warm generator as Sark enveloped my blanket around me, then kissed my temple softly.

"You scared me to death," he said, his voice hushed and anxious in my ear.

"I'm sorry."

"I care about you." His hand reached underneath my blanket and found mine. "I care about you a lot." He kissed my cheek. "I can't lose you. I just can't." Then he just held me and buried his face in my neck, breathing me in like I'd disappear again at any moment.

"I'm sorry," I said again. "About everything."

I closed my eyes and tried to focus on him instead of me. The tingling on my skin grew more and more uncomfortable, especially on my arms, until it was outright painful. There was a pressure inside me somewhere, making it hard to breathe.

After a few minutes, Sark growled something under his breath, then sighed, lifting his head to talk in my ear again. "I've got to go. I hate to, but…"

"Don't get in trouble," I mumbled, wincing as the heat on my body seemed to turn up four notches. "Then you couldn't come back."

"Exactly. Please be careful. Just stay here and try to sleep. Call Ellen if you need anything. I'll be back in a few hours, okay?"

I nodded. "Thank you."

Sark kissed my head before carefully standing up and heading for the window. I heard his feet against the metal as he made his way down the ladder. Then I started shaking. Badly. I couldn't control it. That shouldn't have been a huge deal, but for some reason it brought a wave of foreboding uneasiness over me. I opened my eyes and forced myself up, taking shaky steps to the window with the hope I could catch Sark.

My brain felt mushy. The world slid back and forth in my vision, like it was made of mush too. Something exploded inside of me, and I nearly screamed, crumpling to the ground.

Something was wrong. Something more than the drugs.

Dragging myself up, I kept going, calling Sark's name as loud as I could and hoping he was still close enough to hear me. Somehow I lost control of my movements and fell to the ground again.

I felt my body convulsing as though I were having a seizure. My skin was scalding, melting my insides. A sense of familiarity washed over me, and I forced my arm to the collar of my sweatshirt, yanking the fabric over my shoulder. Horror overwhelmed me as I saw the blue lines from my arms continue on their rampage. I watched them grow over my shoulder, feeling them burn onto my neck, my chin, my face. I tried to scream, but I choked on liquid instead. My eyeballs singed and everything turned blue, like a filter had been placed over my vision. I choked and thrashed and melted and clawed at my face to try and get the burning blue off.

An image formed in my head. An image of her. Vanessa. Where had she been?

She gave me a triumphant smirk as she watched me writhe. *Say goodbye, princess. Your reign is coming to an end.* Then she flipped a switch on my consciousness and I went out like a light.

13

When I opened my eyes, I saw my arm stretched out. It was nearly bare, the blue symbol on full display, several IVs inserted into it. I could smell the disinfectant soap wafting from the crisp hospital gown I was in. It only added to my wooziness. Farther down my arm I looked to see a strap around my wrist. I pulled against it. Nothing gave.

Next to me was another table with what looked like a body on it, but it was covered in a plastic tarp. The hair on the back of my neck stood up on end.

Where am I?

I tilted my head up to look at the ceiling and screamed. The ceiling was a mirror, reflecting my body strapped to a table, the blue lines running over me like vines, from my legs, up my calves, arms and neck to crossing over my face in various patterns. My eyes shone bright blue, almost solid, but I could barely make out small pupils. Small pieces of humanity.

Something brushed my arm, and I turned to see Cyrus standing next to me, a counter of tools and needles and flasks set out behind him. "Well done, dear," he said, a triumphant grin on his face. "I'm happy to see you're finally accepting your fate."

My whole body went numb. "No. No, you can't do this. Please. You don't know what you're doing."

"On the contrary, I know more than anyone else in the world." He tapped my wrist twice, as though that would reassure me.

"No you don't. You've failed before—with Xander, your last key. You don't know how this will end."

"Oh, but I might. Xander's body was unable to sustain the full power and burned up from the inside, showing me a vital mistake: I have to take the key essence out of you—the part you now hear in your head—and put it in something else. It's a rather tedious, complicated process; I won't bore you with the scientific details of it all." He shook his head once gravely. "Unfortunately, you will not survive the process, but it will be an honorable death. One to be proud of. That's much more than most people can say."

I pulled against my restraints, my panic threatening to take over. "You can't do this. You think you can control her, but you can't."

Cyrus raised an eyebrow. "Her? My, she's quite developed, isn't she?"

"No!" I shouted in frustration. "You don't want her. You want order. She'll give you chaos. This is so far out of the realm you are looking for, I swear."

"She will bring me perfection," Cyrus answered, his tone hardening. "She will bring perfection to a corrupted, imperfect world. She will bring peace."

"No she won't! She'll bring death. She just wants to kill everyone. She's not going to listen to you."

Cyrus clamped his hand down on my thrashing arm with more force than I thought possible. "Stop fighting it. You are talking about things that you don't understand."

"*You* don't understand!" I thrashed harder though it did nothing. "You're not getting a soldier or a general or a weapon. You're unleashing a monster." My voice broke in exasperation. "Can't you see that? You're being stupid! You're letting yourself be blinded by a perfect world that *can never happen*."

"I am not the blind one!" Cyrus shouted, squeezing my arm harder, rage boiling in his eyes. "The world is blind! Humans are blind! They refuse to see what's right in front of them! They turn against the very things that would cause them to grow and prosper. I am sacrificing to show them how they have been living in contradiction."

He turned and retrieved a facemask and began hooking up tubes to it. Anesthesia. He was going to put me out.

Tears stung my eyes and fell down my face as I resorted to begging. "Please, don't do this, please! You don't understand."

I frantically flipped through all of our conversations we'd ever had, trying to pinpoint something I could use. Then I remembered.

"You told me once you had a family," I said, desperation on full display. "You told me the worst experience in your life was seeing their bodies on the floor, dead. She'll kill everyone she can. So many others will lose their families. How can you knowingly unleash that?"

That was the very wrong point to bring up. Cyrus exploded, his small body shaking with rage. "Because I was the one who put them there! They didn't understand! They shunned their hideous brother, their damaged son, and tossed him out like the rest of the world did. They were too blind to see the vision and I realized their uselessness! Caring is weakness and weakness is death! I will not have weakness! *I am not weak!*" He bent halfway over, panting, as though he'd exerted himself too much.

I just stared at him in horrified shock. "You're insane."

He took a last deep breath to steady himself back to calm and straightened up. "Knowledge will always be insanity to the ignorant, Arie. Always. Enlightened people like me bear the cross of knowledge to bring about the future. That's how it is." He glanced down at his scarred hand, the first time I'd ever seen him acknowledge his disfigurements, and his voice hardened. "And I've borne my cross for too long."

I started hyperventilating. He was crazy. He was crazy and that was terrifying because there was nothing I could say that would break through that. I was going to lose everything. After years of running, fear, nightmares and dread, I was here, strapped to a gurney, powerless, about to watch my brittle world crumble into nothing.

"Please, don't," I cried, borderline sobbing. "Please, please, please. You can't. You just can't." I lifted my head up and started shouting. "Help! Somebody, please stop him! Help! Please!"

Nobody heard. Nobody came. It was going to end. I couldn't stop it.

Cyrus seemed oblivious to my shouting or pleas. He went on working with the oxygen mask until all the tubes were in place. Then he moved toward me.

"No!" I shrieked, shaking my head violently back and forth. "No! Stop! No!"

"Sweet dreams, dear," Cyrus said. He grabbed hold of my chin and held me still as he secured the mask over my face.

I held my breath—a short-term solution, but still something. I continued to pull on my restraints. Nothing. I could only watch helplessly as Cyrus injected something into my IV and I felt myself fading away, giving one last scream before I was pulled underneath the blackness.

To my surprise and terror, I didn't go all the way under. Instead, I remained in between, aware of myself and my body but unable to do anything, like I was lying in a pile of drying cement. I heard faint sounds of a heart monitor, some possible footsteps and occasional metal clank. All was still. All was quiet.

A burst of heat came from what I thought was my arm—my IV. The heat coursed through me, bringing burning hellfire, and I felt myself scream. I'd felt this hellfire before. This was how it felt to be infected. This was how it felt when that horrid formula intruded my body and stole my life.

The distant sound of the heart monitor sped up, announcing my torture to the world. Then I saw her. Or, rather, I felt her. A blue essence filled up my awareness, an eagle spreading its wings before it took off and soared. She was bragging. She was leaving. The blue essence started dimming as though it was being sucked up in a vacuum, taking my energy with it.

I fought through the burning to grab onto her, gripping the edge of the essence and refusing to let go, to let her escape.

She got angry, flaring up and pulling harder against me. The burning got hotter. I almost lost my grip and drowned in the flames, but somehow I held on. I had to hold on. She pulled on me and I on her. She'd edge me closer to the exit and I'd yank her back inside. She would not win. I'd been fighting this war for too long, given up too much, to see it all go now.

We fought for eternal seconds, the stakes as high as they'd ever been. I felt myself stretching, popping, overexerting myself in a desperate attempt to keep her at bay. To keep her locked up. She used the burning against me, yanking herself away toward her freedom and ultimate revenge. The fight was close.

But this was war. The fight could be close, but someone had to lose.

Something snapped and I flew backwards, like a rubber band stretched so far until it broke. I slumped with a small piece of blue in my grip. The rest of her essence was sucked up into oblivion, taking the burning with her. My awareness went numb, dull, stiff, and I heard the distant sound of a heart monitor flat lining.

It was gone. She was gone. It was over. I lost.

The key was free.

I felt light and airy, ready to float up into nothing, but something held me down to my corpse. A weight tied around my ankle. I realized it was the piece of blue essence I'd yanked off and kept for myself. It was heavy. It was holding me here. I knew that, but I couldn't let it go. I should. It was over.

But I was stubborn. I didn't let go. I clamped onto the blue with hopeless ferocity, as if that could make up for what I hadn't been strong enough to do. It couldn't. It never could. It was all over. But I still wouldn't let go.

The last thing I heard was the restarting of a heart monitor, slow and steady.

look for part 2: